Victoria was onstage, in her street clothes. Enigma was again playing over the speakers. Victoria looked right at Brett, sending heat flaming through her, pulling her all the way into the auditorium. Victoria slowly began unbuttoning her blouse and pulling it off. She seemed to be stripping just for Brett, again.

Brett wanted her so much it was a physical ache. She could almost feel exactly what Storm—no, Victoria—would feel like in her arms. She wanted to bury her head in Victoria's hair and breathe her scent and feel the warmth of her body pressed against her own.

Brett took a deep breath, trying to calm herself, and leaned back against the wall with her eyes closed. But in her mind's eye, she could see Storm moving to the mysterious music. She tried to focus on other things to overcome this reaction: someone was out there, on the streets, knocking off strippers, hookers, her girls.

Visit

Bella Books

at

BellaBooks.com

or call our toll-free number

1-800-729-4992

WHEN GOOD GIRLS GO BAD

A MOTOR CITY THRILLER

BY

THERESE SZYMANSKI

Bella
BOOKS
2003

Bella Books, Inc.
P.O. Box 10543
Tallahassee, FL 32303

Printed in the United States of America on acid-free paper
First Edition

Editor: Greg Herren
Cover designer: Bonnie Liss (Phoenix Graphics)

ISBN 1-931513-11-2

This one is for an incredibly intelligent, strong, and attractive girl I had the privilege of meeting this past year — may her life be filled with happiness, success and fun!

And let's all hope my brother Bruce and his wife, Amy, raise Peyton Elizabeth Szymanski (the lil' Peanut) the right way — as a Democrat!

Acknowledgements

Dear Sir Gregory brought many a smile to my face for more than a year—and also brought a new member to my family, Little Sir Gregory. I am now up to thirteen bears in the house!

Love and kisses to both Barbara Johnson and Karin Kallmaker (in no particular order—and I hope neither of their loving partners beats me up for that statement!) Thank you to two very special ladies!

Finally, for a very special femme who found me through Brett. Thank you for not finding me lacking, and for helping me find my own butch swagger.

1

Thursday

The black Jimmy veered off Woodward, crossed Six Mile and slid right into a parking lot. The dirt and gravel lot was littered with used condoms, food wrappers, empty beer bottles and chip wrappers. At night, after closing, with bums, dealers, and addicts skulking about, and no light present to illuminate the corners, it was a frightening place.

But Brett Higgins couldn't help but park in one of the seediest parts of town. She worked there.

She stepped out of her vehicle, dropped her cigarette, and ground it out fiercely with her black leather boot. She tipped her sunglasses down, looking toward the lot's back corner. A large Dumpster sat against the back of the Paradise Theatre.

"Damnit," she said under her breath and looked around. The only person near was the security guard. "What the hell is that?" she asked, pointing toward the pile of trash next to the Dumpster.

"Dunno."

Brett made a mental note to fire the lazy jerk's butt as soon as she found a replacement. She was sure a trained chimp could do his job better. But a trained chimp would probably cost more per hour than she paid her loser employees—after all, they didn't exactly need a physics degree to work at the sleaziest adult club in town.

Brett walked back toward the Dumpster, figuring someone had dumped their trash sometime in the night. Either that or she needed to can her closing clerk as well. It was a bad morning, and this was just adding to it. She kicked the pile.

Everything went quiet. All she could hear was the blood pounding in her ears. She felt cold.

"Oh, Nicola, baby . . . what'd you go and do now?"

Brett had seen Nicola in all her glory more times than she could count, but this was . . . wrong. She wanted to reach down and pull the young woman into her arms. Sweet and innocent Nicola was stark naked, buried only in her own blood.

Brett knelt down and felt for a pulse she knew wasn't there. "What did this one offer you couldn't say no to? Huh? I always told you to watch out for them, they never meant you any good."

She reached over and closed Nicola's eyes.

An overwhelming feeling of sadness consumed her. Nicola was a good girl. She didn't like to see the girls she liked hurt. She went back to her Jimmy, grabbed a blanket out of the back, and tossed it over the corpse. "The parking lot's closed this morning, keep everyone out," she told the guard.

"What's going on?"

"Nothing. Nothing at all. Frankie and I'll take care of it." She pulled her wallet from the breast pocket of her blazer, selected a

2

twenty and gave it to him. "Nothing to worry about, just keep everyone out."

"Gotcha boss," he said, pocketing the money.

She started to leave, then went back to him. "When was the last time you saw Nicola?"

He shrugged and put down the Hustler he'd been looking at. "Last night when she left." A thick stack of porno magazines sat on the small desk in his guard shack. The trash was over-flowing with coffee cups and fast food wrappers.

Brett grimaced at the foul smell. "Clean this joint up."

Frankie's car, a 2003 black Toyota 4Runner, was in the lot. She entered the building and asked Tim, the daytime clerk, "Where's Frankie?"

"Upstairs," he mumbled through a mouthful of Egg McMuffin.

"Frankie, we got a problem," Brett said, going directly into Frankie's office. "Nicola's out back, dead." She said it in her most detached voice, but couldn't help the chill that ran up and down her spine.

Frankie looked up at her. "That is a problem," he said slowly. "Whatcha wanna do about it?"

She sighed and sat down in a chair across from Frankie. "I guess we oughta report it to the police."

"Yeah."

Neither moved.

"This sure is a different way of doing business, isn't it," Brett finally said. She and Frankie weren't accustomed to calling the police for any reason. Back in the old days, they would've just taken care of the body themselves. If the police were involved, Brett knew who the only two suspects would be.

Frankie pushed the phone across the desk to Brett.

Brett put her hand on top of it, then looked at Frankie. "We can't call 'em. They'll think we did it."

"That don't make no sense—why'd you wanna go cappin' one of your own girls?"

"So you think I should call?"

Frankie shook his head sadly. "Ain't got no choice." He looked at her for a moment, "but you should see if Allie's got any friends can help us out."

An hour later, Brett was standing behind the theatre, talking with Detective Chris Vargas. "Look, I've already told you everything I know," she said. "I got here this morning, saw this trash lying here, outside of the Dumpster, so I came over to see what it was and found Nicola."

"And then you did what?"

Brett sighed. How many times was she going to have to tell the same story? "I checked for a pulse and then I ordered the guard to keep everyone out of the lot."

"So what about this blanket?" he said, pointing toward the corpse.

"I couldn't just leave her lying here, naked!"

"Keep moving, there's nothing to see here," Brett heard a cop saying at the foot of the lot.

"It's all right, I'm one of you," Randi replied, flashing her badge as she ducked under the yellow police tape and walked to Brett. "Chris," she said with a nod to Detective Vargas.

"What do you need, McMartin?" he asked.

"Ms. Higgins is a friend of mine, and so I thought it might be best if I stopped by so you didn't start thinking that maybe she's behind this."

"Just 'cause she's a friend don't mean she's innocent."

"Chris, isn't this the third dancer to get hit recently? Now what reason would Brett have for knocking off all these dancers?"

4

Detective Vargas stood and looked at her with his arms crossed over his chest. "Besides, I already know she's got an alibi." Randi laid her trump card. "It's provided by an ex-cop."

"Huh." He glanced sideways at Brett.

"I can also say, without knowing the time of death, when I called Brett's house at eleven last night, Brett answered the phone. That might not be relevant, depending on what time it happened."

"But then why was she messing with the crime scene? She admits to closing the corpse's eyes, and covering it with a blanket! Why else would she be disturbing the body except to cover something up?"

"What would you do if Nicola was one of your friends?" Brett asked.

"I wouldn't disturb a crime scene," Chris replied, "no matter what."

"So if you found your mother, your grandmother, stark naked, with her throat slashed, you would just let the cops and the photographers and everyone else see her? You wouldn't do a damned thing to show her your respect, to acknowledge all she'd done for you?"

"Listen, this is a damned hooker—don't . . ."

"C'mon Vargas, give it a rest," Randi interrupted.

He glared at Brett, jotted in his notebook, and said, "I'm sure I'll have more questions for you later."

Brett nodded respectfully and said, "Yes sir, I'll be available." She remained in place while Vargas turned and walked over to talk with the crime-scene technicians. Just how many goddamn photos did they needed to take?

Randi, too, watched as Chris joined his partner, before she turned to Brett.

"Thanks," Brett mumbled. "I was getting really tired of that. You helped me out. A lot. So thanks." It was awkward for her. She and Randi had never gotten along well, she wasn't used to thank-

5

ing people, and she didn't care much for any cop. She pulled out a cigarette and lit it with a gold-colored Zippo, which had been a gift from a woman. She couldn't remember which one.

"Yeah, well, Allie called me. I have to admit I was pleasantly surprised you decided to report it to the proper authorities."

Looking down at the ground, Brett toed the dirt. "I called Allie 'cause I'd promised her to clean up my act. The only way I could not call the cops was if she gave her okay."

"Which she'd never do." Randi pulled a stick of gum out of her pocket, popped it into her mouth, carefully folded its wrapper and pocketed it. "I'm assuming you didn't have a piece on you by the time the police showed up?"

"Of course not. I knew I'd be in enough trouble without having something like that on me—just because some little piece of shit decided to do this to poor Nicola here."

"So you knew the girl?"

"Yeah, she was one of my dancers, her real name was Karin Frost. Did you say that two other girls got hit recently?"

"Yes . . ." Randi glanced over and saw the other two detectives watching them. She began walking Brett toward the entrance to the theatre. "I've got to get going . . ."

"Do you want to come upstairs to my office?"

"No . . . no, I don't think so. Can I stop by your place later for a drink maybe?"

Brett stopped. She figured Randi didn't want to be caught talking with her too long. And she assumed Randi wanted to come by later so she could see Allie.

But Randi was helping her out. And Brett did want to pick her brain, probably as much as Randi wanted to pick hers. "Yeah, why don't you come by around seven? You know where we live."

"That'll work." She glanced at her watch. "I gotta get back to it." She began to walk away, then turned back to face Brett again. "By the way, Brett, thanks."

"For what?"

This time Randi was the nervous one apologizing. "I know how you feel about the police, so thanks for being the way you were with Chris."

Brett shook her head slowly. "Randi, you came out here to save my butt. I wasn't going to dis' you by being disrespectful to him after you said what you did."

Randi shrugged, embarrassed. "It was all true."

"Except about us being friends."

"You saved my life once, so I still owe you." She looked at Brett. "But you have to know that it won't count for anything if I ever catch you not toeing the line."

"I know," Brett said with a slight grin, going back inside.

She could keep an eye on the cops from her window while she used the phone and surfed the Net. She hadn't seen anything in the papers or on the TV news about the other murdered girls, but hadn't been looking for it. And the death of a hooker usually didn't warrant the front page. But if some loony was out there killing dancers, Brett had to make sure her girls were safe. Losing Nicola was bad enough—she didn't want to lose any more.

But as soon as Brett entered the lobby of the theatre and saw the woman, all thoughts of cops and dead dancers left her head.

Thick black hair cascaded down her back like a luxuriant waterfall, throwing off blue glints in the dim light. It stopped just above nicely rounded hips and long slender legs. Faded blue jeans, worn through in a few strategic places, clung to her body like a soft, pale, cotton skin. Without even thinking, Brett ran her hand down her silk tie, straightening and smoothing it. She adjusted the silk handkerchief in her pocket and buttoned her jacket.

Just as she donned her most charming smile and opened her mouth to speak, the woman turned and Brett's flirtatious speech was lost. She didn't believe in ghosts. But one was now standing directly in front of her.

Brett's heart fell to the floor.

She blinked her eyes, imagining a trick of the light. But when she re-opened them, everything was still the same.

A dead woman stood directly in front of her. Close enough to touch. Brett roughly grasped the turnstile that stood between them, using it to stay upright.

Storm was dead. She'd seen Storm's body. This could not be Storm. But the olive skin, dark hair and eyes, and curvaceous body were the same.

"You're Brett," the woman said, with Storm's voice.

"I'm Brett," Brett replied, finding her voice. "Can I help you with something?"

The woman smiled. It was a lovely thing. "When the clerk said I'd have to audition for Brett, I thought he was talking about a guy." She reached over the turnstile and straightened Brett's lapels. "I find it exciting that you're a woman."

Storm was sweet and shy. This woman was bold and brazen. Brett looked deep in her dark eyes. This was not the woman she'd loved so many years ago. "You knew I was a woman?" she said. Most people assumed Brett was a man.

The Storm clone tidied Brett's tie and handkerchief. "How could I not know?" She ran her hand over Brett's hair, pulling a lock rakishly down over her forehead.

Someone was playing a cruel joke on Brett. That was what this was, a cruel joke. Storm used to play with her hair, her tie, her jacket, just like this woman did. She had the same full lips, sensual movements, and teasing grin.

The woman was already toying with her. People didn't toy with Brett unless she wanted them to.

"Do you just want me to audition here, or is there somewhere . . . more private . . . where we can do it?" Her breath was warm on Brett's cheek when she whispered into her ear. Storm was sweet and naïve. This woman wasn't.

8

This woman was nothing like her Storm. "What's your name?" Brett said, pulling herself together and pushing through the turnstile as the clerk released it.

"Victoria, baby."

"Victoria what?"

"Just Victoria."

The dressing room door banged open. "Hey baby," Chantel said, putting an arm around Brett's waist as if it belonged there. Her full breasts pushed against Brett's side. Brett just kept looking at Victoria, reading every reaction on her face.

Chantel glanced at Victoria and ran a hand proprietarily down Brett's leg. "What's say we make some noise later, huh baby?"

"Chantel, did Nicola have a date or anything after work last night?"

"Nah, you know her. I 'spect she went right home after work."

Brett had overheard the guard telling the cops that Nicola had a date the night before. "So did you two walk out together?"

"What is it with you and that girl? Is she the reason you don't pay no attention to me anymore?" She had her hand possessively on Brett's ass. "I left soon's I got done, and I was up first."

The cops must not have questioned her yet. Some of these girls wouldn't notice anything unless you forced them to. "Did you happen to notice what the guard was doing when you left?" She was wondering if he had fallen asleep.

Chantel laughed. It was a deep, throaty sound. "I ain't got a clue—he was long gone by the time I left."

Tim's voice boomed over the loudspeaker system in the auditorium, "And now gentlemen, she's out to rock your world —Chantel!"

"Gotta run now," Chantel said, kissing Brett briefly on the lips, then, "Don't I know you from somewhere?" quickly to Victoria, before hurrying into the theatre without waiting for an answer.

"Brett, what're we gonna do about Nicola?" Tim, the clerk,

said, sticking his head out the door of the box office. "She was supposed to go on next."

Nicola was dead. Christ. Brett took a deep breath. "The show must go on," she said to herself. She couldn't bear to think of Nicola's lifeless body lying out back. Instead, she could focus on what she could do something about—business.

She thought about the hundred-plus girls on her call sheets who would love to do an extra shift at the Paradise. She looked at Victoria, making the decision, even as the words came out of her mouth. "You want to work here? Then you go on in half an hour."

Victoria's eyebrows shot up. "You don't even know if I can dance."

"Yes, I do. I know everything about you." This woman could dance and turn boys on. In fact, she knew everything this gorgeous woman was capable of. "The rules here are simple: dancers pay us two-hundred bucks for each schedule, whether it's a three-day weekend set, or a full week. You pay fifty bucks extra for each tardy, and a hundred for each absence. If you owe a fine, you pay it before you dance again. But you can charge whatever you'd like for lap dances."

Victoria looked nervous. Brett wondered why. If she was a dancer, or wanted to be one, she should be excited Brett was giving her a chance without having her audition. This was what she wanted, wasn't it? "Well, do you want the job or not?" Brett asked.

"Yes, but—I just got to town . . . came up from Indiana."

Storm was from Indiana.

"Okay, I'll postpone the start-up fee just this once. This is the only break you're getting, got it?"

Victoria fluttered her long eyelashes. "Maybe I can find a way to make it up to you?"

"You can by paying me the two hundred in three days."

"I don't have a costume."

"Do you want the job or not? I ain't got time for this shit. You don't wanna dance, I'll find someone else."

Victoria's chin went up. "I'll wear what I have on. Problem with that?"

Brett looked her up and down. "The boys'll love seeing you strip out of what you're wearing." She turned to the clerk and spoke to him through the thick bullet-proof glass that separated him from the lobby, "Tim, find her some music to dance to."

Tim leered at Victoria. "How 'bout some Prince?"

Brett shook her head. "Do you have any Enigma?" Enigma was more sensuous and imaginative than Prince's bold and blatantly sexual music and lyrics.

Storm had always stripped to Enigma.

"Enigma?" Victoria asked.

"You gotta problem with that?"

Victoria stared at Brett. "How did you know?"

"Got it right here," Tim said to Brett, holding up a CD.

"That's what she'll dance to. And she'll just use her regular clothes. Seeing her take off so much clothing ought to really get the boys worked up. They'll love it for today. Just get a real costume for tomorrow." Most girls didn't have a costume. They were more likely to use cheap lingerie.

"Should I just call her Victoria?" Tim asked.

"No. Call her . . . Tempest." Brett liked hot dancers because they brought the men in. After all, dancer's fees were only a part of how she made her money. She made more charging men ten bucks a pop to get into the theatre to see them.

"Now, do you want the job or not," Brett asked, "or are you getting cold feet?"

2

Brett walked into her office and went to the window facing the parking lot. She wondered how long the cops would keep it cordoned off as a crime scene. Police on the premises was not conducive to business.

She only stepped away from the window when she saw them zipping Nicola into a body bag.

She hadn't wanted to see that. She'd liked Nicola, who'd always been a good girl. Brett walked to the other wall of her office and looked out the window toward the same scene she saw every day, with one key difference: people were behaving better. Normally, Brett would see hit and runs, drug deals, muggings, and other forms of petty illegalities, but the police lights blinking on the surrounding buildings had people behaving. This was a bad neighborhood, where a single woman didn't dare to walk alone after dark, unless she had a death wish or was packing some major fire power.

She tossed the Yellow Pages from her bookshelf onto her desk, quickly finding the listings for security companies. If someone was killing dancers, the least she could do was spend a few more bucks to get a reliable security guard on the premises. She usually just hired guys who looked like they could walk and chew gum at the same time, and paid them minimum wage, under the table. After all, there was no reason to cut unnecessarily into her profit margin.

It wasn't until the third agency that she was able to get an armed guard for that night. They would have someone there at 6 p.m. that night, and every day from 9 a.m. until the last customer and employee left at night.

She would pay through the nose for this, but if she didn't protect her dancers, she wouldn't have any profit at all.

She turned on the power strip for her computer, kicked her feet up on her desk, and started searching the Net for information on the other murdered dancers Randi had referred to.

As she added and deleted search words and phrases, her mind kept wandering. She looked across the room at a picture of herself, Storm, Frankie and Rick that was almost a decade old. Since that long-ago day, she had changed into a different person, with a different life. How different her life would be now if she had believed then that she had been in love with Storm. She admitted to herself that she hadn't thought she was capable of love, and hadn't thought anyone could love her. Really love her. Flaws and all.

Brett continued to gaze at the picture. Storm's long, black hair fell back over her shoulders, and her beautifully flawless olive skin covered well-defined features. She remembered how each time her Storm had learned something new about her, she had not looked away. Instead she looked at Brett with more love and devotion, no matter how rotten and evil Brett felt.

They'd had so much in common that everything each learned about the other brought them unbelievably closer still. They had the same nightmares, the same gruesome memories of abuse, and the same dreams of success. Brett could look deep into Storm's eyes and see her own soul reflected there. Storm was a mirror image of her—mirrored through their differences, but reflected through their sameness.

Brett cleared her throat and grabbed a Kleenex from the box on her desk. She hated how allergies sometimes made her eyes water.

She pushed her hand through her thick, dark hair. She glanced toward her office door, ensuring that it was still closed.

Brett enjoyed pleasing Allie and giving her pleasure. But when she looked into her eyes, Brett realized, she didn't see a reflection of her own self. But she did see love there, and shouldn't love be enough?

It had been about a decade since Brett had dumped Storm for Allie. She'd realized to be with Allie, she had to be monogamous. She had to be faithful to Allie, so she'd dumped Storm.

First she'd dumped the exquisite stripper Storm, then Rick, her old boss, had been killed. Brett had given up her life of crime and went on the lam, hiding away with Allie until it was safe for her and Allie to come back home to Detroit, something that only happened recently. Now she was back in business, but only on the legal side of things. At least she still had Frankie, who had worked with her, Rick and Storm those many years before.

She had done all she could for Allie, and to ensure they could have their happily ever after.

Brett looked at herself in a mirror, holding up her façade. She let her shoulders droop, and looked at herself frankly. She didn't know why any good femme would go for her as she really was.

Storm had loved her the way she was, but how long would Allie?

• • •

Allie leaned back in her chair and stared at the computer screen. She was searching for a job online, but couldn't seem to keep her mind on what she was reading. She was wondering what had happened at the Paradise.

She called Brett.

"Paradise Theatre."

"Tim, this is Allie, is Brett there?"

"Yeah, just a minute, let me buzz her."

He put Allie on hold, then came back on. "She's not in her office. Let me go find her." He put the phone down on the desk. Allie could hear loud music playing in the auditorium. It sounded like Enigma. Allie tried to remember the last time she heard Enigma. It had been years ago. Brett never played it. Not anymore.

"Allie?" Brett answered. "What's up?"

"Did Randi get there all right? How is everything going? Is everything all right?"

"Randi was a real sweetheart—got the cops off my back, at least for now."

"Are they still there?"

"Yeah. Got the whole parking lot sealed off as a crime scene and they're questioning everyone. Business is gonna suck today —who the hell's gonna want to come to a strip club crawling with cops?"

"Brett, you did the right thing, that's what's important."

"Easy for you to say, what are my girls gonna be thinking? I

15

mean, if there ain't no customers, they can't make any money, and they're not just here for the kicks, you know."

"Brett, Randi said something about this being the third one in about a week. If it continues, you won't have any dancers left to bring the customers in with. They'll all be running scared."

"Do you know anything about these girls who have gotten it?" she asked, her voice tight and angry.

"Randi didn't really say much of anything. She wanted to get down there right away. She was sure the detectives in charge would be suspicious of you."

"And I'm grateful to her for that, because that's exactly what happened. She didn't mention anything about where the dancers were, or their names or anything?"

"No, Brett, she didn't."

"Have you read anything about these murders? Has there been something in the newspapers that I missed?"

"No, Brett, I haven't. I don't think there's been any news about it at all."

"Goddamnit! I still should have known!"

"Listen, I have to get back to looking for a job," Allie said. She couldn't talk to Brett when she was in such a mood.

"Hey, Allie . . . wait a minute."

"Yes?"

"I love you."

Allie smiled. "I love you too."

After she hung up the phone, Allie got up to find a CD. It took her a while, but she found and inserted it into the computer. She hit the play button and then rotated around in her chair to continue the job search while she listened to the eerie yet sensuous tones of Enigma. It was the music she'd heard at the Paradise.

The last time she heard Enigma was the last time she saw Storm dance.

Her smile faded.

She wondered what one could do with a Criminal Justice major besides be a cop or detective? What did she want to be when she grew up?

She looked again at the jobs open in the Detroit metro area. Of everything she could be doing right now, looking at these sites and jobs was the least interesting of them.

Allie surfed to detnews.com and could only find one short article that had run about the first dancer's murder.

With a shiver, Allie imagined how Nicola's body had been discovered. Brett walked out there this morning and stumbled across it. Her wake-up call to a brand new day. She imagined Brett closing the dead woman's eyes and covering her naked body before going in and calling her, then the police. Allie knew Brett shouldn't have touched the body, but Brett wouldn't be able to help herself.

Most of society thought girls like this one gave up their rights when they had the audacity to do things that got them murdered. A lot of people would think it was the victim's fault. She was obviously an unsavory woman in an unsavory business. No one to care about.

Allie pulled out a notebook and started jotting down questions. What, if anything, had the other dancers been wearing when they were found? Had they been sexually assaulted? How had they been murdered? In fact, she wanted to compare everything about the crime scenes she could.

From the article, Allie had noticed that the first girl was found within twelve hours of her murder. She wondered if the killer was flaunting his trophies, or if there was another reason for the quick discovery of it?

She reached for the telephone and left a message for Randi to call her. She would have more details than the cursory article in the newspaper.

17

3

Brett glanced around the dirty theatre. It was an exact duplicate of the theatre Brett had first seen Storm in so many years ago. You walked in from the grimy streets of Six and Woodward into a dingy hallway leading to the straight or the gay side. On either end you'd walk into a corridor with a turnstile, which the clerk's booth looked onto through thick, bullet-proof glass.

It was in that area on the straight side that Brett had met Victoria that morning.

The same sorts of movies that had shown at the original Paradise were still showing constantly on the huge screens at the front of each auditorium, sound muted when the dancers performed. Although the titles changed from week to week, different from the ones that had cast shadow on Storm's olive skin so many years ago, they might as well have been the same. Brett had stopped being able to tell one from another years ago.

Standing at the back of the auditorium, Brett shook her head to pull herself back to the present.

It was all the same. Except now it was Tempest onstage, with the lights from the movie flickering over *her* body, the eerie, sensual music of Enigma setting *her* scene.

Victoria had hesitated just a moment before going onstage, pausing and looking out over the faces of the men who grew restless, wanting to see pussy *now*.

But she was a true professional. She boldly strode onstage, looking out over the men as if she owned them. Her gaze went from man to man as she moved to the music, gyrating her hips while she unbuttoned her shirt, slowly, teasingly. She wasn't wearing a bra, so a beautiful expanse of rich skin was revealed. She left the shirt on, unbuttoned, while she unzipped her jeans. Wearing her normal street clothes, but undone like this, she looked extremely erotic. The combination of so much revealed, but so much hidden, lit a fire deep within Brett.

Victoria looked directly at Brett, a slow grin spreading over her face, as if the thought of Brett watching her made her happy. Some people thought that someone onstage couldn't see the audience, but Brett knew they could.

She stared right at Brett when she eased her jeans down her long legs, taking her underwear with them. She danced about the stage. Every time she faced front, her eyes met Brett's, as if she were aware of only Brett. This intimacy fueled the fire within Brett. It was almost as if the two of them were the only people in this theatre, and Victoria's dancing was just foreplay.

When she spun around, her shirt opened, revealing even more of her beautiful, curvaceous flesh. Then the shirt dropped to the stage.

Victoria ran her hands down her body, then back up, holding her breasts, teasing the nipples while looking right at Brett, as if she were imagining Brett's hands on her. Brett knew she wanted her hands on Victoria, feeling the silkiness of her skin and exploring her luxurious curves.

Brett loosened her tie, her breathing becoming heavier by the minute.

Victoria's feet were slightly apart, opening her beautiful thighs invitingly, showing off the dark triangle of hair nestled between them. She reached down to brush that hair with her fingertips, slowly moving her hips side to side, still looking at Brett, then she thrust her pelvis forward, opening herself further, just for Brett, who ran her hand nervously down her tie.

She could imagine what Victoria would taste like. Every inch of Victoria's sensuous body was burning its mark on Brett's mind, and Brett didn't like it one bit. She didn't like losing her rock-hard control, the control she'd developed through her years in the industry. She'd learned long ago how to hide her lust when she saw a naked woman. She had to remember she was no longer a free agent, able to do whatever she chose. She belonged to Allie.

Victoria licked her lips, then reached down between her legs and touched herself. Brett wanted to climb onto stage, take those wonderful hips in her hands and bury herself between Victoria's legs to drink deeply of her essence.

She had thought Allie was what she wanted. She had made her decision after meeting Allie's parents. But had it been simply because of the familial love and devotion so apparent in the Sullivan family and so entirely absent from Brett's own life?

She looked at Victoria onstage. She always stuck by her choices. And, after all, it was now a moot point—Storm was dead.

But Victoria wasn't.

Angela walked up as Brett stood outside the auditorium, leaning forward against the door, and laid a warm hand on her shoulder.

"Is there anything I can do?" Angela asked, her quiet voice comforting.

"No, just thinking about the new girl, and how she reminds me of someone I knew once."

"Good or bad?"

Brett grinned. "Probably good, I guess you'd say."

"Then why do you look so down?"

"Because you might say very good," Brett replied with a wink, trying to regain her composure. She couldn't believe a dancer had caught her like this.

"Anything I can do about it?" Angela replied, running her hand casually over Brett's bicep.

"No . . . no. I'm all right, really." Angela, unlike other dancers, respected Brett's commitment to Allie.

"Okay then." Angela turned and began walking away from Brett.

Brett reached out to touch her shoulder. "By the way, what do you think about this new girl?"

"She seems alright." Angela seemed somewhat hesitant.

"But what?" Brett prodded.

"Well, but . . . I can't help but think that I've seen her around before." Angela stood meekly looking down at the floor, like some sort of Catholic school girl confessing to Mother Superior. The only time she really acted like a dancer was when she was onstage, stripping for the men.

Well, then, and when she was giving lap dances.

"Where?" Brett asked.

"I'm not sure. I just can't shake the feeling, though, that it was a while ago."

"Think about it. Any idea where?"

Angela slowly shook her head. "I can't place it exactly."

Brett took a deep breath and looked at Angela. Victoria was lying about being new to town. "Let me know if you remember."

"Brett, there wasn't anything goin' on between you and Nicola, was there?" Frankie asked when Brett came back upstairs, needing to cool down from seeing Victoria dance.

Brett sat in a guest chair. "No. Shit no. You know I don't do dancers anymore."

"But you did once." He grinned. "Well, more than once."

Frankie's knowledge without condemnation sent a whirlwind of images, feelings, and women flying through Brett's mind. Long legs, full breasts, soft skin . . . and Storm, always Storm. She knew she needed to find out what Victoria's story was, because she'd be bugged by memories of Storm until she knew everything. Something about Victoria rocked Brett's world to its very core.

But then Brett's mind rocketed back toward what had started this conversation: Nicola. The dancers Brett liked she took the time to get to know. She knew Nicola. And she didn't deserve this. And no matter how sleazy or drugged out any of them were, none of them deserved to be killed.

Brett jumped to her feet. The authorities wouldn't be working very hard to solve these murders. If she wanted to keep her dancers alive, if she wanted to save the few good girls like Nicola and Storm, the ones who had merely wandered off the path, she had to get involved. She would have to figure out who was doing the killing and stop him. "It's all up to us," she said to Frankie. "If this is the third one, we have to stop it, before we ain't got any business left at all. The cops ain't gonna do crap to help us."

"How're we gonna do it?"

Brett stared across the desk at Frankie. She had been back in town long enough that she should've heard about this. She was out of contact. Frankie wasn't working the streets as much as he should, and she wasn't networking enough with the other bar owners.

This would have to be rectified.

She needed to get her ears back to the pavement. "The old-fashioned way. I'll check with the owners, you hit your connections. I've already hired a guard service to replace that dip shit we've got now. The girls are not to leave at any time by themselves. I don't want anything happening to any more of our girls."

● ● ●

Randi looked down at her desk when she returned to the station and smiled to see the message from Allie. She knew it was irrational, but anything with Allie's name, smell or memory attached to it drew her in. She couldn't help but long for the feel of Allie's soft, warm, naked body curled up next to her again. It had been many years ago, but those few months she'd shared with Allie were the happiest of her life. They had only been possible because Allie had broken up with Brett because of Storm. Allie and Brett had been separated for several years when Randi hooked up with Allie, but then Allie went back to Brett.

She shook the memories from her mind and picked up the phone, dialing the number she knew by heart.

"Hello?" Allie said.

"You rang?" Randi answered, smiling at the sound of Allie's voice.

"Randi?"

"Your ever-faithful servant," Randi said. She always tried to be her most charming with Allie. Part of the reason Allie was with Brett was her supposed charm.

Allie laughed. "I was wondering what you're doing later on tonight?"

23

"Why? Did you want to arrange a little tryst?"

"Randi! I just want to get together to talk about the girl who died this morning—and the ones before."

"Hm. Maybe I can squeeze you in. I'm meeting Brett at seven for drinks at your place, so maybe I could talk with you after?"

"You little shit. Why didn't you just say so in the first place?"

"Because then I wouldn't have an excuse to keep talking with you."

"Seven o'clock for drinks at our place. I'll see you then, Randi."

Randi wanted to tell Allie she loved her. Instead she said, "I'm looking forward to it."

Randi sat looking at the far wall for a few minutes, remembering how many times she and Allie had to rewind and rerun the video tape of some *Nightmare on Elm Street* movie. Allie would get scared when Freddie showed up, scream, and then hide her face in Randi's shoulder. Randi would comfort her, wrapping her arms tightly about her lithe figure, and then they'd start kissing and end up making love, missing most of the movie.

The same thing happened over and over again. Randi wasn't sure if they ever made it through the movie.

Randi shook her head, knowing she shouldn't be dwelling on the past. She was dating again—in fact, she was dating a particularly lovely woman named Danielle, who was far more compatible with her, in all actuality. Danielle wasn't the extraordinary beauty Allie was—her features were soft, whereas Allie's were finely sculpted; her curves were so soft and supple she never felt, like she sometimes did with Allie, that she had to encourage her to eat more; and, perhaps best of all, she was much closer to Randi's own age.

Randi sometimes felt like a child molester, or a dirty old man, lusting after someone 15 years younger than herself.

There, she said it, she lusted after Allie. Pure and simple. She didn't love her, she just lusted after her. That was all. Danielle was much more her speed.

24

The sound of raucous male voices behind her brought her back to reality.

"I think she's the hottest one so far. I wouldn't mind spending some time with her—when she was alive, that is."

"Thank god, man. I'd hate to have to start worrying you gettin' a boner during an autopsy."

There was a deep, heart-felt sigh, and then Chris said, "Well, I suppose we'd better go notify the next of kin. God, I hate this shit!"

Randi stood up and looked at Detectives Phil Norberg and Chris Vargas, whose desks were right behind hers. "Hey, you two, how's it going?" she asked, approaching their side-by-side desks. Chris was rifling through a stack of folders on his desk. She was surprised to see them back at the station already. Had they already finished questioning everyone at the Paradise?

"Shit, Randi, this is a mess," he replied, looking up at her. "Third one in about a week, and all of them found by Dumpsters, and you know what that means."

"It must be a nightmare to try to find any sort of a lead in all that garbage."

"You got that right. We're hoping that now the bodies are piling up, they'll pull us from some of our other cases to focus more on this one. I mean, this asshole ain't showing a single sign of stopping—in fact, it looks like he's gaining momentum. I mean, if it gets down to one-a-day, even the newspapers around here will have to start to notice it."

All too often crimes in Detroit and its suburbs were investigated in a priority ranking. Rich white men were at the top of the list, poor women of color were at the bottom. Hookers ranked even lower. Randi could think of more cases than she liked that were assigned time and resources using this unwritten rating scale.

Because these recent murder victims were considered unimportant, the department would not allocate sufficient resources toward finding their killer. Randi had to live with such sad truths every day of her life. She fought against racism, sexism, homophobia and classism—not only to protect her job, but to protect and serve the citizens of this city equally.

Randi looked from Phil to Chris and back again. "Listen, I was wondering if you could do me a favor?"

They exchanged glances, and Chris said, "What is it?" Randi already knew that they would probably readily agree to anything she asked for, because she always found time to help them out. She'd also saved their lives once in a drug bust that went bad.

Randi leaned back against her desk. "Well, I told my friend Brett I'd look into this. The dancer killed last night was one of her favorites, and Brett's pretty pissed about it." She shrugged. "And since I got in early this morning and cleared off my desk, I've got some time to maybe go with one of you to notify the next of kin?"

Chris shot Phil a grin, and kicked his feet up on his desk. "I was just telling Phil I was surprised you haven't started poking around in all this yet. I mean, hookers are often connected with crime bosses." Randi was assigned to the city's organized crime unit.

"Any involvement I'd have in this would be on my own time. But as a favor to Brett, I'd like to look into it. Just so long as I'm not stepping on your toes."

"Must be some friend for you to go so far out of your way," Chris said. It was well known throughout the station that Randi was a dyke, but she was still respected. She was a damned good cop.

Randi just shrugged. "We've known each other quite a while. And I worked with her girlfriend years ago."

"Her girlfriend?" Chris asked with a raised eyebrow.

Phil stood up and pulled on his jacket. "Chris, looks like this is your lucky day," he said. "Randi can come with me to inform the girl's family."

"Thanks a lot," Chris said, pulling over a large stack of manila file folders.

26

4

"You've got it made, Randi," Phil said, as they climbed into the car. "One case at a time. Man, I'd like to be in your shoes."

"One case at a time? Hardly," Randi replied. She had to be constantly vigilant, looking for anything that would help pull those in power down. "So, what can you tell me at this point?"

"The only real thing we got so far is those strange rosaries the killer's using to tie their hands together."

"Rosaries?" Randi asked.

"Oh, man, you really didn't see the body this morning."

"I just stopped by to help out a friend."

"Well, all three of these girls—and this is the third in a week—

have been found naked with their hands tied together in front of them with a strange sort of rosary."

"What's so strange about it?"

"Well, you gotta understand, I was raised Catholic, y'know, and I used to have a rosary myself." He nervously glanced at Randi. "So anyway, these rosaries are longer than normal. There's a couple of extra decades to it. It's got seven instead of five." He let his voice trail off and gave a shrug.

Randi wasn't surprised to hear Phil refer to the decades of a rosary so casually, nor was she surprised to find out he was Catholic. After all, this was Detroit. "Is there anything else different about them?"

"Well, they're made out of a strange green glass."

"So they're not reinforced or anything?"

"No. Why?"

"Well, rosaries aren't too strong—I mean, they're corded together basically with string." Randi herself came from a good, Irish Catholic church-going family. "So they couldn't be used to restrain the girl prior to death."

Phil was nodding. "Yeah. They had to have been tied up like that after they're killed, 'cause those things ain't strong enough to rope together a baby's wrists. Plus, well, the hands are in front of them, instead of behind . . ."

"And so they're probably not being tied for some kinky sexual reason," Randi said. A lot of times people would be tied spread eagle, or with their hands behind their backs. Those positions open up the sexual organs, as well as keep the victim from being able to cover herself from the assailant. "But it must be for some religious reason they're being killed. I mean, given the facts, that's the only logical explanation."

"Yeah," Phil said, "or more specifically, it's a Catholic reason."

Randi looked at him curiously.

"Nobody else reveres the Virgin like we do."

28

Randi put her head against the headrest and closed her eyes for a minute. "So now we've got it narrowed down to what? Half the area's population? I mean, think about how many Irish, Polacks, and all the rest we've got here?"

"I know, but if the killer is leaving a rosary, I'd stake my reputation that it means he is Catholic. And that this is being done for some perverted religious reason. Most likely. So at least we know that much."

"So this could be, more specifically, something to do with the Virgin Mary. I mean, if the rosary is about Mary, and these killers usually think everything through down to the detail, then . . .?"

"That's a very good point, especially since we've discovered that this type of rosary is specifically known as either a Rosary of the Seven Joys of the Blessed Virgin Mary, or of the Seven Sorrows of the Blessed Virgin Mary. That's why it has seven decades, with an ending of two Hail Marys, and then an Our Father and one last Hail Mary."

"So tell me, detective, is there any significance to the green color of the beads? I know they come in a lot of different materials and colors, but most of the ones I've seen are made out of little black beads."

Phil shook his head. "Not anything that we've found. But we did track down where the killer got them from."

"What?"

"One Catholic supply shop in Hamtramck had rosaries exactly like these in stock. We found it."

"Did they remember who they'd sold them to?"

Phil grimaced. "They had them in stock," he continued as if Randi hadn't even spoken. "Someone came in recently and bought them all one night."

"So? What'd you find out?"

"The clerk who worked the next morning had noticed they were all gone, and that's how we found out about it. The woman said they'd had them for years, never selling a single one, and suddenly, one morning, she got into work and they were all gone."

"So did the clerk who sold them remember anything?"

"We don't know."

"What do you mean?"

"She's dead. All we know is that about a month ago, this one little old woman sold all of their green, Seven Joys rosaries, and, since that time, she dropped dead of a heart attack."

Randi paused, not believing this sort of rotten luck. How was it possible that they could have a killer leave such a memorable calling card, and be unable to track it down?

"He paid with cash, so there's no paperwork trail to follow."

Randi couldn't look at Phil when she asked, her voice trembling, "How many rosaries were there?"

"Two dozen."

Randi stared straight ahead. Any hope she had that the killer would just stop, suddenly, on his own, vanished. "Are there any other commonalities between these victims?"

Phil shook his head. "Nope, none at all. Different hair colors, body types, races, ethnicities and socio-economic backgrounds. Etcetera. I mean, they are all dancers, which probably means they're also hookers. The murder weapon seems consistent— they've all had their throats slashed, but . . . nothing more than that, except . . ."

Randi waited for him to continue, and when he didn't, she picked it up, "Except?"

"There's no defense wounds on any of them, Randi, which means that the girls probably knew whoever's doing it."

"And that's why you were harassing Brett this morning."

"Hey, we weren't harassing her. Just questioning her thoroughly—and you can't blame us, can you? I mean, you'd blame us if we didn't make sure her story stayed the same—especially since she admitted to interfering with the crime scene! But anyway, why didn't she mention you calling her last night?"

Randi turned away and looked out the window. "I didn't call her, I called her girlfriend. I'm more her friend than Brett's. Brett's the one who answered the phone, and she probably didn't remember it this morning."

"Her girlfriend's friend?"

"Yeah. Allie's. Brett and I really don't get along well."

"And why is that?"

"I did a major stakeout on her a while ago. I'm pretty sure she's cleaned her ass up now. Regardless, I know how much her dancers mean to her, so I know she's not behind this."

"Well, we obviously don't have the autopsy results back yet, so I can't tell you if your alibi clears her for sure."

"I'm telling you, Phil, she's not behind this. To be honest, she wouldn't call the police if she was—and we wouldn't be finding the bodies this quickly either."

"That's honest." He turned and grinned at her. "So, you got the hots for her girlfriend? She must really be something to write home about then, huh?"

Randi laughed. "Okay, so you mentioned the murder weapon—what's it look like?"

"It's a short blade. They all got it right across the front of the throat, hitting the jugular. Although they die fairly quickly, it's not quick enough that they shouldn't have any defense wounds. Even if this guy is sneaking up behind them and slashing their throats, they should still hear something, or at least react when he cuts them, but they don't."

"How do we know it's a short blade?"

"The cuts aren't very deep, but are surrounded with bruising, as if the hilt of the knife and his hand hit the skin almost immediately following insertion. Like it's an X-acto knife or something. Short and sharp. But he cuts all the way across the throat to ensure he hits all the major arteries and veins to make sure they die."

31

"And since there're no defense wounds, they must know him. Any evidence about how he approaches them or anything?"

"Nothing," he said, shaking his head. "We've talked to everyone we can find who was around at the time of the murders, and we have absolutely nothing. But you know how hard it is to find witnesses for crimes like these."

Randi sat back, thinking how nurse's shoes don't squeak. This guy must be wearing shoes that didn't make a sound—or else, Phil was right, the girls did know him.

The lack of defense wounds showed the victims were caught by surprise; they trusted the killer so much that even as they died they were unable to fight back.

That, or he was too well covered for anything to rub off on him. Either way, he was very ingenious.

"Yeah, all these girls," Phil was saying, "different neighborhoods, different backgrounds. Just dancers, going home when they got it. But it was always at night, after closing."

"And they were always found outside, by a Dumpster, with their hands tied together in front of them with a seven-decade rosary, naked, with no defense wounds," Randi said. "Same murder weapon, short and sharp, so there's bruising and a lot of blood."

"That's about it. But your *friend* Brett might want to look out."

"Why?"

"Well, the first two did get it at the same place." He shrugged. "Might be a pattern, might not be. But if I were her, I'd watch it. He might be planning on hitting victim number four at her place as well."

"You don't know Brett, then. Anyway, were these women dancing at the same place, or were they found at the same place?"

"All of the above."

Randi slowly drew in a breath, thinking about this. "So it looks like he might do two in one place?"

"Yeah. Maybe." He shrugged again. "But there's another reason your friend oughta watch out."

"And why is that?"

"These women weren't found *in* the Dumpsters, but next to them. This could be for a lot of reasons, and one of those is that maybe the killer ain't strong enough to lift them into it. So maybe it's a woman."

"What are you saying, Phil?"

"I'm saying that Brett Higgins is a woman."

"Phil, I've known her for a long time, and I can tell you . . ." Repeating herself about Brett's innocence wouldn't have any further effect. Phil needed evidence. "If that's the only reason you have to suspect her, then you'd better keep digging. I've seen her do bench presses, and she'd have no problem heaving these girls into the Dumpsters."

"She's the best suspect, the only logical suspect, we've got."

"Are you planning a stakeout at the Paradise?"

"He hit the same place twice only once. There's not enough to justify the expense of a stakeout." He shrugged and looked apologetically at Randi. "You know how it is. He's done it once, so it's not a pattern. Besides, he might see a stakeout or whatever. We just don't know enough yet about who he is or what he's after yet. I'm guessing our best bet is to watch the customers. He must go to these places first, after all. You know, check the place out before he chooses his victim."

"So what we do know is it's a religious murder, because no one else would lay out a body like that, placing the hands in front of the body is obviously a tie-in to the Catholic ritual of laying out bodies, like they do at the viewing before burying the body." She sat back, staring up at the car ceiling, thinking. "We also know that the girls most likely know the murderer, and so we have to figure out why these girls, why now, and why like this?"

"Yeah. You're more than welcome to look over the files and

anything else. Chris and I have got several hot cases, and with how we're under-staffed, I just don't see them reassigning any of them so we can focus more on this. We need to catch this creep, but there's not a lot we can do. You know how it is." They pulled up in front of a neat house, on a street of neat, cookie-cutter houses. "You do the talking, I hate doing this sort of thing. Her real name was Karin Frost. Daughter of Emily and Paul Frost."

Randi gave him a nod and led the way up the neat sidewalk, carefully edged and surrounded by thick, green grass.

"Mrs. Frost?" Randi said when the door was opened by a frail, elderly woman.

"Yes?"

Randi wished Allie was with her. Allie was good at things like this. Randi herself never had been. She knew too well what it was like to receive bad news. So did Allie, but it gave her greater empathy. Randi couldn't get past her own sorrow and fear.

"Ma'am, I'm afraid we have some bad news for you," Randi said, flipping open her badge. "We're with the Detroit Police Department. I'm Detective McMartin and this is Detective Norberg. You do have a daughter named Karin?"

"No. No, I don't have a daughter," Mrs. Frost said, fearfully looking about as she stepped back into the house.

"Karin Frost isn't your daughter then?" Phil asked, his eyebrows knitted together in confusion.

Randi peered into the house. "You are Mrs. Emily Frost, correct?"

"Yes, yes I am."

"We discovered information that led us to believe you are the next-of-kin for one Karin Maria Frost. Is this incorrect, then?"

"What's happened to Karin?"

"Ma'am, I am sorry to inform you that Karin expired sometime this morning." Mrs. Frost continued backing into the house. Randi followed. "Are we incorrect in that you are the next of kin?"

34

"No, no, I am . . ." She gasped, turning from them. "Tell me, what happened to my little girl?"

Randi followed Emily and looked around the modest living room. Half-hidden on the TV in a small frame was a decade-old family portrait. Randi walked over and picked it up.

The picture showed a much-younger Emily next to a dignified man with close-cropped hair. Two children knelt before them.

"Karin had always been such a sweet girl," Emily said, taking the picture from Randi and looking at it for a long moment before placing it face down.

"I got two girls myself," Phil said.

Emily looked at Phil, then glanced around before saying, "She really was a beautiful child."

"Why don't you tell me about her?" Randi said.

A tear fell down Emily's cheek. She looked up into Randi's eyes. "She really is dead, isn't she? I mean, why else would you be here?" There was a tone of desperation to her voice.

Randi wanted to pull the short, white-haired woman into her arms and pat her back, but she couldn't. "Mrs. Frost, Emily…" Perhaps using the woman's first name would create an intimacy between them and get her to talk. "I know this is a difficult time for you, but . . . I need to ask you some questions."

Emily nodded, then said. "What happened to her?"

"Somebody slit her throat, ma'am," Phil said.

"Oh, god . . ."

"Sit down, Emily," Randi said, leading her to the sofa. "Can I get you anything? A glass of water?"

"No, no, I'm fine."

Phil glanced down at his notes. "Tell, me, ma'am, is there anybody you can think of who would want to see Karin dead?" he asked.

Emily shook her head. "I . . . I don't know. I really just don't know." She looked up at Randi. "I haven't seen her in years, to be quite honest."

Randi met Phil's eyes, telling him silently to leave this to her. If she had a rough touch, his was more like a sledge hammer. "Why don't you tell me what happened?"

Emily nodded. "We were always a close-knit family. I always thanked the Lord that we were safe from all the troubles of this world. Paul Junior and Karin stayed away from drugs. We had no teen pregnancies. They did well in school. They were model children. Always in on time, taking jobs during high school by their own choice. I believe that working gives children good values so they learn early that things don't just come to them, that they must work for them." Emily looked into Randi's eyes with such eagerness that all Randi could do was nod in agreement. "I knew we had to be doing something right. But then . . ."

"What happened?" Phil asked.

"Dad, Paul, Paul Senior that is, came home early one evening and found . . ." Emily pulled a handkerchief from her housecoat pocket and wiped at her eyes. When Randi didn't prompt her, she continued, "He found Karin and another girl . . ." she again dropped off.

This time Emily needed prompting. "What did he see, Emily?" Randi asked.

"He saw Karin and her best friend Jenny together . . . naked . . . in bed." Randi wouldn't prompt her again. Not this time. Emily looked up at her in desperation. "They were doing things together that only men and women are supposed to do together!" She said it as if she expected Randi to agree. She wanted consolation and coddling.

"What did he do?" Randi said.

"He told her to repent and ask the Lord's forgiveness—for we all know He forgives. But she wouldn't. She wouldn't repent her ways, she wouldn't pray with him. She was an evil child."

"When did you last see your daughter?" Phil asked.

Emily found her resolve. "Tell me, what was she like at the end? Was she still under those evil influences?"

36

"I don't know ma'am. I didn't know her," Randi said, honestly. "I just know that nobody should die like she did."

"If you want to know who did it, then, I'd look into those evil . . . lesbians. I bet they did this to her." Emily looked up into Randi's eyes. "She died because of them. I bet she didn't confess either. She's gonna rot in hell because of it you know."

"Can you think of anybody who'd want to kill her?" Randi asked.

"Anybody who knows right from wrong," Emily answered, her eyes filled with righteous conviction as she looked up into Randi's. She reached forward as if to take Randi's hands into her own shaky, wrinkled ones.

Randi pulled away. "So you and your husband only started having problems with Karin when you caught her with another girl? When you realized she was a lesbian?"

"She was no such thing! That Jenny girl got to her—recruited her! They did something to her! Brainwashed her..."

"Do you happen to know Jenny's last name, or have her or her parents' address or telephone number?" Phil asked.

"No, of course not. I wanted nothing to do with anybody who could raise their child in such a manner."

"So your husband blames you for it, and now—" Randi said.

"Of course it was my fault, I did something wrong! I didn't respect her father enough, I didn't go to confession enough. It's my fault, all my fault that she's dead." Emily dissolved into tears, holding herself in abject misery, pulling lamely at the tissues in her pocket.

"So Paul Senior got very upset when he saw Karin. Did he hit her? Or her friend?" Phil asked.

Emily looked aghast. "Of course not! He would never do such a thing!" Randi had a feeling she was telling the truth.

Phil looked over at Randi. "Are you sure, ma'am? Has he spoken with her or any of her friends lately?"

"He's not spoken to her since he ordered her out of the house. It's been years."

"Are you sure about that?"

"Of course I am. He'd tell me if he did."

This was obviously a dead end. They'd have to question the father directly.

"Can I look in her room?" Randi asked, knowing the only details she would get were from Karin's personal possessions. This woman would give nothing more than further recriminations and guilt.

Emily looked up. "We cleared it out the moment she left. We wanted no more of her sin in this house. We have a son after all. Somebody to carry on the family name. We didn't need that evil influence touching him as well."

5

Brett climbed into her Jimmy and headed north on Woodward to check with some of her old contacts. This would also afford her the opportunity to start looking around town for new dancers to recruit to the Paradise. After all, she did have to start rebuilding the enterprises she and Rick DeSilva had originally developed. Granted, now they had cut down to the purely legal activities: a dozen adult bookstores in and around Detroit, the theatre, a phone sex service, a LesBiGay book and gift store, and a distribution service, supplying a number of small, independent adult bookstores with pornographic magazines, videos and devices. The only illegal things they now did were cooking the accounts—keeping two sets of records. Since they dealt largely in cash, they only needed to claim a few employees at each business, and didn't have to claim much of their trade. Why pay more taxes than they had to?

She headed to a topless bar that served food. There were a few of them in the area, mostly along Eight Mile. There was also one up on Mound in Warren as well. Of course, up there, to make it easy for the natives to look the other way, they called it *Businessmen's Luncheons*.

She parked her car in the lot of Charlie's and went in. There weren't many folks around because of the time, but the bouncer looked Brett up and down as she entered.

"Hey. No women," he said, sticking a beefy arm out to stop her. She grimaced and took a step back, quickly glancing down at her attire. She couldn't remember the last time she had been IDed as a woman twice in a day by total strangers. Maybe she needed to change cologne?

She looked up at the guard and ran her hand back through her hair (maybe she needed a haircut?) Even from a foot away, he smelled as if he hadn't taken a shower in a week. She was sure most of the patrons never saw this ape. As a businessman's place it had to hold to a higher standard of decorum.

Brett looked right at him, trying to breathe as little as possible so she wouldn't gag from his strong body odor. "What's the point of a topless bar if there ain't no chicks?"

"Girls gotta be with a man."

Brett reached into her pocket and pulled a twenty from her money clip. "I got a few men with me."

The bouncer glanced around, and left his arm up. "Ya can't bribe me."

Brett saw what had given him sudden morals. The owner, Jeff Perkins, was heading their way. "Well, you just blew your only chance for a decent tip today," Brett told the bouncer when Jeff grinned and stretched out his own hairy arm.

40

"Brett Higgins!" Jeff said.

"Jeffie, how the hell ya doin'?"

"I've been known to be better. Especially since you're probably here to try to steal somma my girls." He frowned at her, acting all big and tough. Brett and he had come to a rough understanding of each other years ago, when she still worked for Rick. Jeff, like most of the men in this business in Detroit, had a problem with Brett, a problem only marginally lessened by the fact she was a dyke. Brett and her .357, with its six-inch barrel, finally prevailed. The bosses grudgingly learned to give her her space, if not respect, after she roughed up some of their boys. They should've just been glad she didn't put out hits on them or their employees.

Of course, aside from Brett, who had a B.A. in business, most in this profession didn't have much of an education. A few did have both degrees and business-world experience. When they realized how much money they could make in the adult industries while having a helluva good time as well, they kissed the white-collar world goodbye.

Jeff wasn't one of them. He and his brother had taken over the place when their dad kicked the bucket. His brother, whose name Brett couldn't remember, was dead. Killed in a random drive-by shooting. Brett was one of many who thought it wasn't quite as random as the cops and Jeff wanted people to think.

"Hey, Patty, bring my friend Brett a burger and a beer," Jeff said to a cute redhead who was waiting the few occupied tables. She nodded while Jeff led Brett to a table in the corner. He pushed some of the papers covering it to the side and said, "Just gimme a second here." He waved toward a chair. "Take a load off."

Brett sat, looking around. The place was exactly the same as the last time she saw it. The waitresses were still topless, their pert white breasts bouncing lightly in the air-conditioned room, chilly enough to cause their nipples to become hardened and erect. It was a pleasant sight. Brett knew that when the show started, the patrons would have even more visions to fill their eyes.

41

But not as much of a show as they'd get at the Paradise. Brett's place wasn't as nice, and she couldn't serve alcohol, but her girls took it all off. She couldn't legally have naked dancers and alcohol, and, since most places chose serving $10 beers with topless dancers and waitresses, Brett found her niche with having the girls naked. She could charge a much higher cover to make up for the lack of over-priced alcohol.

Brett and Jeff had sat down and lit their cigarettes when Patty arrived with Brett's burger, fries and beer. Just as Brett took a healthy mouthful of the burger, the brawny bouncer came up to Jeff's shoulder and murmured just loud enough for Jeff and Brett to hear, "Boss, there's another chick who wants to come in."

"Give me a minute," Jeff said, standing and following the bouncer back to the door. Brett leaned back to enjoy the view and her burger while she awaited Jeff's return. It was probably just a nosy wife.

"You got great timing," she heard Jeff saying as he returned. "I got somebody you might wanna meet."

Brett looked up and saw a nubile body, topped with a head of fiery red hair. "We've already met," she said, standing and pulling out a chair for her.

Tina O'Rourke brazenly looked her up and down. "Brett Higgins. Fancy meeting you here," she said, sitting.

Brett grabbed her hand and kissed it. "A moment is too long without your beautiful smile, Tina m'dear."

Tina laid a stare on Brett.

Jeff stood watching them with a smirk on his face. "Tina's learned about you the hard way too, huh?"

"But you'd think she'd thank me for her sudden promotion," Brett said.

This got Jeff's full attention. "You had something to do with what happened to Jack?"

"I don't see how you'd really care, Jeff. All that should really interest you is that I've just about called it even on Jack for putting that hit out on me a coupla years ago," Brett replied.

Tina jumped to her feet. "I don't give a shit what happened between you and my father—all I care about is you and me!" The few patrons glanced toward them.

"Oh, baby, there ain't no you and me, no matter how much you might want there to be." Brett remained seated.

"Tina," Jeff said, taking a healthy swallow of his scotch then lighting up a cigar, "if you're gonna stand a chance in hell of playing the game in this town, you'd better be watching Brett carefully. She's the only reason you've even gotten a foot in the door."

Tina glanced over at Brett, who was wolfing down her burger and liberally dunking her fries in catsup between gulps of beer. "I don't really think you should be giving me business advice, Jeff. After all, you run a bar and I'm in charge of my father's entire operation."

Brett signaled Jeff to keep his seat. "Yeah, that's just it, babe, you're trying to run your daddy's business, but unless you get a clue, you'll just be running it into the ground." If Tina could ever learn the ropes, she might be a worthy business opponent.

"But I'm not the one who had to go on the lam," Tina said.

Jeff started to say something, but Brett interrupted. "She's nice," she said, referring to the latest dancer to take the stage. She kind of liked Tina, and liked that there was another woman in the game, but the girl needed to learn a few things. Brett had to work her way into the scene and make her mark in Rick's eyes to get where she was.

"Yeah, she is," Jeff said. He looked up to the stage and gave a nod to the long-legged brunette. She came off the stage and headed toward them. "Princess, I'd like you to meet an old friend of mine, Brett Higgins."

Princess turned toward Brett, with slow, soft movements. She was fairly tall with nice curves. Her full, tanned breasts were accented with pert nipples that were just inches away from Brett's face. "Any friend of Jeff's is a friend of mine," she said, her voice deep and husky.

Brett stood up, ran a finger along the girl's jaw, and pulled a business card from her pocket. "We'll be having an amateur night next Friday, you're welcome to come."

"Amateur night," Princess replied, "do I look like a fuckin' amateur?"

"Yes, you do. But you might end up being worth my time." With a huff, Princess turned to walk away, but Brett reached out, running a finger along the woman's arm. "Just keep in mind if I decide to give you a booking, you'll make five times what you make here in a week, easy."

"And just what've I gotta do to get a bookin' with you?"

"Make the customers, the men, tell me they want you." She turned back to her meal without waiting for a reply. Princess was a good dancer and a good looker, but she had a lot to learn. Brett wasn't about to let any dancer think she was something special and act like a diva.

Tina, watching all this, pulled a cigar out of her purse, bit down on the end and looked for a lighter. Brett yanked the cigar out of Tina's mouth and properly took off the end with her Xino cigar guillotine. She then stuck it back in Tina's mouth. "Straight girl, of course you'd like cigars," she said, holding her lighter just below it. Tina gently puffed on the stogie.

"And you don't like them, wandering around with that chopper in your pocket?"

Brett merely grinned. She turned back to Jeff. "So do either of you know anything about some dancers going down?"

Jeff shrugged. "So what's new?"

"What do you mean?"

"Somebody's always takin' down the girls. Nobody ever gives a rat's ass, either."

"Have *you* lost any dancers?"

"Ah, just some bitch got her brains bashed out while ago."

Brett did a double-take on him, but Tina pulled herself up close to the table, placing the cigar in the ashtray. "It's not the same guy." Brett figured the cigar was Tina's way of trying to fit in with the boys. The boys liked cigars, and so should she.

"What makes you so sure?" Brett asked.

"Oh, c'mon, it's so obvious even a copper'd have to see it," Tina said.

"What do you mean?"

"Oh, c'mon, this one, what's her face, got her head bashed in. The others had their throats slit. This one was six months ago —and there weren't any killings in-between. They're not related."

Three months was too long for a serial to wait, yet . . . "There hasn't been anyone else targeting dancers around here lately, has there been?"

"Damn, you really are out of it," Tina said, shaking her head.

"Well?"

"No. And nobody got nabbed for Luscious's death, either," Jeff said. "It was probably just some jealous john."

That made sense. "Okay . . ."

Brett searched her memory for any names previously mentioned. There were none. "There were two others before Nicola."

"Sylver and Desiree," Tina said.

"Which girl got it first?" Brett asked, trying to hide how out of it she was.

Tina smirked. "These girls live a dangerous life. None of 'em ever live to a ripe old age."

"So how did your girls die?" Brett asked Tina.

"Both of 'em had their throats slashed."

"He got two from you?"

"Yeah, last Friday and Sunday."

"Okay, so we've got three dead dancers. We got ourselves a serial on our hands," Brett said, not standing, not moving one inch.

"Dancers. Hookers. They're a dime a dozen," Jeff said, picking up Tina's forgotten cigar and puffing it.

"Not my girls," Brett said.

"Still grieving after your beloved Storm, are you Brett? My father told me all about that one."

"I'm a businesswoman Tina, so I know there are some girls who pull the men in, who do a good show, make me money, and ain't no trouble at all. I hate to lose those."

Tina looked into Brett's eyes. "Well, my girls, Desiree and Sylver, were pains in the ass. They thought they were doing me a favor by showing up to work."

"Luscious was no better," Jeff added.

"Did they get done when they were dancing at your places?" Brett asked.

"Yeah," Tina said. "They did. Carcasses left right near by."

"Yeah. Good riddance to bad rubbish I say," Jeff said, and Tina nodded.

"Good, bad, indifferent, I don't care. I know what I lost, and I don't like losing anything," Brett said. "Do you remember anything about your girls and how they were found?" she asked Tina.

"What are you, a fuckin' cop now?" Tina asked.

"Listen, if we don't do something, the cops and reporters will come knocking, and that'll be bad for business for all of us." Brett had to leave. She was losing her cool. The last thing she needed was for anyone to think she cared about her dancers more than she would any other business investment.

"They were all found right nearby." Tina said, staring right into Brett's eyes. "Out back behind the places by the Dumpsters. My girls were Desiree, Kelly Roberts, and Sylver was Maria Teresa Siciliano."

46

Brett nodded, wishing she could take notes, but nothing made folks in the business so scared as having someone write down their words. Perhaps they were afraid of such a blatant show of literacy. "Which one on which day?" she asked.

"Sylver was Friday, Desiree was Sunday," Tina replied.

"Which bar?" Tina ran a number of strip clubs.

"The Naked Truth."

Brett nodded. "Eight and DQ, right?" she said, referring to Dequindre Road by its nickname.

"Yeah, both were at the same place."

Brett nodded, then tossed back the rest of her beer. She looked over at Jeff. He'd been eyeing them both during this entire exchange. "Let me know if you hear anything else." She got up and left without another word.

6

"So, you're new in town?" Angela said to Victoria as they were getting ready for the next show. The first dancer had just gone on and Angela was up next.

"Yeah, and it appears I got lucky showing up here when I did."

"You certainly did. I mean, not only showing up when Brett needed a dancer, but also being one she would pick up just like that." She snapped her fingers.

Victoria shrugged. "What can I say? It's time I had a little luck."

"You know, I just can't help but have the feeling we've met somewhere before."

"I must have that kind of face," Victoria said, staring into the mirror as she applied her mascara.

"And body?" Angela was pulling up her thigh-high stockings, trying to appear nonchalant.

"What do you mean by that?"

"You just remind me a lot of some other dancer I've known."

"Who?"

"I just can't quite place her."

"Hm. Let me know if you remember, 'cause I'd like to meet this supposed twin. So do you want me to pick up the last spot again, or should we try something different?"

Angela stared at Victoria for a moment. "That's kind of you to offer. If you don't mind, I'd like to go last. Lunch took longer than I expected, so I'm not quite ready yet." She still needed to get into costume and put on her make-up, but she kept watching Victoria. The woman was hiding something.

"No problem," Victoria said, heading toward the door. "Was it a hot date, by the way?"

"What?"

"A hot date? Your extended lunch? You know, the sort you make a few bucks from?"

"I don't do 'dates,'" Angela said. "Brett doesn't like hooking or drugs."

"And you're just the teacher's pet, huh? Well, let me know if you remember where you've seen me before," Victoria said, blowing a quick kiss to Angela as she left the dressing room.

Angela stared at the door long after Victoria had left. The girl wasn't up to any good. She knew she was lying to Brett, and didn't like it. There had to be a reason she would lie.

• • •

While Phil drove them from the Frost's, Randi looked through the Karin Frost file.

"Do you want to come with me to check out Frost's apartment?" Phil asked.

Randi glanced at her watch. "Yeah, I would. You got her address?"

"Yeah . . ." he grabbed the file from Randi's hands and glanced at his almost illegibly scrawled notes, "Frankie . . . Lorenzini? found it for me in Frost's file. Thanks for helping us out on this. Chris and I ain't no good at shit like we just went through."

"No problem."

"Randi, I saw the way Mrs. Frost looked at me earlier. I just keep sticking my foot in it, y'know?"

"I'm just surprised that you found time to track down the rosaries. I mean, they can't allow you much time to investigate this."

Phil stared straight ahead at the road, both hands firmly glued to the steering wheel. "Chris and I had some patrolmen help us, and we did what we did on our own time. The rosaries were the clearest thing we could track down."

"And you did. On your own time."

"Yes. We did. Chris helped me. I mean, the department really doesn't give a shit, you know?"

"Then why do you?"

Phil was silent so long Randi thought maybe he was ignoring her, but then, finally, he said, "My sister's two years older then I am, and so she hit college before I did." He thrust his chin out. "The folks wanted her to get an MRS degree, if anything, so they didn't help her as much as they did me." He stopped at the light and looked at Randi. "She wanted her degree, and I was so young, I thought it was cool. Except when my friends saw her—she was a dancer. She took her clothes off, just like these women, Randi."

Randi didn't want to ask, but she had to. "Did something happen to her?"

"No. But it could've. She's married now, with two kids. She

50

went all the way—got her M.B.A., and sometimes, sometimes, I think she did it to spite our folks. Here I am, a cop, and she went on to run some company . . ."

Phil was now, again, staring straight ahead. Randi was amazed he'd revealed what he had. She wondered if Chris knew why Phil had such an interest in this case.

"Phil, I wish I coulda had a brother like you. Let's go see what we can find in Frost's apartment that'll lead us to a killer."

• • •

Brett drove back to the Paradise Theatre and was just walking in when she remembered why she didn't want to be there.

"And now boys, we've got the little storm you've been waiting for—Tempest!" Tim's voice blared over the loudspeaker.

Brett didn't hire these guys for their talents. But Tim's choice of words made Brett open the door and look inside, wondering why he had chosen to refer to Tempest as a storm. He hadn't even known Storm.

Victoria was onstage, in her street clothes. Enigma was again playing over the speakers. Victoria looked right at Brett, sending heat flaming through her, pulling her all the way into the auditorium. Victoria slowly began unbuttoning her blouse and pulling it off. She seemed to be stripping just for Brett, again.

Brett wanted her so much it was a physical ache. She could almost feel exactly what Storm—no, Victoria—would feel like in her arms. She wanted to bury her head in Victoria's hair and breathe her scent and feel the warmth of her body pressed against her own.

Brett took a deep breath, trying to calm herself, and leaned back against the wall with her eyes closed. But in her mind's eye, she could see Storm moving to the mysterious music. She tried to focus on other things to overcome this reaction: someone was out there, on the streets, knocking off strippers, hookers, her girls.

51

These were her girls. She knew what they played with daily; the diseases, maniacs, drugs. She did what she could do to protect them, but those who died usually had already died years ago from something else. They had given up their lives and souls to some other power. Allie could never understand that. Randi understood it to some degree, having lost her own brother first to drugs, then the street, and finally to death itself. But she would never know what it was like to lose all hope.

Brett opened her eyes and saw that Victoria, Tempest, was now wearing only her panties. And still she danced for Brett. Brett could imagine her full breasts in her hands, could feel the hardened nipples teasing her palms, smell the sweetness of her arousal . . .

Tempest hooked her fingers into her lacy black underwear, slowly pulling them down, looking directly into Brett's eyes.

Brett decided she had tested herself enough for the day, she turned and walked out of the auditorium. How convenient that Victoria had suddenly appeared that morning. Had the girl somehow known she would have a sudden need for another dancer?

If Angela was right and had seen Victoria in the area sometime before, then Victoria lied when she said she'd just come to town from Indiana. If she had lied about that, then what else she was lying about?

● ● ●

When no one answered their pounding, Randi and Phil found the landlord and got him to let them in. A stooped old man with bushy eyebrows that dominated his face, he saw their badges and handed them his passkey. Too many people didn't want to get involved in anything they didn't have to.

The apartment was simply furnished with milk crates acting as bookshelves, a folding table posing as a dining table, and a ratty old sofa positioned opposite an old black-and-white television.

No one was home.

"I'll start in the bedroom, and you can start out here," Randi said to Phil.

"Sure. Not that I think we're going to find anything." He shook his head. "I doubt she knew him away from work."

"I know, but we've still got to check it out," Randi said.

The bedroom housed a full-sized mattress on the floor, with what looked like handmade blankets. Two cheap dressers were set against the walls, and there was a closet.

Stacks of books abounded. Milkcrates served as bedside tables, each with its own clock. One had a picture of a femme woman Randi recognized as Karin standing next to a very butch woman. They had their arms around each other and were smiling.

Randi was struck by a wave of sadness. Karin lived with her lover. Some woman had just lost her lover.

She wondered who the strange butch was as she looked through the dressers and closet. It was easy for her to tell which dresser and which side of the closet belonged to Karin, and which to the butch. The butch favored jeans, T-shirts and flannel shirts; Karin owned several sets of lingerie, which were probably for work, and a few blouses, skirts, and jeans. All of the clothes looked old or from the Salvation Army. Interestingly enough, the butch owned more clothes.

Randi's questions about the identity of the butch were answered when she came to the bottom drawer of Karin's dresser—there she found a shoebox full of more pictures of the two women together, some apparently from a few years ago, as well as little love notes Jenny had written to Karin.

Jenny and Karin must have been together ever since Karin's father had found them together. Randi picked up one of the books nearby and flipped through what was obviously a college text-book. Karin was an exotic dancer, but someone who lived here was in college.

"Hey, Randi!" Phil called. "I just found something."

Randi closed the box and dresser drawer, and went to where Phil was in the kitchen.

"What do you think this means?" he asked, indicating a University of Michigan course schedule next to a calendar on the kitchen wall.

"It confirms what I found in the bedroom—I think, Karin and Jenny moved in together after Karin's parents kicked her out." She went again to the living room. "Did you finish searching out here?"

"Yeah, except for the answering machine," Phil replied, nodding toward the small black box near the telephone. A red light on it was blinking. "I haven't found anything—except an interest in computers and literature. Kind've a strange combination."

Randi felt almost guilty when she hit the play button, but she needed to figure out where Jenny was.

"Hey sweetie," said a butch voice. "You were right, I'm exhausted. I was up all last night studying for my Calc exam, and I've got both Physics and Spanish tomorrow. I think I'll take your suggestion and spend tonight up here with Amy. She can help me study. I expect I'll need to sleep tomorrow night, so I'll see you on Saturday. I love you. Deeply. Desperately. Wholly."

Randi suddenly understood. Karin was working to put her lover through college now—and Randi expected that once Jenny had her degree, she in turn would put Karin through school.

Randi picked up yet another picture of Karin with Jenny. No wonder Mrs. Frost thought Jenny had recruited Karin. Randi could almost laugh—Mrs. Frost apparently didn't realize that the femme always had to make the first move.

Karin was a lesbian, and she had a lover. Someone who loved her. Randi looked over at Phil, imagining it was he telling her that the woman she loved had died.

She took a piece of paper from the computer printer—the

computer alone explained where quite a bit of Karin's earnings went to—and scratched a note, asking that Jenny contact her as soon as she got home. She put it with a business card on the futon.

"I think we're done here for now. If you don't mind, I'd like her to contact me," Randi said. Poor Jenny would be lost without Karin.

"No problem," Phil replied as they left.

• • •

When Brett got home that night, Allie had dinner ready and waiting for her. Over dinner, Brett reviewed the newspaper articles Allie had printed off the Internet. She wouldn't tell Allie much about what she had learned during the day. She needed to let it go for a little while.

"I only stopped by the house quickly to change, so I didn't have a chance to pick up a bottle of wine or anything," Randi explained when she arrived at seven.

"Relax, it's not like it's dinner or anything," Allie said.

"Besides," Brett said, "this is really just more work. What can I get you?"

"You got a beer?"

"Coming up," Brett said, heading to the kitchen. She rejoined them in the living room a few minutes later, carrying a Miller Lite for Randi, a glass of white wine for Allie, and scotch for herself.

Randi sat next to Allie on the beige leather sofa, put her briefcase on the coffee table, and pulled a thick file from it. "I made copies of everything they had on it." She quickly launched into a recitation of the salient facts of the matter—the dates, times and locations of the murders, where and who found the bodies, the cause of death, and the known facts about the victims.

"Is that all you've got?" Brett asked, as Allie took the folder to glance through it. She quickly found the girls' bios and pictures, which she pulled out.

"It's more than you've got. I mean, when I saw you earlier, you didn't even know about the first two girls." Randi replied.

Brett didn't like or trust the cops. But she did have to admit that Randi seemed to be totally forthcoming. After all, it was a thicker folder than she had expected.

"I haven't had much time to dig up anything. What do you want to know?" Brett said, wanting to keep something up her sleeve just in case Randi decided to play any games with her. She could still be withholding information until she had to barter an exchange of info with Brett.

"Tell me everything you know about the girl who got hit this morning," Randi said.

"Her name was Karin Frost. She went by the stage name Nicola. She was working for me this week."

"How long has she been working for you?"

Brett shrugged. "I'm not sure. Remember, I just got back to town, and just started back at the theatre a few months ago. I can tell you she'd already been dancing there for a while before I returned. She was a good girl. Frankie told me she's putting her lover through school."

"Sounds like you liked her."

"I did, like I do any girl who keeps clean, comes in on time, and works hard for what she wants. You don't know what that's like, but I do. She knew what it was like to have to fight out of the hole one was born in."

"You liked her," Randi repeated.

"I just said that I like any girl who stays off the drugs and is heading toward something better than the theatre. I clearly admitted this morning that I liked her," Brett said. She could feel her temper already rising.

"Randi . . ." Allie tried breaking in. She knew Brett's history with the cops, and how she was likely to react.

"You sound defensive," Randi continued, either not picking up on Allie's hint or ignoring it.

56

Brett took a moment to pull out a cigarette and light it slowly with her ever-handy Zippo. She let its flame dance over the tip of her smoke. "She did a few tricks, not a lot, she mostly just danced. Her other customers were . . . they weren't your usual perverts." She leaned forward to meet Randi's eyes. "When she was alive her eyes told you everything about her—her hopes, fears, dreams. Her parents kicked her out for being who she was. We mighta all grown up in the same neighborhood, Randi, but you don't share what she and I, and so many others, do. The horror of not even being safe in your own home."

"The past is the past Brett," Randi said. "And right now I'm trying to deal with the present. I know you grew up in an abusive household." She took a deep breath. "I want to stop whatever is going on."

Any interview with Randi was an unpleasant experience for Brett. Whenever she was in a situation like this, an interview with Randi or some other officer, she had flashbacks of prior experiences. Though they'd never been able to charge Brett with anything, that didn't mean they hadn't tried repeatedly.

Brett glanced at Allie and decided to try to hold her temper. Randi was Allie's friend, so she'd keep herself from attacking Randi. "We each have our own tactics. Now, I've told you who she is, was—what else do you need?"

Randi looked over at Allie, and Brett stood up.

"Nicola was a good girl," Brett said. "She saved her money for school, for living. Didn't do drugs. Didn't do many tricks." She was pacing like a caged animal.

"For such a bad ass, you do have on your rose-tinted glasses," Randi said with a slight grin. "What was she doing in that back alley if she didn't do tricks?"

Brett studied Randi for a moment. "She had to go through that alley to get to her car. To go home." Brett shrugged. "But yes, I already said she probably did some tricks . . ."

"You said she did—not *probably did.*"

"Frankie thinks she did some. Not a lot, but a few. We don't really know for a fact sometimes, we just see the signs."

"There's a history behind this sort of thing, you know," Allie said. "Back in, like, the 50s or so, a lot of femmes supported the household because they could find work more easily than their butches could."

"And sometimes that work was as a secretary, and sometimes as a whore," Brett said.

Randi stood up to confront Brett. "We're both on the same side. I met her mother this afternoon," Randi shrugged. "And to tell the truth, I didn't care for her much. I know her parents put her into her . . . *profession* . . . forced her into it."

"Do you really now?" Brett asked.

Randi sat down and said, "We spoke to her mother this afternoon. She told us what happened."

"Have I missed something?" Allie asked, flipping through the file quickly, but not seeing notes on the interview. "What are you two talking about?"

Brett sighed and sat down, her head in her hands. "Nicola's parents are strict Catholics. Very homophobic. They kicked her out."

"But she has done some tricks?"

"Just about everyone in the business does at some time. I don't think she has any priors for solicitation, because it really wasn't her style at all." Brett got up, pulled on her smoke and then suddenly turned back and leaned on the table, in Randi's face. "She was a good kid, and I'd like to string up the bastard that done her myself."

"So she might've picked up a customer last night, then?"

Brett stood and shrugged. "I'm sure you'll find out all you need to know through the autopsy. It's possible." She met Randi's eyes. "I know my dancers, and there are some I like better than others, but I'm always honest about them."

"Yes, I remember," Randi said. "You do know your dancers quite well if I recall correctly."

Brett stared at her, then downed her drink. "Do you need another?" she asked Randi with a nod toward her beer.

"Yes, please," Randi said, handing the empty bottle to Brett.

Brett picked up Allie's wine glass and went to the kitchen.

● ● ●

Allie turned to Randi. "I thought you were going to be nice."

"I am being nice!" Randi replied in a loud whisper.

Allie turned away. "Sorry. You were. Are. Being nice." She hefted the file folder in her hand. "I mean, thanks for this."

"Allie, if you two want me to look into this, then I've got to ask her some questions. I thought you two would want to get to the bottom of this as quickly as possible. The only way to do that is to ask questions."

"Yes, I know. Thank you."

"It's not easy—I've got a full load."

Allie put her hand on Randi's shoulder, looking into her eyes. "You have to know, Brett had nothing to do with this."

Randi ran her hand down Allie's cheek. "Yes, I know."

They stared into each other's eyes for a moment. "Is there anything else you need, Randi?" Brett asked.

"Did you know Maria Teresa Siciliano or Kelly Roberts?" Randi asked, turning around to face Brett. Her face was pink.

Brett shook her head, handing Randi and Allie their drinks. "No, I didn't. I spoke with Jeff Perkins and Tina O'Rourke today, though, and they didn't have a very high opinion of them. But I don't think they care about any of their dancers."

"You said this woman, Nicola, was supposed to dance for you this week. Do you have somebody to cover for her yet?"

"Yes."

"Already?"

"I'm a businesswoman, Randi. You know that. The show must go on, no matter what."

"So what happened?"

"Some girl just showed up this morning."

"What's her name?"

"Victoria."

"Victoria what?"

"I didn't ask."

A small grin wove its way across Randi's face. "Not a very thorough employer, are you?"

Brett stared at Randi. They both knew that dancers didn't fill out all of the information required for I-9s, W-2s, and all that other stuff. Brett would be hard-pressed to come up with a single social-security number for any of her dancers. And Randi knew this.

It was the same with most people in the industry.

"I was busy this morning," Brett said.

"But you'll get all the proper forms filled out when you see her again," Randi said.

"Of course. As soon as I get back to work."

"Do women often just show up at the theatre looking for a job?"

"Yes. I usually make them come back for amateur night, where the guys themselves let me know who they want."

"But you made exception for this Victoria. She must really be something."

Allie was silent.

"I've been doing this long enough to know who can do it, and who can't. Plus, I had nothing to lose. I couldn't find another dancer at such short notice."

Randi sat back and crossed her legs. "What's this new girl's stage name?"

"Tempest."

"Tempest? Did she come up with the name herself?"

"No, I gave it to her," Brett admitted.

7

Allie looked away from Brett and Randi, and down at the pictures of the dead women, studying them, learning them, knowing them.

Maria Teresa Siciliano was the first to be killed, last Friday. Twenty-years old, she danced as Sylver, was 5'6", slender with jet black hair. She lived in Southfield at Ten and Lahser.

Kelly Roberts, the second victim, lived in Detroit, at Six and Woodward. A forty-year-old African-American, she danced under the name Desiree, had nice breasts, with a few more pounds on her than Maria. She was only 5'2" with dark brown rasta locks. She was killed Sunday night.

Both women were found behind Tina O'Rourke's bar, The Naked Truth, near the Dumpster. And now, just three days later, it was Karin Frost, 21. Nicola. Danced at the Paradise Theatre at Six and Woodward. At 5'10", she was a shapely redhead with long hair. Worked for Brett Higgins and Frankie Lorenzini. Lived in Detroit in the Cass Corridor, miles away from where she was found.

"What are you looking at, babe?" Brett asked.

"The girls. I'm wondering what ties them together, besides the obvious? I mean, is there anything besides the fact that they're all dancers—prostitutes?"

Brett stood up to look over Allie's shoulder at the pictures of the girls when they were alive.

"Well, they're all pretty hot."

"Yes, but their age, hair color, height, weight, race, and breast size all vary," Randi said. "Usually serial killers have a type. Ted Bundy like brunette coeds. But our guy's victims are all over the board. There isn't a type."

"Yes, there is. They all do the same thing for a living," Brett replied.

All three women began digging through the file, first comparing the bios and recent pictures, then looking at the layout of each corpse, Randi and Allie sitting next to each other on the couch, with Brett crouched on the far side of the coffee table.

"We need to track down where all these girls danced at during their careers. Where they all hooked," Allie said, grabbing her notebook and starting to write in it.

"But why did this bastard choose these particular girls out of all the other dancers—I mean, what did they do to get his notice?" Randi asked.

"Yes, what put these women apart? What made them the chosen ones? Out of the sea of dancers and hookers in Detroit, why had they been killed? They didn't even all work at the same club," Allie said. "I mean, there had to be some reason."

"Why they were picked instead of one of their co-workers?" Randi asked.

"Maybe they were the first one to leave on their given nights?"

"No," Randi said, shaking her head. "If it was that, somebody would have seen something, and nobody saw anything. The bodies weren't found until the next morning, although it looks as if they were all killed shortly after the club closed the night before."

"Then maybe they picked up the killer, and that's when it happened? Not all dancers prostitute themselves, so maybe it's just that he chose the ones who did."

"Dancers work at different places," Brett said. "Any girl liable to dance at one location might very well show up at another a week, or a few weeks, later. So maybe all these girls had danced at the same place, at the same time?"

"Maybe something happened one night with one of the patrons—and on that night they really pissed off this guy? Like, it's all part of one bad night for some geek boy? I know I've met some men who are such total losers, I can easily see them losing it and going over the edge." Different psychological profiles went through her brain. They wouldn't do squat to help her. She needed answers, and she needed them now. Before anybody else died.

Allie knew any murder not solved within 24 hours wasn't likely to be solved.

"One thing that doesn't work with that, though," Randi said, "is that none of these girls seemed to have been sexually molested prior to, or following, their death. You'd think a rape or something would play into that sort of scenario. Especially if it was some john."

"But they were all found naked, weren't they?" Allie asked.

"Yes, but the forensic evidence so far shows no sexual contact of any kind," Randi replied. "Plus, none have defense wounds, so it seems likely it's somebody they knew."

"Someone they knew?" Brett repeated, looking up at her.

"Yeah, I mean, normally in a knifing like this, the victim would fight her assailant and so would have cuts on her arms. At the very least, she'd probably have some nice tissue samples under her nails, but there's nothing."

"Which means that the bad-night-for-a-geek-boy theory doesn't work." Brett looked up at the two women from her crouching position. "The other interesting thing is that we know it's a religious murder."

"You mean because of the rosaries?" Allie asked.

Brett flipped a picture from the files. It was a close-up of a seven-decade rosary. "Yes."

Randi explained about the rosaries and everything she and Phil had discussed earlier that day.

"Oh, by the way," Brett said, once Randi had finished, "I found out today that another girl got it a while ago in Warren."

"Do you think it might be related?" Randi asked.

"No. It was at least six months ago at Charlie's. Leslie Newsome got her head bashed in."

"Thanks for letting me know," Randi said, nodding while she jotted in her own notebook. "Though I think you're right, it probably isn't related." She looked up at Brett. "I really do think we can help each other out on this one."

Allie was happy to see Brett nod. "Since we're both on the same side, it'd do us both best to work together. After all, I'm in the best position to tell you if this is a gang war thing, owner versus owner, or, in fact, in any way related to the bad guys going after each other."

• • •

Victoria pulled a piece of lingerie from the rack and held it against her in front of the mirror. She felt the texture of the material under her fingers, and imagined she was wearing the flimsy negligee.

The street clothes she was wearing now were a novelty. She knew she needed to stay one step ahead of everything and everyone else to keep her job and meet her primary objective. She needed to follow Brett's orders, and Brett had told her to get a costume. But she needed to do that as Tempest, as the storm that was brewing.

She looked all around the store at things that would make her look just like all the other dancers. She picked up a teddy, a sheer negligee . . . nothing was right. She wanted to tease and please. She needed something special. She needed to stretch the boundaries. She'd go to another store. This place didn't have what she needed.

She had a long overdue dance with a certain five-ten butch.

• • •

Brett stood up and stretched. "I need to go do some work on the computer," she said, having had enough of Randi. She would only work with her on this for the girls.

"I should probably leave myself," Randi said, not getting up. "I have to go into the station early tomorrow. Since I'm not officially on this case, I can only spare it a little time, and whatever I can do on my own."

Brett looked her right in the eye. "Thanks."

"No problem. I'm as worried as you are that this won't get the attention it deserves. But, Chris and Phil have really done a lot more work on it than I would have suspected."

"There are some good dancers out there," Brett said. She leaned down to quickly kiss Allie, and noticed that Randi turned away at this obvious intimacy. Regardless of their temporary truce, Brett wanted to make sure that Randi knew to whom Allie belonged.

• • •

"Randi, I know you think you and Brett are nothing alike, because you think she's a bad guy and you're a cop, and that she only cares about these girls because they work for her. But these are her girls, and people just don't . . ."

"People don't mess with what belongs to Brett."

"That's what she wants people to think. Regardless, she wouldn't want to lose her employees, especially not the good ones. If somebody's targeting dancers or hookers, then it's pretty damned likely that Brett'll know half of the women who are gonna buy it."

"Why are you saying this? I'm already helping out, aren't I? Didn't I even show up this morning to help keep Brett out of trouble?"

Allie remembered how the first time she ever saw Randi she briefly thought she was Brett. When seen in the full light of day, however, the two women looked nothing alike. Like Brett, Randi was a butch, but she was only 5'6" compared with Brett's 5'10", her thick hair brown instead of black, and she was almost a decade older than Brett. And she looked it. Both were slender, fairly muscular, with an incredible intensity. But still, it was their resemblance that originally attracted her to Randi. "Yes, I know. You've been a good friend."

"I do remember that I owe her my life, after all."

Allie reached forward to again caress Randi's cheek.

Randi couldn't help herself. She took Allie's hand in her own and tenderly kissed the palm.

"Randi," Allie said, pulling her hand away after a moment.

"Sorry." Randi looked at Allie. Her arms were at her sides, and she had a helpless look on her face.

Allie put her hand on Randi's. "I know, Randi."

Randi looked away. She glanced again at her watch.

"So do you have any insights on this case?" Allie asked.

"I want to look in on this rosary angle a bit more closely. Maybe question the families again, check out the bars." She shrugged.

"Basically cover all the bases that have already been covered again. See if anything's been overlooked. With everything else they're working on, Chris and Phil might have missed something."

Allie stood up to walk Randi to the door. "Keep me posted, okay? Maybe we can meet early tomorrow so that I can help out. After all, I've got some time on my hands right now, being unemployed and all."

"Allie, you know if you just ask, I'll put in a word for you."

"Randi, I can't go back to being a cop—let alone with the Detroit P.D. C'mon, I helped a criminal."

"Brett has never been charged with anything."

Allie smiled. "Am I hearing right—are you actually defending Brett?"

"No! I'm just . . . I mean, we never got anything on her, so you really didn't help a felon. C'mon Al, I know how much you want to be a detective, and how much you should be one. Why don't you let me help?"

"Randi, thanks for your offer, but I'll find my own job, thank you."

"Well, then, maybe you should stop looking for a job and just figure out what you want to do with your life instead." She shrugged. "You could go back to school—maybe take some classes at Wayne State or something." Before Allie could say anything, Randi again looked at her watch. "Oh, god, look at the time—I really should get going."

"You keep looking at your watch," Allie said, pulling Randi's watch arm down. "You got a hot date or something?"

"Not a hot date, but... I am meeting somebody for drinks."

"Where?" Allie asked, straightening a picture on the wall.

"La Dolce Vita."

Allie paused. She knew the restaurant. It was pretty nice. "So it's serious then?"

Randi didn't look at her. Instead she looked at the wooden

floor. She shrugged. "Not really. I mean, we've just gone out a few times."

"Randi. We're lesbians. A few times is serious." Allie tried to find her sense of humor, her compassion, her happiness that her friend was working on finding somebody else, but all she could find was an emptiness within herself. "Is she nice?"

"I think you'd like her," Randi said, looking at Allie.

Allie pulled Randi into her arms, hugging her tight. "I hope she makes you happy."

Randi took in the hug, then said, pulling away, "We're not engaged or anything, c'mon."

Allie lightly touched her cheek, then put a hand on her shoulder and directed her out.

She watched Randi's taillights disappear in the distance, listening to Brett in her office. And felt very alone. Even if she never thought so, somewhere deep inside, she had always known Randi was her back up, in case anything happened with her and Brett. Now she was going, if not gone.

Allie also knew a tempest was a type of storm.

The real question though was, was Tempest really a type of Storm?

8
Friday

"Dear, dear—wake up!" Angela's grandmother yelled while knocking on her door.

"*Babcia,*" she moaned, rolling over in bed and pulling the covers over her head. She was in the middle of a good dream.

"You'll be late for work dear," *Babcia* said, opening the door to peer in at her granddaughter. "I've got your breakfast ready for you, my little angel."

When Angela emerged from the bathroom, she discovered *Babcia* was as good as her word. She always was. No matter what hours Angela worked, she was always there with her breakfast, and to make sure she got safely into bed each night.

Angela entered the kitchen, pinning her hair into its neat bun, having washed up quickly in the bathroom. *Babcia* had breakfast waiting for her.

But as soon as Angela sat down and started eating, *Babcia* began ranting about something she had found buried deep within the newspaper, which was nothing new. *Babcia* got up as soon as the paper was delivered. She never terrified herself enough with the horrific headlines. She dug deep to find the worst. "You wouldn't believe what this world is coming to. A bunch of hookers have been getting themselves killed lately. Serves them right, I say. Any woman who makes money debasing herself, appealing to men's lower instincts . . . Well, I just don't know what this world is coming to."

"*Babcia*, some women don't have a loving grandmother like you to watch over them. They're not all as lucky as I am. They don't have someone like you to teach them right and wrong." She reached over to take *Babcia's* hand in her own, but wished she could remember what she had been dreaming. It really had been a good dream. She had done really good things in it, and *Babcia* had been so proud of her.

"And this is a sign right from Revelations. We've been studying that in my bible class, you know."

"Yes *Babcia*, I know. I'm blessed that you have always been here for me."

Babcia walked up to Angela and patted her hair lovingly. "Well good riddance to bad rubbish is what I say. I'm glad you're such a good girl I don't have to worry about you at all."

Angela wondered what *Babcia* would say if she knew what Angela was really doing. It didn't matter—she knew she'd be proud of her for all her hard work.

"A woman like that deserves what she gets, Angela," *Babcia* said.

"I want to nail this bastard," Brett said, walking into Frankie's office.

"I know that." He looked up from what he was working on. "I wanna nail his ass too. But I couldn' find shit last night."

"How far'd you go?"

"A ways, but there's still lots more to do," he said.

Brett studied Frankie's dark features. She figured he'd be considered handsome, in a rough, masculine way, if one was into that sort of thing. "So you didn't uncover anything, which means we don't know anything."

"And you know what else it might mean that I couldn' find anythin'."

Brett knew Frankie was thorough. If he didn't find out anything, it wasn't from lack of trying. "Yeah, it means that nobody's bragging about it. So . . ." She paused, thinking about what everything meant. "It ain't no pro, because this sorta thing would be both stupid for a professional, and not worthwhile. And it ain't someone who's excited about it, because then he'd be bragging about it. So we have a bona fide maniac on our hands."

Frankie looked over the desk at his longtime friend. "You got that right. So you got your work cut out fer you, sweetcheeks." He grinned at her.

It seemed as if a slightly lighter touch than Frankie's might be required for this investigation. But Brett didn't know quite what to do at this point. She did know it wasn't good for business if someone was killing off their dancers. It also wasn't good for business if many TV reporters came calling around the Paradise. Their clientele wouldn't want to be on the five o'clock news. "I guess this sorta crap is part of the reason you brought me back, huh?"

"You got that right, bud," Frankie answered.

"So you're saying I need to get to work figuring this out."

"Right again."

Brett looked down at Frankie, who was still comfortably reclining in his seat, even though she was standing. This was the only sort of position from which Brett could look down at Frankie. At 6'4" and close to 300 pounds, he was almost a behemoth. "You're a cocksucker, you know that?"

"Yup. And I'm good at it, too."

Brett grinned at her friend, knowing full well she was the only person who could say such a thing to him and walk away with her knee caps intact. "Randi stopped by last night, by the way," she said, filling Frankie in on the little bit of information they had.

"You know why she wants to nail your ass so bad, doncha?" Frankie asked. "She's tasted heaven and now she wants it. She tasted it the first time ya messed up with Allie, when she got her first chance, and now she's just waitin' for you to fuck up again."

"I ain't gonna fuck up again, Frankie."

"You better not," he said. "But Brett, tell me you ain't ever screwed around on her again."

Brett lit a cigarette and went to stare out the grimy window at the grimier scene below. "You know me too damn well Frankie." She couldn't count how many petty crimes she'd seen on the streets below. She had even once witnessed someone mugging a nun.

Frankie stood and Brett leaned against the windowsill, looking up at him. "You gotta discuss this crap with Kurt," he said, referring to his boyfriend, "'cause we don't talk like this. Kurt's the only reason I even bring it up. But the one thing I will tell ya is that Allie's like family to me, and if you two break up then I'm gonna hafta deal with Randi like she's family, and there's no way in hell I want some copper in the family."

Brett smiled. The Frankie from a decade ago never could've said that. Still he had to use street language to keep up his tough-guy image.

73

"I love you too, Frankie. Now let's go nail this asshole before he knocks off any more of our chicks."

He grabbed her hand. "Nobody fucks with our girls. And you don't screw with Storm Junior either, huh?"

"So you think she's a dead ringer as well?" Frankie had known Storm, so, she wasn't hallucinating the resemblance or just hoping it.

"I think you'd better stay as far away as possible 'til we know more about her is what I think. She's up to no good, that one. Nobody good comes on the way she did." He sat back down at his desk, returning to work. "No good is all she's gotta be up to."

• • •

"Okay, so there are several avenues of inquiry available," Randi said between bites of breakfast. "Someone could talk with the families of the other girls, check out the clubs they were dancing at when he got them, try looking into their pasts, see if they could find any common variables. Basically, double-check the work Norberg and Vargas have already done." She shoved some toast, sausage and egg into her mouth.

"Randi, you're forgetting one thing. I'm not involved with this case."

"Neither am I." She took a sip of her orange juice and sat back, holding the glass. "And, quite frankly, I don't have the time to do it anyway. With the recent cut-backs, we're all over-worked."

"And under-paid, I know. So that means we're just here on a social visit." Allie leaned back with her own orange juice, studying Randi. "So how was your date last night?"

Randi went back to eating her breakfast, not looking up, not meeting Allie's eyes. "It was okay."

"Just okay?"

"Yeah, it was okay."

"Are you going to share any details?"

"Like what?"

"Like . . . is this the first time you've gone out with her?"

Randi looked down at her food. "No. I told you last night we've gone out before."

"What's she look like?"

"Tall, blonde. Why are you so curious?"

"You're my friend, I worry about my friends." Allie reached across the table, took Randi's hand into her own, and caressed it.

"If it was just friendly curiosity, you would've asked what she's like, not what she looks like."

Allie pulled away and refocused on the remains of her breakfast. "I was planning on leading into more detailed questions later, okay?"

Randi reached across the table to gently touch Allie's chin. She tilted her face up toward her own. "I can't, couldn't, wait forever, you know. And I'm not the sort to break up a seemingly happy couple." She took Allie's hands in her own. "If you're really, truly, happy with Brett, then I'm happy for you. Otherwise . . ." She leaned back and looked deep into Allie's eyes. "Otherwise, as they say, speak now or forever hold your peace."

Allie didn't say a word for a while. Finally, she found her voice. "If you're not working on this case, and I'm not working on this case, then what shall we talk about next?"

"Perhaps your job search? Have you looked into college classes yet?"

Allie rolled her eyes toward the ceiling. "I've thought about it. But I don't even know what I want to be when I grow up."

"Then why don't you just take some classes for the fun of it?"

"Classes for the fun of it?"

"Yeah, like women's studies or something. Allie, you're smart, and since you don't really need a job, it would be nice if you'd put your intelligence toward something better then just hanging out."

Allie sighed.

"Just think about it, okay?"

"Okay, fine. I will. But back to the situation at hand. What are we going to do about it?"

"The situation neither of us is working on? The one I really can't do much on?"

"Yes, that one."

"Really, Allie, I'm hard-pressed enough as it is."

"So what are your thoughts on it?"

Randi sighed. "Okay. I might know where someone could get some passable credentials. Not that I'd tell them, but maybe if they looked at the right notes, they'd find out. So, if I were you, I'd start talking to folks. I know Phil and Chris haven't been able to focus on this case." She shrugged. "They'd be called on the rug if they spent too much time on this. They've already done far more than what anyone in the department would expect of them."

"So I need to go over their footsteps. Need to reinvestigate every nook and cranny. And you won't be able to help me."

"I'll do what I can. Call me if you need help," Randi said, putting some money down on the table to pay for their meals. "I'm sure Brett will want to get involved with it all. I mean, she already is."

"Yes, she is."

"What I can do, however, is help you out today. And divided up, we'll be able to cover more ground. I'll take the strip clubs, since that's where you'd have the biggest problems."

Allie smiled and ran a hand over Randi's cheek. "I knew you couldn't just walk away so easily."

"One thing though," Randi wasn't sure how to broach this topic, but she knew she needed to. "I think we both need to check into this new Victoria as well. I don't like that she just showed up out of the blue right after this latest murder. I mean, it's pretty suspicious that she showed up at the exact time Brett needed her."

Allie looked at Randi, remembering how she heard Enigma on the phone the day before. Music she hadn't heard since Storm died. She knew Brett would find this new girl's timing suspicious, if something else wasn't going on in her head.

• • •

Allie had met Randi at the station that morning for breakfast, so Randi took her back there, and had her come in to pick up some information.

Armed with two cups of lukewarm too-strong coffee, Randi pulled Allie into a conference room. "Allie, we need to talk again." Allie had been looking through Randi's files, seeing if there was anything that she hadn't seen the night before in Randi's photocopied files.

"What's going on?" Allie asked, taking the proffered cup of slime and sitting. She knew Randi would prefer to have the height advantage. It was a tactic that worked on criminals and femmes alike.

Randi pulled out her notebook. She had thought about this during her sleepless night. She knew what she needed to know. "I've been thinking this through. Even though we all talked quite a while last night, I've still got a lot of questions." She hadn't wanted to interrupt their breakfast with this.

Randi looked at Allie and tried to remember Danielle. Randi wanted nothing more than to fall in love again. Danielle might be the one, with her long willowy legs and blonde hair... Just like Allie...

"Okay."

"You might know this stuff." Randi opened the notebook, then looked into Allie's blue eyes. She looked back down at the notebook. "Okay, one of the things that's bugging me is that this guy isn't just going after hookers, he's going after hookers who dance."

77

"Yes . . ."

"So we need to think about this," Randi said.

"Okay . . ."

"Allie, I know a little about a lot. I need you to fill in some blanks. Like why women dance."

"They dance for the money," Allie said, matter of factly. She looked up at Randi, who was now perched on the plain table. "Some of them are students, just paying their way through school. Some, like Karin Frost, have to suddenly make their own way. Maybe they get kicked out of their homes, or they're runaways. Maybe they've been beaten or abused, so they've got to get out."

Allie fell silent and stared at the dirty-white wall. Randi said nothing, so Allie said, "Storm was a runaway. Her father abused her. She didn't have much of a choice. But she was also working her way through school, through college." She shrugged. "There are some who also get a morale boost from it—the boys want them, look at them like they need them. But, basically, they just need the money for drugs, because they've got kids, because they need to eat. They don't have any jobs skills or have low self-esteem and can't see anything better for themselves." She stood up. She needed to pace to think through this. She suddenly realized she wasn't jealous of Storm—had never been jealous of her, in fact. She was jealous of Brett's feelings for her.

"They usually need easy money for some reason," Allie continued. "School, kids, drugs, rent, food. Not necessarily in that order." She walked to the end of the table, turned and looked back at Randi. "I think there's also the few odd ones who dance just to escape from life. They want to freak out their parents, or else . . ." She looked Randi right in the eye. "Have you ever noticed how so many dancers look drugged out? Some are, but there're those who just go bye-bye from life. They can check out from their life while they're onstage."

Allie had thought about the dancers the night before, wonder-

78

ing what it took, what would drive a woman to dancing and hooking. Desperation? Thrill seeking? Fear? She already knew the basic logistics from Brett. Still, she wanted to get inside their heads. And she thought she had, to some extent, but there was a difference between just *understanding* and really *knowing*.

She concentrated on the dead girls. She imagined their lives and tried to get in their heads and feel what they had gone through, because that was the only way she'd be able to visualize their last moments on Earth. The only way she could recreate their deaths enough to see their killer.

"I get it," Randi said. "And remember, I want to save them."

"Okay, so what else do you need to know?" Allie asked, sitting back down and looking up at Randi, who still sat on the edge of the table.

"I assume they choose to be dancers because it's less of a violation than hooking. Superficial sexual contact only. And they get dancing gigs because of something the club owners see in them. I also know something about how dancers work, how they do lap dances for money, how they actually pay to dance at a particular establishment."

"What more could you need to know?" Allie wondered just what Randi wanted to know. How deep she wanted to embed herself in it all.

"Why do they do tricks then? If they can make so much just dancing?"

"Because some nights they don't make so much dancing, and they need more money for their drugs, or they can't find enough dancing gigs, or they've lost that last bit of self esteem. Or maybe because they're so wiped out on drugs, they just stop caring, or somebody makes them an offer they can't refuse." Allie sighed. "The bottom line is, women do it because men will pay them for it. It's easy money. And if you feel you don't have any options, it's the only route. It's not a good way of life. But men still hold too much of the power."

79

Allie was tired of talking about it. She felt worn down, thinking about women reduced to selling their bodies. She wondered how Brett could put up with it, day after day. "Okay, what's the next step? You said you'd help me question people today."

"We question everybody—three dead dancers; two clubs. We talk to staff, customers, family. We need to find out who the girls were likely to pick up as a closing trick. Did they go for certain types of men? Who they last saw, who they were last with. It's a good starting point. It's likely to give us some ideas. Vargas and Norberg had officers question people at all the places." Randi took a sip of her so-called coffee. "But I'm sure we can do a much more thorough job." She grimaced. "Is this asshole just randomly walking into places and killing girls?"

"Seems to be."

"What do you think? What do you really think?"

"You want to know what I really think? What I really think is that you're looking to me for easy answers. Easier than what you perceive other answers would cost." Allie stood up, feeling angry. "But the fact is, the easiest answers could be found with one phone call."

She dialed the private number she knew by heart. Randi tried to stop her from turning on the speaker phone, but she brushed her hand away. "Yeah babe, what you need?" Brett's voice sounded loud and clear in the near-empty room.

"Brett, I've got you on speaker. Randi's here with me," Allie said. "We're trying to figure this out. Our killer's only apparent type is dancers. Now why would somebody go for dancers, as opposed to cruising Woodward for pros? There's something key in this simple fact."

"You got me. I've been bugging on that myself. There's got to be something about these gals that's got him."

"Okay. But have you found any other pattern in the killings?" Randi asked, breaking into the conversation.

Allie opened Randi's case files, which she'd brought into the conference room, and began to flip through them. "I haven't found much. Like we said, they're pretty good looking. More your type than mine." They were all femme. Or at least played that role to get the money.

"So why's some John out popping these chicks?" Brett said.

The girls' photos were all lined up neatly on the table, one girl next to another. A butch's dream come true.

"Oh, shit," Brett said.

"What is it?" Allie asked.

"I've got all these pictures lined up in front of me too, and, well . . ."

"What is it?" Allie asked.

"You're not going to like this."

"What is it, Brett?" Randi asked.

"I think they've all worked here."

9

"Frankie?"

"Yeah boss?" He held the dancer book in his big paws, flipping through it to the pages Brett had marked. He was looking at the photocopied files from Randi that Brett had brought with her into the office. Brett wanted him to look at the pictures, since they were none-too-clear photocopies.

"Talk to me, my man."

"Well, y'know now Brett, they didn't technically work for you and all that crap."

"But?"

"It does look like they've all danced here. At some time or

'nother." He was also double-checking her comparison of the known facts about the girls."They'd hafta be stupider'n shit to think we're cappin' our own gals. Those girls pay the rent."

Brett flipped around in her chair, kicking her heels on her desk while she looked up at Frankie. "You know I don't mind free publicity, but I do like to be prepared. We need to make sure we, and all our employees, are covered. I don't want any problems, though any news can be good news—so long as it just brings in the customers and doesn't scare them, or the dancers, away."

• • •

Allie started off by going to a place she knew well—a street near the Paradise Theatre. She had her Polaroid with her because she wanted to get a picture of Victoria to show around.

She didn't have to wait long.

She had worried whether or not she'd know which girl was Victoria. But there was no question as soon as she saw her—and neither was there any question why Brett had hired her without an audition.

• • •

Victoria got off the bus and hurried into the theatre. She looked forward to getting enough cash put together to get a decent set of wheels. Detroit was definitely behind other major metropolitan areas in the public transportation department. Since coming to town, she hadn't danced at any one place long enough to develop a following, let alone save much money. She had merely been learning her job and how to do it well. Along with a few other things.

She stopped just before going into the theatre. She had the feeling someone was watching her; there was a set of eyes on her.

She shook off the feeling, rearranged her purse and the bag on her shoulder, and walked into the theatre.

"Nice to see I'm not the only one getting here early these days," Angela said with a smile when Victoria walked into the dressing room. "What's that?" she asked, indicating the bag.

"The boss told me she wants me in costume, so it's my costume." She lit a cigarette and headed upstairs, leaving Angela to get dressed on the lower level.

When Victoria came back down again she was wearing sunglasses, a black leatherette body suit unzipped just enough to show a hint of cleavage, black spike heels, and a low slung leather belt with a black toy pistol in it. She carried a CD.

Angela gave a low wolf whistle.

"Wait'll you see the rest of it," Victoria said with a wink.

"But you know, Brett thinks the johns come here for tits and ass, not for a show."

"Actually I think they want to see tits, pussy and ass. And just so long as I show them all that, and play with myself a bit, I don't think they give too much a crap what I do." She left the dressing room, closing the door behind her, and knocked on the door of the box office.

"Whatcha need?" Tim said through the bullet-proof glass.

"I wanted to give you my new music," she held up the CD and raised an eyebrow, inclining her head toward him.

He inched the door open slightly saying, "Brett doesn't like any dancers being in here."

She pushed the door open. "And what about you? Do you like us being in here?" She inched her zipper down, exposing still more cleavage. "Kinda warm in here, isn't it?" she said, stepping into the box office.

"Yeah, it is." He leaned against the desk, his eyes glued to her body.

"How 'bout playing this for me today?" Victoria asked, handing him the CD.

"You don't like Enigma? Brett picked it out for you."

"I think she'll like this."

"Prince?" he said hopefully.

"You'll find out."

"What's going on here? No dancers in the box office," Brett said, coming downstairs. She stopped in the doorway and looked at Victoria. Her look was like a caress. It was the look that told Victoria she was making the right impression. No matter what Brett said or did that indicated otherwise, Victoria had her attention.

"Like what you see?" Victoria asked, running her hand along her opened zipper and dropping it down below her breasts.

"I'm hoping you'll move out of the way so I can get what I need. I have things to do today." She reached for the dancer's schedules from the desk.

"I'm hoping I'm one of them."

Brett roughly pushed by Victoria, keeping her hands in front of her, but her arms out, slightly away from her body, so she could negotiate her way through the fairly small space without coming into bodily contact with anyone.

"I hope you're at least planning on catching my show today," Victoria said, blocking Brett's passage. "I think you'll enjoy it."

"Black's not a good color for a dark stage," Brett said, assessing Victoria.

"It'll look hot under the stage lights."

"Like we got real theatre lights here. You want me to blow tons of green on shit like that that don't even matter?" Brett grabbed the papers from the drawer and returned upstairs.

Victoria felt a surge of anger at Brett's dismissal, but let it go quickly. She was sure Brett would come to her once she'd seen the new act. How could she not?

"Brett?" Angela said timidly from the doorway to her office.

"Yes? What is it?" She tried to hide her frustration as she looked up from her desk.

"It's about what we were talking about yesterday."

"Which was?"

"Well, I think I remembered where I've seen Victoria before. At the Rainbow Room."

Brett grinned. "Angela, is there something you ain't been telling me?" Angela always said she was straight, and the Rainbow Room was a lesbian bar. She leaned back in her chair.

"You know how a lot of dancers do shows there at some time or another."

"I didn't know you had."

Angela bowed her head shyly. "Well, it can be kinda fun. It doesn't pay much, but it's nice to have women buying you drinks for a change." She sat down in a visitor's chair across from Brett. "And they don't treat us like sluts."

"I understand."

"Anyway, I think I saw her dancing there a while ago. Victoria." Angela was looking at Brett with a deadly serious expression.

"Really? But she said she just got to town?" Brett stood.

"Yeah, that's kinda why it bothered me so much I had to remember."

"Because it looks as if she's been lying about that, and no telling what else."

"Yeah."

• • •

Allie, armed with her Polaroid of Victoria as well as pictures of the other dancers, headed north on Woodward to Eight Mile, and over to The Naked Truth. Even though Randi was in charge of

86

checking out the bars, Allie wanted to get a feeling for what had happened at each of the crime scenes.

Allie drove up to The Naked Truth, parked her car and got out. There were only three other cars in the lot. She went behind the bar, pulling out her notepad to double check the facts she had jotted down. She wanted to be able to visualize everything as precisely as possible.

She started down the alley from her car, carefully looking for anything out of the ordinary. She wasn't holding her breath because it had been a few days since the bodies were found. Anything the killer had left had probably either been washed away in a rain, or picked up by some street person.

She was surprised there were so many cans back here. She could understand the trash and grime, but pop and beer cans were worth a dime each in Michigan. Some people made their living collecting these returnables.

She continued down the alley, alert for anything, however small, that might have been overlooked when the bodies were found. Nothing. She reached the Dumpster and tried to visualize where the bodies had been. The front of the Dumpster faced her, and her notes said that both bodies were found on the right side. The side closest to the parking lot.

Near the Dumpster, but not in it. She glanced through her notes and saw that Nicola had also been found next to a Dumpster.

Why weren't the bodies in the Dumpsters? It would take longer to discover them buried in the trash, and more evidence would be destroyed. But . . . maybe the killer wanted the bodies to be found?

Or maybe he couldn't lift the bodies up and into the Dumpsters?

But . . . was there any other reason the bodies wouldn't've been tossed into the Dumpsters? Perhaps the murderer was some sort of 98-pound weakling who needed the Charles Atlas program?

Allie wrote these notes in her book, then went back to her car, looking for any other evidence.

She found none.

10

When the butch woman answered her knock, Allie's eyebrows shot up. "Anna Siciliano?" She had decided to start double-checking Vargas's and Norberg's work by speaking with the families. If all the Detroit P.D. would allow them time for was a cursory investigation, there was no telling what a little more time and energy might turn up.

"No, just a minute. I'll get her."

Allie stood on the porch, looking around at the quiet, suburban neighborhood. Why had poor Maria Terese run away from home and become a prostitute? Who had done what to her to force her into such a life? And just who was that obvious butch who answered the door?

"Whaddya want?" The woman who came to the door was tall—about as tall as Allie—with thick, black hair and a buxom figure. She looked like a typical Italian mother. Allie could almost smell the spicy marinara sauce in the house.

Allie took a deep breath and said, "My name is Allison Sullivan, and I'm here investigating your daughter's death." She quickly flipped out the forged P.I. license she had obtained that morning. Randi left just enough information, lying on her desk, for her to know how to do so. Just as she had intimated.

"Private investigator? Why're you interested in my daughter?"

"Your daughter was one of three girls killed so far. The family of the last one hired me to look into her murder—"

"Three girls? I didn't know any other girls had been killed!"

"There have been three girls murdered, apparently by the same man. The parents of the latest victim don't believe the police are taking it seriously enough."

Anna snorted. "Imagine that. The cops that came by earlier didn't seem to care much about anything. Don't know why they even showed up." Her face was stony.

"I wouldn't have taken this case if I didn't care."

"I don't know that there's anything I can tell you," she said.

Allie knew she had to get Anna inside. "Mrs. Siciliano, could we step inside? I have some uncomfortable questions to ask you, and I think it would be better if we weren't half out on the street."

Anna Siciliano looked her up and down and, as if deciding she posed no immediate threat and allowed her in.

Allie knew entry into the house was only the first step toward getting the woman to talk with her. "Mrs. Siciliano . . . I know this is a really difficult time for you—"

"What would you know about it?"

Allie thought about what this woman was experiencing, and, although knowing there was no comparison, she said the only thing that came to mind. "I've lost both my parents, Mrs.

Siciliano, and I know that's no comparison to what through . . . and that's part of why I'm looking int one else loses their daughter before their time."

Anna Siciliano gave her a hard appraisal. "You're ~~young to~~ have lost both your parents."

Allie looked down at the tiled floor. It was identical to that which her own parents had had in their entryway. "They thought they couldn't have kids. They were in their early forties by the time I showed up. First one died, then the other followed." She was trying to lighten up her words, but it still hurt too much.

Anna took her by the arm, gently, like a mom, and led her to the kitchen and a plate of cookies, "Would you like something to drink? I have coffee, tea, soda?"

"I would love a glass of water."

Anna pulled a Coca-Cola glass out of a cupboard, filled it with water from the tap, and placed it in front of Allie. "There you go. Now have a cookie, just come out of the oven. You look like you're about to fade away right in front of my eyes."

"Thank you, ma'am," Allie said, feeling almost as if she was in her own mother's kitchen again. A wave of sadness swept over her.

"I know how this other family must feel." It was as if she intuited that Allie didn't need to talk about her parents, so Anna dived into the very thing that could distract her from her misery. She was such a Mom. "I miss my little girl, and I wish the police would do something about finding whoever hurt her." Anna stood with her hands on her hips, daring Allie to defy her. "So, what is it you want to know?"

Allie pulled out her notebook and a pen. "Can you think of anybody who would want to kill your daughter?"

Anna shook her head slowly, tears running down her cheeks. "I lost touch with Maria a few years ago, so I really don't know the type of woman my daughter became."

The first woman rushed into the kitchen and pulled her into her arms. "Georgie, Georgie," Anna sobbed into her shoulder.

"What's going on? What happened? What did you do? " Georgie demanded, holding Anna close to her, stroking her hair. She was shorter than Anna, with short, straight, white hair, a slender, wiry frame, tanned face, and dark brown eyes.

She's an old-fashioned butch, Allie realized, and she and Anna are lovers. "I'm sorry, ma'am, but I'm just here investigating Maria Teresa's murder."

"Get out," Georgie demanded.

"It's all right, Georgie." Anna pulled Georgie back to her, and wiped at her eyes. Georgie kept an arm around her, glowering at Allie. "What do you need to know?"

"It appears there's a serial killer out there who's after exotic dancers."

"My baby would never have done that. Dancing? For men? Taking her clothes off for them? Letting them touch her? I don't believe it!"

"The police told you that too, Anna. We have no reason to believe they or this young woman are lying."

"But I still don't believe it!" Anna half-heartedly beat at Georgie's chest.

"I'm sorry, ma'am . . ." Allie began, but Georgie cut her off.

"I know you're right, Georgie." Anna turned tear-filled eyes to Allie. "So, she really did these horrible things?"

Allie was ready to lie, give her a vanilla version, but instead she nodded. "Sylver, Maria Teresa, was the first of three so far. I came here to see if I could find anything that was overlooked."

Georgie nodded. "I knew she'd do something like that when she left here. She took too much after her father, no good son-of-a-bitch."

"Who was her father?"

"Donny Capriano," Anna replied, looking up. "I told myself I loved him. It was the only thing a good Italian girl could do." She looked toward a far corner of the room.

"What do you need to know?" Georgie asked.

Allie looked again at her notebook, then looked up to meet Georgie's eyes. "Everything."

"Why?"

"I'm trying to figure out the pattern of his victims. There's no telling what he's thinking, or where he'll go next. There's no telling what's going on in his mind. I need to learn as much as possible, so I can understand. I need to know what he'll do next."

Georgie nodded. She still stroked Anna's hair.

"Maria Teresa's name, and her mother's, are different from her father's. Do you want to tell me about it?"

"No," Georgie said.

"I did what I had to do," Anna replied. "I'm sure you can't understand, but I had to do things that made me sick to survive. I slept with Donny twice, and found out I was pregnant." Georgie held her tightly. "Donny wanted to marry me, but by then I knew it wasn't right."

Georgie looked at Allie defiantly. "We met when she was pregnant. Do you have a problem with that?"

Allie smiled. "Not at all." She loved seeing these older lesbians and knowing that they had been together for more than twenty years.

"Donny turned out to be a no good son-of-a-bitch," Anna said. "He never paid me child support, like he promised, he never did nothin' he promised."

"Except one thing," Georgie said.

"Except one thing," Anna conceded. "He found out about me and Georgie, and he filed for custody." She looked at Allie, meeting her eyes. "And he won. He was a goddamned alcoholic who never did nobody no good his whole life, and he got custody." Anna leaned into Georgie's chest, sobbing, and Georgie held her.

Allie gave them their time.

"He died about five years ago. Shot when he was trying to rob a

Seven-Eleven," Georgie said. "I was surprised Maria Teresa's grandparents didn't sue for custody then, but they didn't, so we got her."

"But it was too late!" Anna screamed, like an animal in pain.

Allie waited till one of them could explain. She was horrified.

"He wasn't a very good father," Georgie softly said. "When Maria Teresa came to us, she was already drinking, doing drugs and having sex. She was—"

Anna pulled away and slapped Georgie.

Georgie held Anna's wrists in her hands. "She was, goddamnit! And I hope his fucking soul rots in hell for whatever he did to that girl!" Georgie yelled at Anna, who collapsed into her arms. Once she was calmed down, Georgie said to Allie, "Kids these days have too much against them. Even if you're a good parent, it's tough to keep them safe. He wasn't a good parent. We tried to set her straight, scare her straight, but she bucked us at every turn."

"I wanted her to go to college and become the doctor my mama always wanted me to marry," Anna sobbed.

Allie felt as if her heart would burst. It was with difficulty that she controlled her own tears.

"Is there anything else you need to know, Detective?" Georgie eventually asked.

"You said you haven't seen her for a few years?"

"That's right. She did graduate from high school, but just barely."

Allie reached into her pocket and pulled out the Polaroid of Victoria. "Have you ever seen this woman before?"

Anna reached a shaking hand forward to take the photo. She and Georgie stared at it. "Is this another of his victims?"

"No, she's another dancer, one who just recently appeared."

"If she only just showed up, why are you asking us about her?" Georgie asked. "What does she have to do with our Maria?"

"Well, she showed up rather suspiciously, so I thought it justified some looking into."

Anna shook her head. "I've never seen this girl before in my life."

Allie nodded, then took in the way Georgie had her arm protectively around Anna. "I can see you two need time alone, but I might have to come back."

"I'll walk you out," Georgie said.

"Thank you for your time," Allie said, pulling out a piece of paper and scrawling her name and number on it. "If you think of anything—"

"I'll call you," Georgie said, taking the paper and pocketing it. If she was surprised Allie didn't have a business card, she didn't show it.

Allie began to walk away.

"Hey."

"Yes?"

"Anna's had a hard enough time already, and all of this is almost too much for her. I hope you find the asshole who did this."

Allie stood still for a moment, the sun on her face, staring at this hardened woman whose heart was soft as the finest down pillow. She swallowed. "I'll do my best."

As Allie drove away, she wondered what instinct, precisely, drove her to say the things she had—to reveal the things she had. She knew it was instinct, and she also knew that instincts were buried deep inside oneself.

Maybe Randi was right. Maybe she needed to go back to school to figure out why she sometimes did the things she did.

But she also wondered why she thought of Georgie as an "old-fashioned butch." What was it about her that showed Allie so clearly what Allie didn't feel with Brett?

• • •

Randi was a few steps behind Allie. She had to take care of some things at the station before going to the Paradise and getting a picture of Victoria. She knew she and Allie would probably have to hit the clubs more than once to get the information they needed. After all, there wouldn't be many people there this early, if any at all. But she could use this time to check out the vicinity and maybe talk to some of the street folks who stayed around each of the locations.

She had a lot of territory to cover in as little time as possible.

After thoroughly searching around The Naked Truth, and finding nothing of interest, Randi approached the entrance. There were at least a dozen cars in the lot. Randi looked at her watch and was surprised to see it was already 11:30.

When she went to the door, the bouncer stretched out a meaty arm. "No unescorted women."

"This is my escort," Randi said, pulling out her badge.

He lowered his arm to catch her before she put her badge away. He carefully looked it over, and she was surprised to see his lips *didn't* move as he read.

"Detroit cop, huh?" he said, handing it back to her with a suspicious glare.

"Yes, I'm looking into the deaths of several dancers. Two of whom were murdered here." She took her badge and I.D. back and looked at him. "I'd like to speak with the owner."

"Huh," he said, still standing between Randi and the rest of the club. "Get Max," he said to the bartender.

While Randi waited, she looked around him, trying to see more of the club. The lights were rather low in the bar, and there were only a few patrons there: three men in business suits with cocktails, one loner in jeans and a T-shirt with a beer, and another man in shirt and trousers drinking by himself. All were hypnotically watching the three dancers on stage gyrate and spin on the poles they used as props.

96

Randi figured the lunch rush should begin soon. She was hoping to witness the infamous businessmen's luncheons (where they only thing they "ate" was liquid) she had heard so much about, where married men spent fortunes on girls and drinks, putting it all on expense accounts.

Of course, this wasn't a very upscale place, its overall ambience was somewhat akin to that of the Paradise, so it wasn't too likely to get too much of the business luncheon dollars. But, then again, there was no figuring out men.

She did figure this would be a good time to try to see a lot of this place's patrons. Maybe get a feel for who the regulars were.

"Yeah? What is it?" a short, stocky, dark-haired man asked the bouncer.

"I'm Detective Randi McMartin, with the Detroit Police."

He gave her a thorough look, nodding to the bouncer that it was all right, although he still didn't invite her into the club itself. "Well, everybody knows I always cooperate with the police. After all, I have nothing to hide, and just want to help you fine folks in protecting us."

"I'm sure," she said, looking around. "Is Tina O'Rourke here?"

"I'm Max Grueber. I manage this joint."

"So Tina isn't here?"

"No. What can I do for you today, Detective?"

"I was wondering if you know anything about the dancers who have been turning up dead?"

"'Turning up dead?' Nice way of putting it. The ones who've been gettin' themselves cut, you mean?"

"What can you tell me about Kelly Roberts and Maria Teresa Siciliano?"

"Desiree and Sylver? They were whores and junkies. They were gonna end up getting it one way or another. Some john, or AIDS, or a pimp or a pusher. It'd happen sooner or later."

"Do you know anything about their pasts?"

97

He shrugged. "They probably came from real messed-up families. Like most of these girls. None of them are worth my time of day."

"They make you a lot of money though, don't they?"

"Hell yes. But that doesn't mean I have to like them or know them or anything." He lit a cigar and blew the smoke right at her. "Hell, I don't even screw the trash I got workin' here. Some guys'll put their dicks in anything, though."

She knew he was trying to get a rise out of her, but it wasn't going to work. "Have you noticed anybody suspicious hanging around? Anybody you think might be behind it?" She tried to nonchalantly step around him, and into the bar, but he kept blocking her way.

"Nope."

"Well, could I possibly get copies of your contact sheets and schedules? I'd like to look through them for any patterns." She glanced around him, but again, he was a man with something to hide.

"Tina keeps that stuff at her main office."

"You know, with the way you're acting, I'm liable to think you're trying to hide something. Perhaps I should come back later tonight? You know, when you're good and busy? And me with a lot of uniformed officers and a search warrant?"

He stepped aside and waved her into the club. Randi had known he wouldn't want cops hanging around and scaring off business. Especially on a busy Friday night when guys who had just gotten paid had money burning a hole in their pockets.

She strode past him and started circling around through the dark club with its loud music and flashing lights.

"If you want, I'll call Tina and tell her you're going to come by to pick up the paperwork."

She glanced at her watch. "I'll come back here later tonight. Make sure it's here."

"Is there anything else I can do for you, Detective?" He knew she was getting pissed, and he'd better kiss her ass to avoid problems with the police.

"Have you noticed anybody suspicious hanging around? Or did you around the time of the murders?"

"Nope. Nobody. Of course, with the sort of place this is, somebody's always bringing somebody new—an out-of-town client, or a new prospect or something."

"So you don't have what you'd call regulars?"

"Oh, of course we have those. They're the ones always bringing me new customers. And some of my dancers have regular followings as well."

"I know that at the Paradise, girls only dance a few days, maybe a week, each month—they're constantly rotating."

"Listen babe, Brett does a few shows a day. This is a different sort of place. I got dancers on that stage every hour I'm open. So I got some girls that just dance for me, and I got some that come and go. I got 'em all."

"Who decides if they're a regular?"

"Well, if they're good, I tell them they can come back as much as they like. Some girls like that—they like having a regular place with a regular clientele and all that. They always know what to expect, for the most part, that way."

"And the others?"

"Some figure they can make enough money not working full time. Others figure they can make more money moving around and dancing at different places. It all depends."

"Are the customers the same way? Either regulars or those who shop around?"

"Yeah. Except for those that are from out of town and get brought in by somebody else. You know, clients of local businessmen, other sorts of out-of-town friends."

Randi nodded, looking around the place. An increasing number

99

of men were coming in now, some of them nodding to Max as they were seated. Max nodded back. No smile or hello, just a nod.

She wondered if he knew any of his customers by name.

On stage there were three different girls going through their motions. One thing she had to give the owners of adult establishments, they didn't seem to discriminate on size or race. Max had as much a mix of races and body types as Brett did.

"So your crowd is always like this?" she asked, sitting down at an empty table.

"It does vary a lot. I'm not as upscale as say Charlie's or Trummpp's, and I'm not in as good a neighborhood, so I get a lot more of the local riff-raff."

"Sounds as if you like your customers about as much as you like your dancers."

He shrugged. "I've got nothing against them so long as they don't cause trouble and they drink up." He grinned wolfishly. "After all, that's where I make my money—on the ten-dollar beers."

"Were there any trouble-makers around the nights Roberts and Siciliano were murdered?" Randi heard a slight commotion across the bar, but didn't want to miss anything Max was saying.

"Nope. Nobody in particular. The night Desiree got it was really pretty quiet, being a Sunday and all, and when Sylver got it we had a few frat boys here getting lit, but Louie took care of them."

"What did he do to them?"

"Nothing much. They just about pissed their pants from him just growling at them." He smirked at Randi. "Louie's so big, he makes Frankie Lorenzini look like a termite, and frat boys ain't got the balls god gave to a caterpillar. You know, I'm curious why the cops are suddenly paying so much attention to all of this? I mean, these girls were just slut-bag whores—nobody anybody'd ever care about. None of them will ever amount to two nickels."

100

"So, you were working both nights?" Randi said, disgusted by his description of the victims. She didn't think she'd get much more detail than that from him.

"Yeah. I'm here a lot. Now, is there anything else, Detective? I do have a club to run."

A rather well-endowed waitress came over, walking so quickly her unrestrained breasts were jiggling underneath her white shirt. "Max? Sorry to interrupt, but . . ." she glanced toward Randi.

"What is it, Susie?" Max said, then quickly jumped up and went to a table across the room, arriving at the same time as the bouncer. Randi hurried after them.

"I told you last time—" Max was saying.

"I wasn't doing anything!" The bouncer grabbed the man in an armlock. He was small, balding, and pasty-faced. The loner who had been drinking by himself when Randi entered.

"Like hell you weren't!" a dancer cried out, but Susie put up a hand, holding her back.

Max glanced over at a seated man, who immediately looked away.

Max nodded at the bouncer, who took the struggling man out. "Somebody's always got to try to spoil the party, huh?" he said to Randi, leading her back to their table. "I've warned him before, one more strike and he's out of here for good."

"What is it he does?"

"He grabs at the girls, tries to put his hands where they don't belong. That sort of thing. Some girls let the guys get away with that sort of shit, some don't."

Randi watched the fellow until the bouncer threw him out of the club. "And he does that a lot?"

"All the time," Susie said, putting a drink in front of Max. "There's some guys who tip well enough that we'll put up with some of that, but he's just plain creepy."

"And he ain't got no money, either," Max said.

"Kinda like the class geek, huh?" Randi asked Susie.

"Yeah."

"Do you know his name?"

"He always says to call him 'Big Jim,'" she replied with a frown.

"Susie, go clean up his table," Max said. "His name is Jim Peterson. I made sure to check his ID the first time we discharged him. Now, if there's nothing else—"

"How long did those two girls work for you?"

He shrugged. "Hell if I know. I'd guess they'd both been here about a year." He glanced at his watch, "I've really got to go now."

"Do you have any written schedules for the time she died?"

"You can get those when you pick up the other stuff from Tina."

"Are your waitresses like your dancers, or do they just work here?"

"Oh, they just work here. I give them security and a good paycheck, which they need since they don't give lap dances or anything." He stood.

"One last thing," she said, stopping him and pulling the Polaroid out of her breast pocket. "Have you ever seen this woman?" she asked, showing him the picture of Victoria.

He glanced at it. "Maybe, maybe not." But his eyes had given him away. Randi knew he'd seen her before. She gave him a few moments to tell her the truth, but when he didn't she said, "Well, then, thanks for all your help." Asshole.

On her way out, Randi looked over the room, and wondered if any of these men could be the killer.

"Huh, I bet you think you're something else," a dancer, finishing her lap dances, said to Randi.

"What do you mean?"

"Max only holds auditions in the morning, before we open. How'd you get such special treatment? Huh?"

102

"I'm not here as a dancer." Randi began, stunned that anybody would think she was. "I'm—" Most of the dancers she had known were not overly fond of the police, and were more likely to clam up when faced with a detective.

"Yeah?"

"I'm a friend of Brett Higgins. I'm here doing a favor for her. Do you know her?"

The woman gave her a thorough look. "Huh. I wouldn't have thought you were her type at all."

"So Peterson was giving you a problem?"

"Yeah, he always does. The creep."

"Any other guys around here like that? Problem customers?"

"He's the worst, but there's another guy comes in some nights—big macho man, thinks he's god's gift."

"What's he look like?"

"Big. Maybe six foot. Beefy, but not fatty, muscular, like he works out all the time 'cause he's not gettin' any. Dark oily hair. Beady little eyes. Why you want to know, anyway?"

"Just curious is all. Do you know his name?"

"You taking a survey or what?"

Randi had learned a few things from Brett. She pulled a ten out of her wallet and held it out.

"Stan."

"What's his last name?"

"I don't know. I'd like to see the bastard busted, so I'd tell you if I knew."

Randi paused, then handed over the money. "Thanks." She turned away from the dancer and found Susie. "I was wondering if you could do me a favor?" She picked up a napkin and wrote her office, pager and cell numbers on it. "Call me if Stan or Big Jim come back." She glanced over to the table where Big Jim had been sitting, but it was cleared off already. "And there'll be something in it for you if you can get me a glass with either of their finger-prints on it."

Randi looked around outside the bar, thinking. Brett was the only one who saw anything other than the obvious in these dancers.

She stopped by the Paradise to look over the crime scene there, but found nothing else helpful. She thought about hanging around, to talk with some of the patrons, but decided to head back to the station and her regular caseload.

She'd go back to The Naked Truth that night, to pick up the information she wanted from Tina. She hoped Tina would be sure whether or not she knew Victoria.

And, after that, maybe she'd stop by the Paradise, when Brett wasn't there.

11

Victoria sat back in her chair on the second floor of the dressing room, inhaling deeply on her cigarette, hoping it would cover the smell of the joint Chantel had just smoked. She didn't like the smell of marijuana herself, and knew Brett would try to track it down if she caught a whiff. She didn't want Brett whiffing around her for any reason she hadn't purposely set up.

She didn't need to be kicked out just after she had found this place and this woman.

She leaned back in her chair, blowing out little smoke rings, and remembered. She could envision each curve of the letters on the sheet of yellow, lined, legal-pad paper.

...Brett, the owner of the theater, is tall, dark and unbelievably handsome and nice . . .

Victoria had now seen just how incredibly handsome Brett was, but she still wasn't buying the nice bit. She didn't think she ever would.

Not that it even mattered. It'd all be over soon.

• • •

Allie decided she needed some time to think after her interview with Anna. She was getting a bit peckish, so she headed to a restaurant for a cup of coffee and a bite to eat. She stared at the coffee and thought about how much like a cop she was. She should've had a donut in front of her instead of a Caesar salad.

Maybe Randi was right. Maybe she should take some classes at one of the colleges nearby.

She needed to go see Brett. Randi seemed to think the tele-conference this morning with her was fine, but Allie wanted to be sure Brett had the same opinion. She didn't like her two butches not getting along. She speared some lettuce and a crouton with her fork and put it in her mouth, enjoying the garlicky dressing. She realized she had just thought of Randi and Brett as her two butches. God, good thing she only had that thought to herself, instead of doing something really stupid like voicing such a notion to Brett.

Enough of that. She had murders to help solve. She sat back, taking a moment before finishing her salad. The first two dancers were killed at the same place. If the killer followed this pattern, the next girl would be from the Paradise.

Allie knew that if the killer was smart, he wouldn't hit again at the Paradise. And if he was planning on it, he'd be sure to notice a stakeout and stay away from it while it was going on.

She finished her lunch, paid the bill, and went out to her car thinking about Brett. She had to go down to the theatre and make sure she was okay.

Well, okay, maybe she wasn't averse to also meeting the new dancer. And taking a look around the place again, because the seed of an idea was planting itself in her mind. After all, there was only one way to do a stake-out without doing a stake-out, so to speak.

• • •

Brett dug around her and Frankie's offices looking for old schedules. Frankie wasn't quite as meticulous as she was. Between their offices and the box office she found what she was looking for: contact sheets, pictures and schedules dating back to the reopening of the Paradise after the building burned a few years before.

She finished the burger Angela had brought her for lunch and downed the last of her soda. It was rather funny, actually. Victoria was the one who looked like Storm, but Angela was the one who acted like her. Storm had always brought Brett food, making sure she ate, taking care of her, watching out for her just like Angela did now.

She shrugged it off, took all of the papers she had assembled and went into the general work area to make two sets of copies of each stack. One was for Allie, the other for her, and the originals would go into a filing cabinet in her office. Properly organized, of course.

She glanced at her watch: 2:10. The two o'clock show would just be getting started.

She sat down at her desk with the copies and pulled a set of highlighters out of the drawer and placed them neatly on the desktop. She went through the contact sheets and highlighted each of the dead dancer's names in yellow. She wanted to make sure that the girls danced at the Paradise under the same name they danced under at the Naked Truth. Hopefully, she'd be able to get copies of the schedules and contact sheets from there. Usually girls just used one stage name, but sometimes they didn't. She wondered if she should double-check with other club owners as well. She stapled those sheets together and put them on a corner of her desk. She got up, poured two fingers of Glenlivet into a glass, tossed in a couple of ice cubes, and went back to her desk.

She looked at her watch. 2:30. She picked up the other stack of papers. These were all of the schedules since the rebuild, which Brett had already put into chronological order. She worked her way through them all, month by month. In blue she highlighted Sylver's name, orange for Desiree and pink for Nicola. They had all danced at the Paradise in the recent past.

3:00. Brett pulled on her jacket, straightened her tie, downed her scotch, and went downstairs.

"Hey, Brett, just in time!" Tim said. "Chantel just left the stage and Victoria's out there about to start. You gotta see this!"

Brett nodded, walked out of the box office and into the darkened theatre. It took her eyes a moment to acclimate to the sudden darkness—the only lights came from the glowing exit signs and the porno movie providing a backdrop for the stage. She could barely make out the shape of Chantel working the crowd, selling lap dances.

"Now boys, you better watch out for this one," came Tim's voice over the loudspeaker, "'cause she's a killer and she's out to get you! Tempest!"

Simultaneously the stage lights came on low with the music, which was loud. Victoria stood in the center of the stage, clad in a black jumpsuit reminiscent of Mrs. Peel from *The Avengers*, and turned around with a gun in her hands. It only took Brett a moment to identify the gun as a cheap toy, and to realize that

108

Victoria's opening music quickly flipped from *The Avengers* to the James Bond theme.

The gun routine only lasted a few seconds, then Victoria put the gun down and sensuously took off the belt, snapping it with a grin while John Forsythe's voice blared through the room, "My name is Charlie." Victoria threw the belt down, unzipped the jumpsuit past her navel, showing off luscious cleavage, and strutted across the stage, whipping around in a high-flying, *Charlie's Angels'* movie maneuver while the theme song played.

Brett enjoyed the graceful ease with which Victoria executed her seduction of the audience. Not many girls these days put on a show. Hell, most of them couldn't even dance. Victoria not only put on a show, one that was quick, aggressive and interesting, but also strutted her stuff. She had a background in either gymnastics or dance, or maybe martial arts. Brett grinned at that thought. She'd be a real tempest in bed, all right.

Somewhere in her mind, Brett was aware that Chantel had left the theatre. Had left rather early in fact.

Victoria teased the top of her skin-tight suit down, revealing her full breasts with their darkened nipples, erect and crying to be teased and nibbled. She dropped the costume down to hang provocatively around her hips while she cupped her breasts, teasing and squeezing the full buds of her nipples. She stretched up, then ran her hands down her body till her thumbs hooked into the leatherette, which she slowly inched down.

She wore nothing underneath it.

She gazed out over the audience, proud of her body, of its nakedness and ability to have such an effect on her audience. And then she met Brett's eyes, a small grin working its way across her face. She winked, sucked the tip of her finger seductively in her mouth, then traced the finger down her chest, around her nipples, and down her stomach to between her legs, all the while keeping her eyes locked with Brett's. Or at least, that was how it appeared to Brett.

There was a cot on the stage for the dancers to use, and Victoria spun around, shaking her booty for the men, before she sat on the edge of it with her legs spread wide. Brett was vaguely aware that Prince's "Darling Nikki" was now playing. She had no idea when the music had changed.

Victoria continued her routine until the last song finally came to a close. She tossed her costume to the side behind the curtains, and donned the g-string she'd left on the stage earlier. Then she went into the audience to start making money.

When she headed right for Brett, Brett got up and left. She didn't trust herself.

"Brett," Chantel said, immediately assaulting her as she left the auditorium, "you know I do good work for you, so how about cutting me a break and not making me dance with that Tempest anymore?"

"What's the matter with her? You went before her, so it's not like you can complain that she dropped lube or whipped cream on the stage." Girls hated when other dancers did that sort of thing, because it left the stage slippery and dangerous.

Chantel pressed her almost naked body against Brett. It felt way too good in Brett's aroused state. "Brett," Chantel whispered into her ear, "you saw what happened in there." She nibbled Brett's ear. "She got goin' and they didn't want anything to do with me. How can I pay my rent with things like that going on? You tell me baby . . ." She was rubbing her big, beautiful self against Brett, using her wonderful curves to their best effect.

"I like a girl who asks nicely," Brett said. She smiled, pushed Chantel gently away, rapped on the window and said to Tim, "Give whoever goes before Tempest a chance to earn some money before you put her on, 'kay?"

"But Brett . . ."

"Timmy," she said, opening the door so she could talk right to him, "I like all the girls to get a fair shake of it. So long as they all behave, you gotta give them a chance."

"But she's good, Brett, real good."

"I know that Tim." She winked at Chantel and entered the box office, closing the door behind her. Chantel walked away. "But guys don't come for just one girl, and if no one wants to dance with her, she's no good for us. You got that?"

"Why should she work so hard if you do this sort of thing to her?"

"She'll still make money, a girl like her can't go wrong. She'll pull in more than her fair share. And the others, if they're smart, will learn from her, and that'll make business better for all of us. Got it?"

"But what if she leaves and don't come back no more?"

"She'll come back—trust me, I know." She winked at Tim and opened the door leading upstairs. "Just don't put her on so soon after they start doing their lap dances."

12

Allie knocked louder, then laid on the doorbell. She knew somebody was home. She could hear the TV in the living room. There
was an old Ford F150 pick-up in the driveway. She glanced at her
watch: 2:15. She wanted to do this interview and go see Brett.

Finally the door opened.

The man was overweight, unshaven, and wearing a dirty
sleeveless, ribbed, undershirt, the type Allie thought was referred
to as a "wife-beater." And she was pretty sure he hadn't bathed in
several days or a week, but wasn't sure if that or the smell of stale
beer repelled her more.

This man could very well be Brett's father, she realized with a start. Brett never said much about her parents or family. But from what she had told Allie, this man fit the bill. Allie felt sorry for Brett.

"Whaddya want?" he slurred.

"I'm a private investigator working on the recent killing spree that claimed your daughter as a victim," she said, flipping out her I.D. for his inspection.

"I don't have no daughter."

"Aren't you Kelly Roberts' father?"

"No, I ain't," he said with a sneer. "She's my wife's kid."

"I'm looking into her murder, and I need to ask you some questions." She hated this man without knowing him. She hated him on sight. He didn't even have the imagination or fortitude to hide who he really was—instead, he was simply a walking-talking stereotype.

"Why? What would I know?"

"You knew her, didn't you?" She was quickly losing her temper. Without waiting for an answer she continued, "Why don't I come in?" The last thing in the world she wanted to do was enter this house, but she knew it was the only way she could get any answers.

"Yeah, whatever. Sure. Wanta beer?"

"No thank you." The entire place smelled as bad as he did. Bottles and cans were lying all over. The ashtrays were overflowing. She was very glad she didn't need to use the bathroom. There was no telling what was living in there.

He turned down the volume on the television. "So what can I do for you, Ms. Private Investigator?" he said with a sneer.

She glanced around the room again, looking for pictures or anything of a personal nature. There were none. "You said Kelly was your wife's daughter. She's been married before?"

"I'm her third husband. And no, I didn't adopt that little whore of a daughter of hers." He went into the kitchen, got another beer and returned to his armchair, where he lit a Marlboro.

113

"So you are Mr . . .?"

"Alfred Meyers. You can call me Al."

"And how long have you been married to Mrs. Meyers?"

"Ah, shit, too damned long. Ten years. Longer. Seems like a life sentence."

"And what do you do for a living Mr. Meyers?"

"I'm laid-off. From Ford. No good scumbags don't keep us working regular no more. Goddamned people keep buying all those foreign cars. Damned Yuppie scum."

Allie could only stare at him. From what Brett had said, Storm had the same sort of jerk for a father as Brett did. She made a show of referring to her notepad while she decided what to ask next. "Kelly was twenty-six when she died, correct?"

"Fuck if I know. You'd hafta ask her mother."

"When did she leave home?"

"I dunno. She ran away some time ago with that no-good scumbag of a boyfriend a hers, soon as she got pregnant. Betcha he dumped her when he found out what a little whore she was, and that's what happened to her."

"So she ran away from home?"

"Hell yes she did. But I woulda kicked her out if she hadn't run away first. Goddamned tramp."

The back screen door banged.

"Bitch, I hope you got me beer!" he yelled without looking away from Allie.

"Yes, I got you beer and cigarettes," a woman's voice called back, staying in the kitchen.

"Then bring me one goddamnit."

The woman, wearing a dirty waitress's uniform, entered carrying a beer and a pack of Marlboros. She took care of Al before she even noticed Allie's presence. As soon as she saw her, though, she looked down. Not quickly enough for Allie not to notice the shiner she was sporting, and trying to hide.

114

"Mrs. Meyers, I'm Allison Sullivan, a private investigator working on your daughter's murder," Allie said, stepping forward to shake her hand, forcing her to look at her. "What happened to your eye?"

"I, uh, walked into a door. A cupboard door. I should've closed it," Mrs. Meyers said, looking down and away.

"She's askin' questions about Kelly," Al said.

Mrs. Meyers looked up at Allie with washed-out blue eyes. A tear formed in the corner of one. Her voice shook as she asked, "Do you have any suspects?"

"I just got on the case, Mrs. Meyers, so I'm just reviewing everything."

"Oh," her eyes dropped. At least Kelly Roberts was loved by someone.

"Loretta, just sit down and answer her goddamned questions. I told you years ago that no-good daughter of yours would come to this, so you shouldn' be surprised." He glared at both her and Allie, then leaned back and turned up the volume on the TV.

"Your daughter was twenty-six when she died?" Allie asked, rather loudly so her voice would carry over the TV.

Loretta nodded.

"And she left home when she was how old?"

"If you two are gonna sit there yimmer-yammering like two old ladies, go to the kitchen where you belong, so's I can hear the goddamned TV."

Allie looked at Loretta, whose eyes had gotten big. She nodded to the kitchen and finally led the way. She didn't like the looks of this.

"She left home when she was fifteen," Loretta said, carefully, silently pulling a chair out from the table.

"What?" Allie said, unable to hear Loretta's low voice over the roar of Cops in the next room.

"Kelly left home when she was fifteen," Loretta said, fingering the edge of her apron.

115

"And why'd she do that?"

"I dunno," Loretta said, shaking her head. "I got home from work one day and she was gone."

"And you have no idea why?"

"No."

Allie stared at the worn woman sitting across from her, unable to determine her age. "How old are you Loretta?" She didn't look too old, but she also looked ancient.

"Fifty this past June."

"And how long have you been married to Mr. Meyers?"

"Goin' on fifteen years."

"And how long has he been laid off?"

Loretta looked away. "I don't see how any of this has anything to do with what happened to Kelly."

"I'm just trying to understand how she and others like her came into the circumstances they ended up in. I'm trying to understand them."

"But how's asking these questions gonna tell you who killed her?"

There was probably no way to get this woman to understand. "How long has Al been laid off, Loretta?"

"Well, you know about those no-good foreigners, coming in here selling cars dirt cheap 'cause they pay their people starvation wages—that's why we always got to be helping them out, all those foreigners, 'cause they don't know how to feed their own people. They only know how to destroy what's good for us, what makes us who we are."

"How long Loretta?"

"Five years or so," she spat. "All those damned niggers, kikes and faggots coming along and taking the jobs hard working men like Al fought for, just 'cause they're younger and ain't got families to support, so they can work for next-to-nothing. Ain't right, I'm telling you!"

"Keep it down in there! Goddamn, can't a man have a little peace in his own house?"

Allie looked around the kitchen. There were beer bottles lined up against the far wall. Allie guessed they had stacked up pretty quickly.

Loretta was staring down at the table. Her fingers were playing with the edge of her waitress' apron.

Probably just like Brett's mother—the eternal victim. But Allie knew that Brett's mother, and obviously Loretta, were both enablers. Both let their men rule their worlds, and abuse them and their children as they would. But Alice Higgins couldn't be troubled to name Brett until Brett was five. Things like those had bonded Storm and Brett.

Allie realized what had probably happened and decided to go for the kill. "Was Kelly pregnant when she left here?"

"Not that I know of," Loretta answered immediately. Perhaps too quickly.

"Did she leave with anybody else?"

"I think her boyfriend talked her into running away."

"So you had no idea whatsoever before that she might do such a thing?"

"No."

"None?"

"None. All right? I just got home one day and she was gone."

"So what was the boyfriend's name?" Allie asked, leaning back in the hard-backed wooden chair, poising her pen above her notepad.

"Boyfriend?"

"You said she left with a boyfriend. Who was it?"

Loretta looked away, then got up. "Can I get you something to drink? I have coffee, tea, beer?"

"Mrs. Meyers, I'd just like it if you'd answer my questions."

"I'm sorry, I'm just thirsty. Are you sure you wouldn't like anything?"

117

"What was her boyfriend's name? Or wasn't there one?"

"Of course there was!"

"Goddamnit! I said to keep quiet in there!"

Allie wanted to get up, walk into the living room, and shoot that son-of-a-bitch dead. It was a good thing she didn't have a gun on her.

"Please," Loretta said, looking scared, "I don't know what I can tell you that those other fellas didn't already ask me."

Allie walked up next to Loretta and practically whispered, "There wasn't a boyfriend, was there?"

"I don't know," Loretta said, looking fearfully about. "If she was pregnant, there musta been, right?"

"So she was pregnant."

"I . . . I don't know . . . You said it . . ."

"No, you just said it. Who was really the father? Why did Kelly really run away?"

"I don't know. I really don't know . . . I didn't see any boys hangin' around . . . I just don't know . . ."

At that moment, part of Allie wanted to feel sorry for her. But not the part that wanted to kill her. At that moment, Allie respected Brett more than she ever had before. After all, Brett not only had the strength to pull herself up from such things, but she also used to think nothing of meting out the justice she knew was deserved.

A beer can flew across the room, just missing the window. "Goddamnit woman, you let my beer go dry!" Al screamed from the kitchen door, slamming his fist against the wall. "And you two lil' gossip-mongers can't shut the hell up long enough for me to hear my goddamned television!"

Allie brought herself up to her full height, so she was looking down at him. "Sir, I think maybe you've had enough to drink."

"I don't need some little girl tellin' me when I've had enough!"

"Sir, I don't think you want to do this."

118

"Please, don't," Loretta pleaded.

"Stop it Loretta!"

"I didn't do anything, Al." Loretta dropped her eyes down to the dirty, old, linoleum floor.

"Loretta, don't piss me off, I'm warning you."

"Sir," Allie said, facing off with him so he ended up backed against the wall. "I am here to try to help track down whoever killed Mrs. Meyers' daughter."

"I know who the fuck you are—you're a goddamned dyke bitch takin' a job from a good man who's got a family to raise and feed!"

He slammed her away from him with his fists. Taken by surprise, she nearly lost her balance, and staggered backward. She steadied herself by grabbing a kitchen chair.

Al rammed his fist into her gut, causing her to double over, gasping for breath. He then slammed his hand against the side of her head, knocking her to the floor. Allie quickly rolled to her back, throwing her feet against his much greater weight as he threw himself down toward her. He went flying back against the wall.

"Cunt!" he screamed, reaching back and grabbing the knife-block to throw it at Allie. She blocked it with her forearm, sending knives falling out of it. Pain shot up her arm. But he was already on the move again, grabbing a chair to hit her with. Seeing the murderous look on his face, the blood in her veins seemed to go ice cold. She pulled her legs up under her, knowing she couldn't fight him off from her back.

"Al! Stop it!" Loretta screamed.

He froze in position. "Bitch! You should know better than that!" He turned and whacked her across her mid-section. Loretta doubled-over in pain.

Allie grabbed him by the neck, throwing backward, causing him to lose his wind. It was a simple move that used his center of gravity against him. She grabbed him by a shoulder and rolled him onto his stomach, planting her knee and all her weight onto his back while she pulled off her belt, which she used to securely tie his hands together.

Then she pulled out her phone and dialed 911. "I'd like to report an assault," she said, when the operator picked up, as Loretta's screams echoed in the small kitchen.

How had Brett ever managed to live through a life like this?

13

"So, what are you working on?" Allie asked a few hours later, walking up to Brett. She was exhausted after her ordeal of the afternoon, and clutched an icebag to her forearm.

"What happened to you?" Brett said, all but running to her from behind her desk.

"It's nothing," Allie said. She almost didn't come because she was afraid Brett would want to race off to go kill Al Meyers.

"What happened?" Brett asked, pulling the ice pack away from Allie's arm just long enough to run her fingers lightly over it, as if assessing the damage. Allie was heartened that Brett's first reaction was concern, and not revenge.

"I went to Kelly Roberts' parent's house. Her stepfather was already drunk, and he's got a chip on his shoulder that's about the size of, oh, say, Oklahoma." She shrugged, but was gratified to see the worry in Brett's eyes. "He started hitting his wife, and I asked him to stop." Before Brett could interrupt, she raced on. "I just couldn't stand back and watch it happen—and I couldn't leave to call the police—he could've killed her!"

Brett shook her head. "Allie, guys like him are totally whacked—there's no telling what he might've done!"

"Aw, he only threw some stuff at me. You know as well as I do that drunks aren't good fighters—they don't think. I had the upper hand across the board. I mean, he weighs more than me, sure, but I'm taller."

Brett turned away from her, shaking her head again. "Allie . . ."

Allie put a hand on Brett's shoulder. "I know Kelly's mom should've just left him, that she's only enabling him, but I also couldn't help but think . . ."

"What?" Brett asked, not turning around.

"How much like your father he probably is. Down to the wife-beater T-shirt."

Brett was silent.

"I tried being nice—I asked him to stop."

"And what happened?"

"He didn't like the way I asked."

Brett turned back around, a bemused grin slowly winding its way across her features. She tenderly ran her hand over Allie's hair, running her fingers through the silky strands. "Since you're still in one piece, I assume he underestimated my fiery lil' blonde?" The worry hadn't left her eyes.

"Brett, I know you're worried, but I was in control the entire time. Worst-case scenario, I would've run—and I know I'm a helluva lot faster than he is."

"So long as he didn't break your leg."

122

"Brett, I went through the Academy. I know a bit about hand-to-hand combat. And I'm in shape. You don't like me always worrying about what you do, so you have to trust me some times, too."

"Touché. Tell me one thing, though," she said, turning around to pick up a paper from her desk. "Was Kelly an only child?" She studied the paper she held.

"Yes, she was."

"Well, that was one thing she had going for her, then."

Allie walked up behind Brett and wrapped her arms around her.

Brett let Allie hold her like that for a few moments before she turned around and buried her face in Allie's hair. "I am glad to see you, babe. Seeing you always brings a smile to my face and brightens my day."

Allie knew Brett was just trying to change the subject. She didn't like talking about her youth, and she also didn't like to remember that time of her life when she felt weak. "I know I just take your mind off work," Allie teased, helping Brett to change the subject. She couldn't help but notice the file folder labeled "Nicola" on Brett's desk. "So who was this Nicola really?" Allie asked.

"Didn't you stop by her house too?"

"No, actually, I didn't. Randi and Phil did that."

Allie and Brett sat side-by-side going through Nicola's file. Personnel files at the Paradise Theatre were hardly a wealth of information. They contained a few handwritten notes, sometimes on Post-Its, about performance, attendance and whether or not the girl owed any fines. There was also a handwritten page of contact info and a picture of the girl. All of the dancers were classified as independent contractors and paid the theatre. There were no reasons to keep track of the money they collected from customers.

"You guys really don't keep very good records on your employees," Allie said.

"Well, c'mon Allie, it's not like this is your usual business. Lots of our girls don't want too much known about them."

Allie frowned and looked around the office. "Nice set up you've got here." She went to the bookshelf and began giving it a thorough investigation. She had only been in Brett's new office once before, when Brett had still been setting it up. She picked up the pictures, pulled a couple of Kleenexes from the container nearby, and began dusting.

She cleaned off the picture of Brett and herself; and the one of Brett, Frankie, Rick DeSilva, and Storm, without saying a word. She also dusted the bindings of Brett's business books. Brett's office was functional, dignified and stylish, done mostly in rich wood and heady leather. Brett fully believed it was well worth paying more in order to get quality goods.

Allie liked the rich texture of wood. She liked the smell and feel of leather. The smells reminded her of Brett. They seemed to indicate strength, assurance and stability.

Brett jumped up and tried to stop Allie from picking up the dancers' book, but she was too late. Allie flipped through the pages that contained pictures of every dancer who worked at the Paradise since it was rebuilt. They were all naked.

"Oh, now she's cute," Allie said, looking up at Brett from a picture of a woman with her legs open wide, revealing herself in her entirety to the photographer. The pictures were the theatre's records. They were used for the marquee inside the theatre, as well as to help schedule the dancers—after all, sometimes you needed booty, and sometimes you needed tits. Depended on who else was dancing to figure out who would round out the schedule.

Some of the women had more fun having their picture taken than others. Some sat bashfully with their legs crossed, while others showed it all. Those pictures more than vaguely resembled some of the disgusting *Hustler Beaver Shots*.

"Do you take all of these? Make all the girls come up here and get naked so you can take their picture?"

"Oh, c'mon Allie, you know me better than that," Brett said, closing the office door and leaning back against it.

"Do I now?" Allie said. She knew what went on at this theatre. She heard the many remarks Brett made about how many diseases dancers could carry. She was convinced Brett no longer had sex with any of them. But still, it upset her to know that women were purposefully stripping and revealing themselves to her lover.

Brett broke into her thoughts with her answer. "Yes, this office is still a virgin. Though it's not like I don't want to take care of that, now that you're here." Brett whispered the last part into Allie's ear while she slowly wrapped her arms around Allie's waist from behind, letting one hand trace its way down over the luscious curve of Allie's hip.

"Brett—"

"Allie, I love you, and I lust after you. You rock my world, baby."

Allie knew she had to ask, but wasn't sure she wanted to know the answer. "Brett, tell me. Have you slept with any of these women?"

"No, I have neither slept with, nor had sex with any woman in this book. You know me better than that." She laid a hand on the album, and turned from Allie. "Storm's picture was never in this book. We had to start a new one when the old theatre burned down."

Allie pulled Brett back into her arms, wrapping them around Brett's neck and kissing her deeply. She knew how much that admission had cost her lover.

Whenever they kissed, Allie was amazed at Brett's softness and gentleness. Brett could be so hard, cruel and calculating. Allie had seen her with a deadly glint in her eye. Allie had seen her kill.

But a kiss from her could always take Allie's breath away. She always knew that Brett was a woman, no matter how butch she was or appeared to be. It was in intimacy that this fact was so wonderfully surprising.

But as their kiss deepened and lengthened, Allie experienced something else about Brett: her passion. Brett's kiss could ignite Allie, and no matter what, she never failed to bring Allie to full flames within mere moments.

Brett pushed Allie against the bookshelf and slid her leg tight against Allie, between her legs. Allie's luxurious 5'9" body fit against Brett's own tall body like no other ever could.

"Brett, you're at work," Allie said, half-heartedly pushing Brett away. Brett reached up and pulled the band from Allie's ponytail, releasing her long blonde hair to float freely around her shoulders. Brett buried her face in the sweet scent of it, again wondering how an incredibly intelligent, beautiful woman like Allie ended up with someone like her.

Allie again tried to push Brett away, and this time Brett backed up enough to see Allie smiling. She could lose herself in those incredible blue eyes. She brought her lips down to Allie's, meeting Allie's with a rush of electricity. Allie tried, briefly, to pull away, but then she succumbed, opening her mouth to Brett's insistent tongue, while Brett's hands gently caressed her through her clothing.

Allie moaned softly and wrapped her arms around Brett's neck when Brett cupped her breasts, teasing the nipples through her blouse and bra until they hardened against her hands. She slid her hand along the front of her blouse, deftly undoing the buttons.

"Hey there, what are you doing?" Allie whispered softly, putting her hand on Brett's.

With one brusque movement, Brett used her other hand to quickly untuck Allie's blouse. She reached up and with a snap of her fingers, undid her bra as well. "I think you know what I'm doing, baby. I want you." She pushed Allie's shirt and bra down. "Here and now."

126

She wrapped an arm roughly around Allie's waist and pulled her in so tight that her feet left the floor and she rested entirely on Brett's thigh. Her mouth was demanding against Allie's, her hand tight on her ass.

Allie loved it when Brett went after what she wanted, when she was demanding and forceful. She knew Brett would stop if she really wanted her to, but of all the things Allie wanted right now— to feel Brett inside of her, be taken by Brett, have Brett's hot tongue on her—stopping her was not one of them.

She knew Brett would never do anything Allie didn't want her to.

Brett had been tormented and teased by Victoria all day long, with visions of Storm running through her head. She would not cheat on Allie again. She WOULD NOT.

Instead, she would give all of her passion to the woman she loved. With Allie in her arms, her heart swelled and felt full. No other could complete her as Allie did.

She reached down and undid Allie's grey trousers, letting them fall to the floor. Allie kicked off her loafers and stepped out of them and into Brett's arms, wearing only her red satin Victoria's Secret panties and a pair of grey trouser socks.

Maybe her heart and soul weren't truly clean and pure, but Brett wanted this beautiful blonde now. Just a smile from her could lift the clouds and brighten even the places where Brett lived.

There was a knock on the door and it slowly opened. "'Scuse me, Brett?" Victoria said, leaning into the office, "Tim told me I should come up here to get my picture taken."

Allie quickly covered herself with her arms while scrambling for her discarded blouse.

"Now is *not* a good time," Brett said, spreading her arms to help cover Allie.

"This seems like a great time to me," Victoria said, strolling in and around Brett to stare at Allie, who was frantically putting on her shirt. "So is this the little woman, or the competition?" She stared at Allie, who stood facing her, clutching her shirt closed. Allie stared back at Victoria.

" . . .and is this a gang bang now or what?" Victoria said. Fully dressed, she picked up the book Allie had dropped onto the couch and looked at it. She saw a spread-eagle beaver shot. "So that's the look you want." She looked up at Brett and Allie, shrugged and began unbuttoning her blouse. "Might be fun."

Brett swallowed.

"What are you waiting for, Brett?" Allie said. "Why don't you show me how you do this?" Allie handed Brett the camera from the shelf and sat down to relax in one of the visitor's chairs in the corner of the room, still holding her blouse tightly closed around her.

Victoria was grinning and unbuttoning her shirt. "I take it you're the girlfriend then, huh? You know this could be a lot more fun if you'd get Butch over there to put on some music. I could give you both the special treatment. Being the new kid on the block, I need to give the boss a good impression." It was as if she had something against Allie.

"I really don't think now is a good time—" Brett began, wondering what the steely glint in Victoria's eye was about. Victoria was making her nervous.

"Now is a fantastic time," Allie said. "Calm down and enjoy the show." She never took her eyes off Victoria.

Although Brett didn't put on any music, Victoria danced nonetheless. Slowly she took off her clothes, moving her hips to the unheard beat, strutting her body for Allie. It was unquestionably Allie whom she was stripping for. Piece by piece all her clothing came off.

When she was naked, Victoria climbed on Allie's chair and straddled her, as if she was going to give her a lap dance. Allie leaned back, away from the woman.

Brett was frozen in place. Victoria had perfect breasts, a tight tummy, long legs, and a shaven pussy. With her legs spread open over Allie, she was hiding absolutely nothing.

"Do you like what you see?" Victoria said, then looked over at Brett, "'cause I think Butch over there would like to see us go at it."

Brett was stunned. She had been thinking just that, that she would love to see these two sultry femmes go at it without restraint. Mouths against each other, on each other. Victoria's darkness against Allie's lightness. She wanted to see it. No matter how much she knew she had the basic male scenario in mind, to watch them do each other until she joined in to make them come, she still wanted it.

Allie stared at Victoria wide-eyed. She couldn't believe the woman's boldness. She hadn't thought she'd take her up on the dare and strip for them both. Victoria took Allie's hands and rubbed them over her own breasts, then started opening Allie's blouse. "Are you anywhere near as wet as I am?" Victoria asked, fondling Allie's breasts and teasing the still-hard nipples.

"Brett . . ." Allie said, looking toward Brett helplessly. But her hands were still on Victoria's breasts, almost as if she didn't know what to do with them.

"Hey baby, I asked you a question, are you as wet as I am?" She took one of Allie's hands and put it between her legs, directing Allie's fingers on her and into her. "Are you this wet?" She leaned forward and ran her lips over Allie's neck, running her hand over the crotch of Allie's underwear while she moved her hips so that Allie's fingers slid in and out of her.

Allie gasped at the feeling of Victoria's wetness. Brett didn't let Allie touch her very often and Allie had longed for the feeling of another woman's hot, wet flesh under her fingers. Brett had also gotten her so turned on that she couldn't help but enjoy the closeness of another woman.

Brett wanted to see where this would go. She wanted to see

both of these incredible femmes naked. She reached up and loosened her tie.

Without thinking, Allie exposed her neck to Victoria's lips, while Victoria caressed her breasts and pinched her nipples.

Allie seemed unable to control herself. Brett knew Allie was enjoying Victoria's touch, but she needed Brett to stop it. Brett steeled herself and walked over, wrapped an arm around Victoria and lifted her roughly off Allie's lap. "Just get over there and let me take your goddamned picture already." She kept her eyes on Victoria, not wanting to see Allie's reaction.

"Okay boss." Victoria stretched out on Brett's desk, opening herself up, while Brett took the picture. She then leaned back further and began touching herself. "You sure you two ain't up for any fun, 'cause I know I'm ready for it. I'd like to get fucked." Brett felt like the mouse to Victoria's cat.

"So this is the reason you have to keep working late," Allie said, still bolted to her chair.

"She just started working here," Brett said.

"You don't deny it then," Allie said, getting up and heading to the door, wrapping her shirt closed around her and grabbing her pants and shoes.

"Allie, Victoria just started working here!"

"No, she's never left you. And if it isn't her, it's somebody else."

The door to the office flew open and a tall, leggy brunette in a high-cut teddy with a plunging neckline entered. "Victoria, I told you, Brett doesn't play those games. Put on your clothes and get downstairs."

"You gonna make me, girly-girl?" Victoria said with a wink as she sat up.

"Better yet, get out of here and *then* put on your clothes." She turned to Allie, "Hey Allie," she grinned, "you should know I don't let *anybody* get away with *anything* when I'm around. I keep Brett in line. Not that she needs me to, of course."

130

Allie smiled back at her. "I should make sure she has you on the schedule all the time, huh?"

"Quit brown-nosing the boss's wife and come keep me company," Victoria said, putting the arm that wasn't carrying her clothes around Angela and leading her out.

"I like her," Allie said, referring to Angela. "She's the sort you should keep around here. She behaves and knows her place, so she won't be causing you any problems."

"Unlike Victoria."

"Yes," Allie went to Brett's computer, flashing an enticing glimpse of red satin as she went around the desk. Brett stepped behind her as Allie sat down and started checking it out, opening up Explorer and going through the Start menu to see what was loaded on it. "You said she just started yesterday?" She was trying to make it look like her interest was casual.

"Yes." Brett knew better than to try to make excuses or say too much when Allie was in a mood. She knew Allie was very upset with her. She could understand why, and she had to be careful. She had thought of doing things she shouldn't have.

Allie swiveled the chair and stood up to Brett. She tightened Brett's tie, almost painfully so, and ran her fingers along her shirt collar. She always loved the way Brett dressed. "So you're saying that just now is the first time you've seen her naked?"

Brett put her hands under Allie's shirt to lay on her bare waist and looked deeply into her eyes. "Yes. It is. You've gotta believe me, Allie, nothing's happening with me and Victoria or any of the dancers." What Allie didn't know wouldn't hurt her, especially with something like this. Allie knew it was Brett's job to be around naked girls, but, unreasonably enough, she still had a problem with it.

"Do you want it to?"

"No."

"Not even Victoria?" She ran her hands down Brett's arms,

squeezing the biceps lightly. "You're telling me you don't want her?"

Brett chuckled, pulling Allie near and burying her head in Allie's neck. "She's not my type." She raised her hands under Allie's still-unbuttoned shirt to gently caress her breasts.

Allie ran her fingers through Brett's hair, then yanked her head back roughly. "Don't give me that. We both know she is."

Brett reached down, wrapped her arms around Allie's hips, lifted her and wrapped Allie's legs around her waist. "But I don't do dancers anymore." She began to lightly kiss, then nibble at Allie's beautiful, long neck. She carried Allie across the room and to her desk, and set her down there. With one swift stroke, she swept away all her desk accessories, except for the computer. She was incredibly turned on, even more now than before. She had to have Allie *now*.

Allie's mind suddenly wandered over Victoria . . . and Randi . . . wondering how they would touch her.

When she had been with Randi years ago, she hadn't been the greatest lover, but Allie thought women could be made into better lovers. At least she knew how to kiss, and that was something Allie didn't think could be taught at all.

Allie was deliberately rude. "Not even this Storm Junior?"

Brett's breath caught in her chest. "What makes you say that?"

Allie pulled away from Brett, but left her legs encircling her. "She looks exactly like her, Brett. You tell me the reason you hired her without an audition. We both know you audition all your dancers because some women might look nice but they can't dance worth shit."

"Most of the guys who come here don't care if the girls can dance or not; they only care about how well they can show their pussy. She showed up at the right place at the right time."

"So the fact that she's Storm's sister had nothing to do with it?"

"Storm's *sister?*" Brett pulled out of the protective circle of Allie's legs.

132

"Storm's sister."

"Storm didn't have a sister, Allie. This chick just looks like her."

"So you know everything about Storm?"

"I did. I do."

"She's obviously Storm's sister." Allie took Brett's face in her hands. "Think about it. She looks just like her, she sounds like her. Except for her age, she might as well be Storm's twin. C'mon, don't tell me the thought hasn't crossed your mind?"

Brett was in some far-off memory. "Storm always had some guilt. I thought it was that she thought what had happened was her fault. I never imagined that she might've left someone behind . . ."

"Brett," Allie said, pulling Brett's face so their eyes met, "all you have to do is look into her eyes and you'll know it." Allie and Brett looked deep into each other's eyes. "You've never looked into her eyes, have you? You reacted purely on instinct."

Allie knew Brett too damned well.

"Who does she claim to be?" Allie asked. She knew also that there was something distinctly un-Storm like in Victoria's eyes. Something cold and calculating.

Brett ran a hand back through her thick, black hair. "You just saw some of our personnel records, Allie. You know we don't exactly run background checks on these women, or bond them for chrissake's."

"Then ask her. You knew Nicola's last name, you know Angela's, you have some information on all of your dancers, why not Victoria?" Allie got up, buttoned her shirt, and picked up her slacks. "I'd better let you get back to work."

Brett pulled her into her arms. "I love you. You do know that, don't you?"

"I've never questioned it, Brett," she said, heading to the door.

Brett followed Allie and in a deliberately obvious move, then

133

reached around her to lock her office door. She leaned down and kissed Allie, pulling her into her arms.

"I don't know what I'd do without you, darling," Brett murmured into Allie's ear.

Allie could find no words with which to respond, so she pulled Brett's mouth back to her own, letting Brett feel her love in that way, and showing her own love in the same gesture.

14

"Allie, I need you," Brett said, when again their bodies were molded as one, with Allie's back against the door. "I need you, I want you, and I love you. More than you can ever know."

Allie pushed Brett back, then lifted Brett's hand and laid it on her breast. It was a gesture that turned Brett on the first time she did it, and still did. The want, trust, and surrender it implied was such a total commitment that Brett, and her body, couldn't help but respond. She laid her hand where Allie placed it, enjoying the softness while searching for the heartbeat underneath.

Allie groaned and leaned her head back against the door. Brett used her other hand to again unbutton Allie's shirt, so the first hand could reach beneath.

Slowly she pulled off Allie's shirt and bra, experiencing the delight of unwrapping a beautiful and incredible present with each movement, until finally she could bear it no more and had to let her lips and tongue taste the beauty of Allie's exposed breasts.

She picked Allie up and carried her back to the desk.

Allie laid back on its smooth surface and lifted her hips so Brett could remove her underwear. She let Brett strip her completely, revealing herself to her woman.

"No matter how many times I see your body," Brett said, sitting on the desk next to her, "it always takes my breath away." She played her fingers lightly over Allie's collarbone and down her arm, then over to her breast-bone, and down her stomach. "You are so incredibly beautiful." She leaned down to kiss Allie, deeply and fully. The lights were on. She knew this would drive Allie crazy.

Allie felt little butterflies of longing in her stomach. Brett knew just what to do to make her long for further touch, to make her feel every whispered caress throughout her entire body. Brett could give her just the right strokes then avoid taking it further, to make her ache deep inside.

"Oh, god, Brett," Allie said, grasping Brett's wandering hand and placing it on her stomach. "You make me crazy."

"Mmmm, I like driving you wild," Brett said, lying beside Allie on the desk. She continued running her fingers over Allie's body, without touching any of the most sensitive areas, teasing her until finally Allie could take no more.

"Brett!" she cried, guiding Brett's hand down to the wetness between her legs. She remembered the wetness between Victoria's legs.

And then, and only then, did Brett allow her fingers to feel Allie's wetness. She ran her fingers over Allie's exposed clit, all the while gazing down at Allie, at the swell of her hips that climaxed with a triangle of light, curly, trimmed hair, at the way her pert breasts flattened against her, giving her even more curves, ones that peaked with hardened nipples. Allie was incredibly beautiful, as was her body. Light fell in shadows across her, accenting her in a way that revealed to Brett all her wondrous curves.

"Look at me," she commanded. Allie opened her eyes. "I want to see inside of you when I'm inside of you." Allie directed her fingers into her.

When Brett was inside Allie their connection was unbelievable. It began with their eyes, went through their bodies, and into their souls.

Finally, Brett's teasing fingers took Allie further than she could bear. "Brett!" she cried, as she closed her eyes and lifted her head.

Brett gently removed her fingers from Allie and kneeled at the foot of the desk, gently sliding Allie down the well-polished surface until her legs were resting on Brett's shoulders.

Slowly, teasingly, Brett put her mouth on Allie. At first she blew gently on Allie's wetness, toying with her, driving her crazy till she squirmed again with longing. Then she finally allowed her tongue to do what it wanted—taste Allie.

Her tongue explored Allie, roaming freely along her clit and up inside of her. Softly at first, and then with a growing urgency that matched Allie's own, Brett's tongue devoured her, searching and dancing across her clit.

Allie started bucking her hips and grasped for the lip of the desk. She needed something solid to hold onto. She knew Brett was going to drive her to the brink and then tantalizingly hold her there. Only when Brett wanted her to, would she get to go over.

"Brett! Oh god, Brett!"

Brett's tongue whipped back and forth over her clit, centered on her, making her scream, taking her to the brink—and finally plunging her over—and even as Allie fell over the edge, Brett's tongue stayed on her clit, moving back and forth . . .

"Fuck me!"

Suddenly, Brett was inside her again, fingers probing deep inside of her, taking her, fucking her, in and out, while her tongue flicked . . .

"Brett!"

15

After Allie left, Brett went into the dancer's dressing area, which was divided into two levels, each one consisting of only one shabby room furnished with a single long dressing table with stage mirror and two chairs. The only way to access the second-level dressing room was through the first-level one.

Angela was in the main room, putting on her regular clothes —a simple blouse, jeans, and sensible black shoes with a fairly low heel. She was a very attractive woman, with long wavy dark hair and nice full breasts, rounded hips and long legs. Now that Brett thought about it, Angela was quite similar in looks to Storm and Tempest.

"Where's Victoria?" Brett asked.

"She's upstairs. Is everything okay with you and Allie?"

Brett grinned, lifted an eyebrow, then raised her hand to her nose and sniffed. "Yeah, it is." She nonchalantly moved her hand down to brush against her chin. "Thanks for that save. I knew there was a reason I kept you around here—besides the obvious." Brett gave Angela a slow, appreciative, once-over.

Brett would almost swear that a frown began to touch Angela's luscious lips before she smiled and said, "Oh, c'mon Brett, we both know you're hopelessly devoted to that woman of yours. Now get up there and fix Victoria. I think she stands a chance, once she knows that her job description doesn't include screwing the boss."

"You seem to know quite a lot about her already."

"I just get this sense about people, y'know? I think she's a good kid who's just had some bad things happen to her is all."

"Do you know anything else about her?"

"Talking about a girl behind her back isn't very nice, y'know," Victoria said, coming down the stairs. She leaned back against the wall and lit a cigarette. She was fully dressed in the same clothes Brett had seen her in and out of all day.

"Well, then," Brett said, "I'll just ask you what your story is, since we didn't have a chance to become properly acquainted earlier on."

"I told you. I'm pretty new in town. I came up from Indiana recently."

"Why'd you come here?" Brett asked.

"I didn't want to do tricks, and figured I could make a couple of bucks dancing in Detroit. There's not much of a market for this sort of thing down there."

"So dancing's your goal?"

"No, I just thought I could make some easy money while I get my shit together."

140

Brett looked at Victoria, assessing her reticence to say anything. It was as if she was being deliberately low life. "You'll need to give Mike, the evening clerk, your contact numbers," she finally said, "and a few other bits of information. But I want to know a few things myself."

"So ask." Angela said, egging her on, while settling back into one of the two chairs in the room.

"Well, for starters, what's your name?"

"You already know that. Victoria."

Brett took a deep breath, not wanting to play this game. "I need a last name." She needed to think of Victoria as a dancer, and nothing more than that.

"Just Victoria is all you need to know."

Brett glared at her.

"What would you like it to be?" Victoria finally said with a sly smile.

"Don't play games with me. I know my dancers. I don't do my dancers, but I do know them." Brett put her hands deep into her pockets and leaned back with her legs crossed in front of her. "I've been very understanding with you so far, but I won't be if I ever catch you on drugs or doing drugs on the premises. Keep any crap away from here. Do you understand?"

"I don't do drugs." Victoria was serious for a change.

"Good. I like that. Now I'm only going to ask you one more time, what is your full name?"

"Victoria Cynthia Jones."

"Just another Smith and Jones. Y'know, Detroit is very ethnic. If you want to be incognito, ya might as well pick a *ski* name. Or maybe a good Italian name." Brett was convinced the name was an alias, and although many of her girls gave her aliases, it still pissed her off that Victoria was so obviously lying to her.

"It's not like I had much of a choice about it. It's the name my folks gave me."

141

"How old are you?"

"Twenty."

"Why did you come here, to the Paradise in particular?"

Victoria shrugged. "It looked like an okay place."

Angela laughed. "If you just randomly picked a place, I'd think you would've found one that looked a lot better than this one." When Brett glanced at her, she smiled demurely and said, "Sorry, but without knowing you, there isn't really a lot to recommend the Paradise."

"So it was almost random that you picked Detroit—" Brett began.

"Not really," Victoria said. "The only three logical places for a gal like me with no money, and not a lot of options are Chicago, Detroit or New York. All a short bus trip away."

"New York's a lot bigger, with a lot more opportunities. Why didn't you go there?" Angela asked.

Victoria laughed. "I'm just a small-town girl. I figured I'd work a big city a while, make some money and lose some naïveté, and then, maybe, move on. To a real *Metropolis* like New York."

"And so you came to Detroit, and this was the first place you came to?"

"Yeah. That's what I said." Victoria said. "I found a room nearby, so that's why I picked this sorry joint, okay?"

Brett wondered what the girl really wanted and why she was at the Paradise. The more Brett thought about it, the more suspicious it seemed to her. She knew the girl was lying, and she'd have to figure out a better way to get the truth from her, so, without saying a word, she left.

Angela caught her as she was about to enter the ticket booth. "She's lying."

"I know that."

"I know it was her I saw at the Rainbow Room."

"I believe you. Just like I know her names isn't Jones. Don't worry, I'm about to make sure no dancer is left alone. I want to make sure the guard walks all of you out at night."

Angela just looked at Brett. "Thank you," she said, staring at the floor. "I really don't like it that all these girls are getting killed, and Victoria's just so obviously lying."

Brett stopped by the office to tell Tim she wanted the guard to come in whenever any girl was leaving and walk her out himself. She didn't want any of the other girls to be alone with Victoria unless they were inside.

● ● ●

"I still need to go back to The Naked Truth," Randi said, sitting down with Allie at a table in the Denny's where they had arranged to meet. "Did you get anything yet?"

"Just one arrest."

"What?"

Allie looked down into the dregs of her coffee. Where were the waitresses when you needed them? "Let's just say I feel as if I've visited all the horrors of the modern world today."

"You said arrest. What do you mean by that?"

"I was assaulted, and so called in the cops. Kelly Roberts' step-father is an abusive son-of-a-bitch who probably raped his wife's daughter."

"What?"

"He obviously raped Kelly. All they'll say is that she was pregnant when she left, but they won't say anything about the boyfriend! Goddamnit! I know the sick shit raped her!"

Randi glanced around the restaurant, wide eyed. "Allie . . . I know . . . Goddamnit, I know. But we have to focus on the case right now. There's nothing we can do for Kelly anymore than find the son-of-a-bitch that killed her."

"I know, I know. But it just pisses me off. She ran away because

143

of him, she left home because she was pregnant. And that asshole won't admit what he did, and her mother won't either!"

"They say the worst thing about incest is that it's someone you're programmed to love and trust who does those things to you. It's the ultimate betrayal."

Allie tried to hold back her tears, but still she felt the wetness on her cheeks. She looked down at the table. "She never had a chance—no decent father, a mother who'd let her boyfriend do that . . ."

"It disgusts me that women find these men and marry them," Randi said, completely missing the point.

Allie looked up, brought back to reality. "He is a son-of-a-bitch. But you know what? After all our talk about why girls do what they do this morning—y'know, about how they get into dancing and hooking and such—I just . . ." She shook her head. "I thought I understood it this morning, but seeing it face-to-face gives me . . . so much more detail than I wanted."

Randi waited for her to continue, and when she didn't, said, "So are you going to tell me what happened?"

"He attacked me. He got drunk and obnoxious and attacked me, okay?"

"Oh my god, Allie! Are you okay? What did he do?"

Allie was thankful to get her mind off where it had been, onto something tangible. "I asked him to calm down, and he attacked me. Kicked me and threw things at me. I took him down, tied him up, and called the police."

"Allie, don't make it sound like nothing—you could've gotten hurt!"

"Randi, I did get hurt!" Allie said, but quickly continued before Randi could butt in again, "I got hurt, but not badly. I'm fine, I'm okay." Allie reached across the table, taking Randi's hands into her own. "We're discussing murder here. Murders, to be exact. Can we try to focus?"

Randi held Allie's hands for a moment, looking deeply into her eyes. Then she said, "I know what we're dealing with. I stopped by The Naked Truth today, but I need to go back there tonight to get copies of their schedules and paperwork."

"So you stopped by there today?" Allie asked, disgusted, though she tried to hide it. Randi was so quick to try to get her attention, to get her gratitude like some doggie begging for a treat. So many butches were so much like men in that they could be easily distracted, that Allie wondered why she even bothered being lesbian.

"Yeah, I did," Randi immediately answered, leaning forward.

"But they didn't have the schedules there?" Allie leaned back.

"No. Tina O'Rourke keeps them at her office."

"So who did you talk to?"

"Max Grueber, the manager."

"Did he tell you anything?"

Randi laughed. "I had Max kissing my butt once I threatened to start paying more attention to his club."

"So he talked with you just because of a threat?" Allie sat back, enjoying the sight of a peacock showing off its plumage.

Randi smiled. "I'm sure even Brett pays off a few cops to make sure nobody pays attention to the little shit."

"You're telling me Brett's still breaking laws?" Why did she like butches who so enjoyed showing off?

"I'd be surprised if she's not helping some girls do so. I mean, you both know some of her girls do tricks on the side. But I'd just about lay money on the fact that there's more than that going on at the Paradise."

"What do you mean?" Allie said, innocently.

"In Michigan a woman has to wear both a top and a g-string to give a lap dance." Randi quickly slid over from her side of the booth to Allie's. "And a man can only touch her . . . here . . ." She ran her hands up the outside of Allie's thighs to several inches

145

below the hip, " . . .here . . ." touched her waist just briefly in neutral territory, " . . .and here . . ." then ran her hands down Allie's arms. "And that's it. The law is very clear cut about it."

"Here . . . here . . . and here?" Allie asked, running Randi's hands over those spots on her own body again. She was disgusted. Randi was being obtuse about what she had learned that day, so she decided to have some fun with Randi.

Randi got up and went back to her side of the booth.

"That's all a man's allowed to touch?"

"Yeah, but at most of these places, they don't exactly enforce that rule, so technically they're breaking the law."

Allie sat back as a waitress refilled her coffee, then said, "So you need to go back to The Naked Truth?"

Randi shrugged. "Tina O'Rourke keeps everything at the main office. I figured it'd be best to just go back there tonight and pick it up."

"Why don't I go with you?" Allie asked. "We can eat here, run home and change, and then go back." She knew she'd see things Randi overlooked.

Randi glanced at her watch. "Actually, I'm having dinner with somebody—"

"The mysterious blonde again?"

"Her name's Danielle."

"So it is her."

"Allie, if I didn't know better, I'd think you were jealous."

Allie looked at her coffee, playing with Randi.

"You've made it perfectly obvious that you're with Brett. When you disappeared years ago, I kept hoping you'd come back. Not a day went by that I didn't think of tracking you down, just to try to get you to forgive me for what I'd done. But now that I know you've always been with Brett, that makes me think that the chances of me getting you back are about the same as me bringing my brother back from the dead."

146

Allie met Randi's eyes, relieved. At this moment, she didn't wonder if she cared too much for her. In fact, at this moment, she wondered why she was with either of her butches.

"With you back in my life, I realized I was starting to hang around like some psycho stalker. I don't know if I can even love Danielle, but I do like her. And I've got to move on with my life."

Perhaps Randi bespoke the truth?

16

Randi and Allie were just finishing their coffee at Denny's when Brett got home. She pulled up into the garage, climbed out of her car, and went inside.

She flipped on the light and looked around. They needed to get a dog. Someone to be home when they weren't. Someone to watch the place. A presence to give life to the place when they weren't there.

They had thought about buying in the city because many great deals could be had in neighborhoods that once again had a bright future, but they wanted to live in the gayest area of Michigan, although it was nothing compared with San Francisco. But still, they had thought it would be nice to drive home on a spring day and pass a few rainbow flags on houses and cars en route, so that left either Royal Oak or Ferndale (a.k.a. Dykedale), which housed Affirmations, the area's LesBiGay community center, and A Woman's Prerogative, the lesbian bookstore. Allie was particularly fond of the bookstore's special-needs puppy, Bella.

She and Allie had found a nice, older bungalow in Royal Oak, just a stone's throw north of Detroit along the Woodward Corridor. The Detroit area was home, and that was what really mattered to Allie and Brett. They had been away far too long, and were happy to be back, regardless of the drug dealers, prostitutes, criminals, gangs and anything else that someone else might hold against the city. Anyway, Brett Higgins was on a first-name basis with quite a lot of the so-called "criminal element."

The bungalow's basement housed the laundry room, Brett's workout room, and a small storage area. On the first floor were two bedrooms, one of which was turned into Brett's study, the eat-in kitchen, the living room, and a full bath. They had made the converted attic their bedroom.

Brett walked through the house, turning on a few lights. As she grabbed a beer from the refrigerator, she heard someone at the front door. She slowly sidled up to it, wanting to catch Allie when she came home.

"Hey darlin'," Allie said, coming in and wrapping her arms around Brett, who immediately melted. She melted any time Allie wrapped her arms around her.

Brett's face was buried in the sweet silk of Allie's hair and she inhaled the beautiful fragrance of the woman—her perfume, soap, skin.

Sometimes images overcome your mind. They play like a little video tape within your head, but there are no stop or start buttons, only rewind, so that once the tape starts, you might be able to play it over and over again. That was what happened suddenly and without provocation within Brett's mind. She suddenly saw Victoria straddling Allie's lap, and she again saw the look on Allie's face when she leaned back from the naked woman opening herself up to her, offering herself to her.

Brett's mind overlapped. She remembered Storm giving Allie a lap dance years before. She remembered Storm leaning forward and giving Allie a deep, long kiss right on the lips.

At that time she had been upset, now she was turned on by the image.

She felt every inch of Allie's long body pressed tight against her own. She was overwhelmed by the scent of this woman. Her hair was silk against Brett's face, her body . . . her body a growing fire within her arms. An ember waiting to be ignited.

"Tell me something, Brett," Allie asked.

"What?" Brett murmured, her face still buried in the heaven of Allie's hair.

"Did it turn you on today?"

"What?" Brett pulled away, holding Allie at arm's length.

"When Victoria sat on my lap earlier today. Did it turn you on?" Allie laid her hands on Brett's hips. "Did you want to see us have sex?"

Brett took a deep breath, wondering what she should say, wondering if a lie or the truth would get her into less trouble, but before she could answer, Allie said, "I thought so."

"What do you mean, you thought so?"

"You want a threesome with me and another femme."

Brett didn't know what to say, so she said, "Why don't I make us some dinner?" With that she took off her jacket, carefully putting it on the back of a kitchen chair, and pulled on an apron she kept handy.

Allie wasn't a very good cook, so Brett ended up with more of the cooking chores, though Allie was very good about cleaning up afterward. Allie also tended to do most of the general housework, so that they shared the household chores pretty equally.

So while Brett pulled out the boneless-skinless chicken breast she had put in the sink earlier to defrost, Allie picked up her jacket and took it upstairs to hang in the closet. By the time Brett had chopped up the chicken into pieces, and cut off the fat, Allie came back downstairs, dressed in a casual top, fairly tight jeans, and black leather boots.

"Going somewhere tonight?" Brett asked, glancing through the fridge and pulling out tomatoes, onions, peppers, carrots and celery. She figured a simple stir fry would be nice tonight.

"Randi needs to go back to The Naked Truth tonight to pick up contact sheets and schedules from Tina. When she was there earlier, only the manager was there, and he said Tina kept those things at her main office."

"Bullshit," Brett said with a grin. "He was just playing with her. Tina can be a control freak, but I doubt she's that obsessive. Max probably figured Tina'd like to talk with Randi herself."

"You know him?"

"Yeah. 'Course I do." Brett pulled out the rice, and put water on to cook it with.

Allie got up and put her arms around Brett's waist. "Is there anything I can do to help?"

"Nope. I got it under control, babe. 'Sides, I don't trust you with my knives. You'd probably slice a finger off."

Allie smiled as she watched Brett's talented hands quickly chop vegetables. Brett was very particular about her knives—not only did she buy the best quality, she also kept them sharp herself. Allie probably would chop a finger off with the razor-sharp edges. Allie sat back down at the kitchen table and enjoyed the view of Brett's tight ass while she cooked. "You're really relaxed today, you know that?"

"What do you mean?"

"I was worried about how you'd react earlier, to that little . . . confrontation . . . I had gotten in. And now . . . It isn't bothering you at all that I'm going out with Randi tonight."

151

Brett turned to her and grinned. "You want me to get all angry and huff and puff and blow the whole joint down?" She walked to Allie and knelt at her feet, taking Allie's hands into her own. "I don't like that you've gotten involved with this shit. I don't like that you keep putting yourself into danger. And I don't like that you're hanging around with Randi, because I know she plays with you just because she wants you. Bad." She ran a hand along Allie's chin. "But I know it's in your blood. I know there's nothing I can do about it. So it's just a lot easier for me to handle if I just accept it as the inevitability it is."

"The *inevitability* it is?"

"Yo, babe. We keep coming back to the same place. When we met, you dreamt of being a cop. You being a cop helped get us back together again." Allie thought it quite tactful that Brett didn't go into details on that matter. "And since then, you just can't keep your beautiful nose out of it." She reached up to tweak Allie's nose, and then got up to finish chopping vegetables. "We bought a haunted house, and you had to look into that. Some guy drops dead in front of me, and you get involved. There's a problem at a high school, and you get us involved—"

"Hey, c'mon, I was just concerned about it when you were a murder suspect!"

"I know, but you're always jumping in. You have to admit, you had to drag me into that entire bloody high school scheme—"

"Yes, but didn't it make you feel good about yourself?"

Brett turned to face her, her right hand, holding a knife, on her right hip. She looked like a fag. "Babe, I've learned who wears the panties in this house, okay?"

Allie decided maybe Brett did have the right idea—just let things lie if they were okay. Why should Allie be trying so deliberately to ruffle Brett's boxers? After all, wasn't Allie getting exactly what she wanted? To be able to do what she wanted, without Brett losing her cool.

152

But she couldn't help but worry that Brett was simply losing her old flair because of what her life had become. After all, Brett in an apron, cooking, wasn't exactly the image Brett had created of herself—that of the street-smart, tough-guy stud.

But still, Allie couldn't help but worry, as Brett stood over the stove stirring the meat and adding vegetables and seasonings, that Brett was bored to death with this all-too-conventional life.

● ● ●

Brett flipped the meat in the pan, adding a dash more garlic powder, coriander and ginger. She liked using an off-the-shelf stir-fry sauce, because it made everything so easy, but she couldn't help dressing it up. She was just thankful Allie liked food as flavorful as she did. "You know, I've been thinking," she said. "Maybe we should get a dog."

"A dog? What brought this on?" Allie asked.

"Well, we've got a house of our own, and I'm hoping we'll be here a while. So why not get a dog?" Brett wondered if maybe she should've gone to a culinary institute, because she did really enjoy cooking. But then she remembered the thousands of hours she had spent in the hot grill area of McDonald's, earning the money to afford college, and thought twice about it.

"Brett, dogs are a responsibility. You have to be home to take care of them. You can't just leave them alone for days."

"Well, we live here. We're here every day."

"But that would mean we couldn't just take off for a while on some romantic little weekend."

"When . . ." Brett began, about to state that they never suddenly ran off on romantic little weekends, but then she turned her brain on. "When we do run off, we could get Frankie and Kurt, or Madeline, to check in on him for us."

Allie stared at her. "Are you sure you're ready for the commitment required of a dog?"

Brett caught herself before words shot out of her mouth too quickly. After all, she wasn't handling the commitment of being solely with Allie too well—and the main thing that kept her from suggesting to Allie that they should adopt a kid was the commitment factor. (She partly wanted to bring a child into their loving household, and she wanted to show a child how you could grow out of the hole you were born in, but she couldn't imagine a child totally fitting into their day-to-day life. At least, not yet.)

"How about a cat?" Allie said before Brett could decide on the words to use.

"What?"

"A cat. Cats are much more independent than dogs."

Brett thought about this as she dished up rice and stir fry onto a plate for Allie. She wanted a Golden Retriever, so a cat seemed tiny and annoying in comparison. "I don't know . . ."

"Think about it as a starter to a dog."

Brett prepared her own plate and sat down across from Allie. "It's just so stereotypically lesbian."

"You say that like it's a bad thing."

"Well . . . I'm a lesbian. I'm a woman who loves other women, so . . . but . . ."

Allie ate, waiting for Brett to gather her thoughts.

"I guess it's that it's so lesbian, and the lesbians I know wouldn't approve of us." Brett thought back over all the PC types who would disapprove of their equal-partner butch/femme relationship, and couldn't imagine fitting in with them. Her friends were gay boys, straight women, and maybe those just coming out. What common ground did she and Allie really have with the overall lesbian community to which they ostensibly belonged?

● ● ●

Angela carefully guided her 1983 Buick Riviera into the single-car driveway. She quickly patted her bun into place and glanced at her watch. She hated leaving *Babcia* alone for so long.

She walked up the sidewalk, being careful not to step on the cracks, while she searched through her handbag for her keys, finally finding them at the bottom of the bag. She pushed her glasses up and slid the key into the lock.

"Thank goodness you're home," her *Babcia* said, looking up from the armchair in which she spent most of her time these days.

Angela bent over her grandma and kissed her forehead. "I'm fine, really. You know how it is down at the center. I can't make up my hours—sometimes they need me there late." The weeks she danced, she tried to make it home to spend some time with *Babcia* before she'd go back to dance her last shows, but she still had to explain her behavior convincingly.

Babcia patted the loveseat next to her. "Sit down, dear, and tell me all about it," and then, without giving Angela a moment to speak or even sit, she continued right along, "You know, I sit here sometimes, reading my paper or watching the TV, and I just can't help but thank the Lord for you. Taking care of your old *Babcia* all this time."

"*Babcia*, you know I'm glad that you're here for me, too. I'm the one who's got God to thank—that the family I do have loves me, and I love her too. Would you like a me to warm you up a glass of warm milk to help you sleep?" She was glad for the moment on the loveseat, during which she could pull off her shoes, which were really killing her feet. They were nice, sensible flats, but they still hurt nonetheless. Especially after a day of wearing come-fuck-me pumps.

Ginny turned the sound on the TV back up, and started pointing at it. "Will you look at this? If it's not here, it's the Middle East . . ." She shook her head sadly. "I pray to Mother Mary for peace, but until people learn to listen to the Lord, I don't have much hope for this world." She reached over and patted Angela's knee through the long, tweed skirt she wore. "I'm just glad I don't have to worry about you. I mean, I sit here and read my newspaper and watch my TV and I keep seeing all of this killing going on. And if it's not that, it's sex. Sex-sex-sex. Can't people even say hello these days without falling into bed together?"

Angela was running her fingers over the crucifix she wore around her neck, the same one she wore every day at the Christian youth center where her grandmother believed she worked. Where she sometimes did work or volunteer. The same one she hid in her purse when she was at the theatre. She knew what *Babcia* would say at first if she knew what Angela was doing, but still . . . Angela looked around the tidy living room and couldn't help but like the fact that she was finally able to give her *Babcia* a few things she deserved. After all, the old woman didn't ask for, or expect, much, and was actually quite satisfied with the smallest things. But Angela knew she liked her television, even more so since Angela had been able to buy her a larger one, which she could see more easily, with a remote, so she didn't have to keep stressing her aching joints by having to get up to change the channel.

Babcia also loved her game shows, especially Wheel of Fortune, as well as the Discovery Channel and different documentaries she found, most particularly those on the life of Jesus and the Bible. Angela's salary from the youth center could hardly pay for cable.

Angela smiled, realizing she was justifying herself again. She knew she didn't have to. If *Babcia* every found out what she was doing, she might pall at first, but then she'd understand—she'd realize Angela was only doing what she did for the best reasons. She leaned forward and took the old woman's hand. "Now, *Babcia*, you know you have nothing to worry about."

● ● ●

After dinner Allie left. Brett quickly cleaned up, and went upstairs, where she changed into a pair of jeans and white socks, then donned her Doc Marten boots and black leather vest. She started to go downstairs when she suddenly turned back and snapped her cockring onto her right wrist.

When she was younger she wore the cockring for its irony. Now, perhaps, it meant something more to her—maybe a return to her younger, wilder days, when all she cared about was herself.

She looked at herself in the mirror and grinned, running her hands back over her short, black hair, smoothing it down.

She slipped a Beretta into her ankle holster and glanced at the clock. Nine p.m. Still plenty of time before she could do anything at the bar. She didn't have to up her 'tude just yet. She didn't yet have to don the persona she had to wear.

She threw her black leather briefcase onto the bed and opened it, pulling out the sheaf of papers she'd brought home from the theatre. She had already given Allie the copy she had made for her and Randi, so now she glanced through her own copy. She hoped Allie and Randi would be able to get copies of schedules and contact sheets from Tina.

She got up, poured herself another scotch, and returned to the schedules. Inside her head, she could hear her old friend Madeline saying, "There's no such thing as coincidence." She knew Tempest was up to no good, and wanted to know why.

She didn't want to think about it before checking on something else, so she went upstairs and opened up a trunk near the outside wall. She only had to dig through it for a few minutes before she found what she was looking for: a small, black case.

She opened it up, and saw what she remembered—the rosary that had belonged to Allie's mother. She sat on the floor, fingering the topaz-colored beads, remembering and thinking. Brett's own

157

mother would hold a similar strand of beads in church while she prayed to a god Brett wasn't sure existed.

Brett liked to imagine there was a god, that something was waiting for her after death, that dying didn't end it all, but she couldn't understand how the secrets of all that were locked into this simple strand of beads with a crucifix.

More people had died during the Crusades than during both the World Wars put together. And people were still dying for a god no one could prove existed.

Another flashback went through Brett's brain, a remembrance of an old sermon, and she made a mental note to look up the exact reference later when she had the time. But then she glanced at the clock and realized it was still terribly early to hit any queer bar.

17

Brett couldn't find the book anywhere, so it must've been placed incorrectly. But she searched methodically from one room to the next, till she ended up in the study, which was her room. She gave the rest of the house to Allie's superior design abilities, but this was her butch den, and she liked it that way. She had a home she could be proud of, but she also had a room she could be comfortable in.

She stopped on her way to the bookcase, suddenly noticing a picture on the wall. It was of her, Storm, Rick and Frankie. She pulled the picture off the wall and stared at Storm's dark beauty, and the tempestuous woman she could see inside.

She missed her. She longed to take her once again into her arms.

She hung the picture back up and walked over to the shelf where she spied the tome she was looking for: *The Holy Bible*. And therein she found, "A new commandment I give unto thee, to love one another as I have loved you." And there she found Jesus admitting that obviously all the others commandments were much too complicated for mere humans to understand and obey, so the system had to be simplified to a basic teaching . . . One that so many still could not grasp and follow.

And if anyone had reread that simple passage, and taken it to heart, so many heartless murders and so much brutality could be stopped before it started.

Brett poured herself two more fingers of scotch and sat on the black leather couch in her room, understanding that there was a lot she would never understand: The Christian Crusade that killed so many in the name of god; a president who allowed the greatest modern epidemic to run amok but still got an airport and other institutions named after him; the farce of democracy that took place in Florida and put the wrong man in the Oval Office —one who claimed to follow the Lord's teachings, but could only think of war; the death of a woman named Storm, and why a woman who looked so like her managed to find her way into Brett's life.

And she looked down at the rosary still in her hand and thought that maybe three other girls had been killed in someone else's judgment. A judgment that, if they really knew and believed their bible, wasn't theirs to make.

She didn't like that Angela had seen Victoria in town before, when Victoria was saying she just arrived. Had seen her at the Rainbow Room, in fact.

And the suggestions Allie had brought up scrambled around inside her head, making her worry all the more.

160

She looked at her watch. By the time she got to the bar, there would be people there.

She quickly adjusted herself and went out to her vehicle.

• • •

"This'll be a lot easier," Allie said to Randi at her house, "if you look like a guy so they won't have problems with the fact we're unescorted."

"You want me to look like a guy?"

"Well, just try to butch it up." Allie ran her fingers through Randi's hair. It had been her idea that they meet at Randi's house. "You got any gel? We can slick this back, you put on some baggy jeans, a loose shirt and a leather jacket . . . We might get away with it. They don't like women going in without men."

Randi closed her eyes for a moment, seeming to enjoy the feel of Allie's fingers running through her hair. Allie stopped, even though she liked the feeling herself.

"We won't have any problems so long as I've got this," Randi replied, pulling out her badge. "I didn't have any earlier."

"But if customers are suspicious, they won't talk with us. We won't find out as much. If we can blend in, if you're my man and I'm your woman, and we're out for a little couple fun, we might be able to find out something. Now let's see what we can do to butch you up." She headed for the bathroom.

"Wait, Allie!" Randi yelled, jumping to her feet.

She was too late. Once she yelled, Allie wanted to know what she was hiding, so she hurried to the bathroom, where she found two toothbrushes by the sink. Smiling, she quickly looked through the medicine cabinet and by the time Randi arrived, she had found the gel.

She wouldn't say a word about it, but she was gratified to know

161

that Randi still cared enough about her that she hadn't wanted her to see the second toothbrush.

• • •

At 10:30, Brett left to head down to the Rainbow Room. She was surprised it was already so busy she had to park in the next-door lot. She paid her cover and went to the bar to get a beer. The barstaff was divided between men and women, and most of them had been there for years. Though she could never remember their names, they remembered her.

The cute bartender, a woman with long, curly-brown hair and Bambi brown eyes, handed her a beer without Brett even having to order. Brett winked at her and left a seven-dollar tip for her three-dollar drink. Both the bartenders and waitstaff of any place she frequented went out of their way to make sure she got served, and she liked it that way. She did what she could to keep it that way. It was her old self reasserting itself.

She had to admit, these bar people probably knew nothing about her, except that she tipped well. All she was to them was a friendly butch who tipped well. Very well.

She took a long drink of her beer and surveyed the room before turning back to the bartender and laying the four pictures she had taken from the dancers' book down on the bar. "Do you know any of these women?" The pictures were of the three dead girls and Victoria.

The bartender looked down at the pictures and cringed. She finally looked slack-jawed up at Brett.

"Do you know any of them?" Brett asked, matter-of-factly. She had taken the pictures out of the dancers' book.

"Yeah, this one comes in here sometimes," the bartender finally said, pointing to the picture of Nicola without looking at it again. "She dances here sometimes." She pointed at the picture of

Desiree, without doing anything more than glancing at it. "She seems familiar, I'm not sure though. In fact, they all look familiar."

"Anything you can tell me about them?"

"Not really. I'll think on it and let you know if I remember anything." She shrugged. "Where did you get these pictures?"

Brett shrugged.

The bartender stared at Brett, probably trying to really remember her. "Like I said, they all look a little familiar. Why are you asking?" Brett wasn't surprised that she was questioning her, after all, they were blatant pictures.

Brett looked into her eyes. "Three of the women have died recently and I'm looking into it." She left the bartender with her mouth open wide. "Thanks for your help," she said with a wink. Flirting came naturally to her, and she had realized a while ago that a little flirting went a long way to get women to do what she wanted. That and money. Though the bartender probably thought she was some sort of freak.

Brett quickly did a tour of the bar, noting the changes since she'd last been there—the dance floor used to be in the corner, flanked on two sides by high, long tables. Now it was moved a little over, so people could sit on three sides of it. A coat-check had also been added.

She recognized some faces in the sea of women. Some had been regulars when she was, and she wondered if, like herself, they were just here for the night, or if they were still regulars, jumping from bed to bed, love to love, in search of something too perfect for this world, or something that would ease whatever hell they were in, making them able to live with themselves and giving them the ability to look at themselves in the mirror each morning.

Now she knew you had to find it inside yourself, but she had to admit that Allie had helped her to find such a safe place. A place free from her guilt over Storm, and from the nightmares her childhood and adolescence had left her with.

163

A voice came over the loudspeakers, temporarily drowning out both the memories and the backbeat that threatened to take over her body by pulsing through her like blood, saying that the show would start in just a few minutes, at eleven o'clock. Brett glanced around and caught a sassy little redhead readying a shot at the pool table. When she missed, she tossed her hair and gave an "Ooops" gesture.

Brett knew Cindy was one hell of a pool player, but was an even bigger player, period. As usual, she had a few butches nearby, vying for her attentions.

"Hey, Cindy, long time no see," Brett said, walking up and looking at her, much to the dismay of her butches-in-waiting. Cindy gave her a long once-over, obviously liking what she saw.

"Brett, how's it hangin'?"

"Have you ever known it to hang?" Brett said, leaning back to show she was packing hard. Cindy grinned at this and ran her finger down a protruding vein in the back of Brett's arm. The butches hovered closer. Brett knew she could either finish this off real quick, or call these peons on their bluff.

No matter what else had changed, Brett Higgins was still not one to turn down a bluff.

She grabbed Cindy's hand and brought it up to her mouth, gently running her lips over the back. She pulled Cindy toward her, leaning her back against the table, shoving her thigh between Cindy's legs, grinding it against her crotch. "I got a question for you," she whispered into Cindy's ear, playing her lips so they almost, but not quite, touched it.

"Go for it." Cindy wrapped her arms around Brett's neck. The women around her bristled, but Brett towered over them, her muscular arms making their own statement as she nonchalantly flexed her biceps and triceps.

Brett reached into her back pocket and retrieved the photos. "Do you know any of these chicks?"

"Oh, sure, I see you for the first time in forever, and you ask me about other girls! Shit, Brett, you got more balls than anybody else I know."

"But do you?"

Cindy pulled away, grabbed the photos and flipped through them, her eyes growing large for only a moment. "You should ask them," she finally said, indicating her pack of butches, non-plussed. "They seem more their type." She stopped at the picture of Nicola. "I do know she dances here sometimes, though." She looked up at Brett. "Still got that thing for dancers, huh?"

Brett smiled at this, then turned to the waitress who was walking by. "Sarah, a round for this group," she said, tossing thirty bucks on her tray. She then looked at the butches and handed out the pictures. "Any of you recognize any of these girls?" No one took the photos. "Excuse me, I asked if any of you recognized any of these girls?"

"Is that any way to treat a friend of mine?" Cindy asked them, meeting each one's eyes, one by one. Years ago, Brett had first put Cindy in her place at the pool table, and then in the bedroom.

One of the butches turned and left, but another took the pictures and conferred with one of the others. "This one dances here sometimes at the shows." They all seemed to be raising their eyebrows at the nature of the pictures. One was staring at Brett as if she was some sort of criminal. Brett was used to such looks.

"And I know this one used to, a year or two ago," another woman added, tapping the picture of Sylver. Her eyes were glued to the picture. Brett was struck by how much like men some women could be.

"I've seen the others around occasionally," the last woman said, slowly looking through the pictures with a leer. She tried to palm a pic to slide into her pocket.

"Here?" Brett asked, catching the picture before it disappeared into a pocket.

165

"Yeah, here," the woman said, slowly giving it up.

"They are all dancers, right?" the first one asked. "I mean, that's the only reason I think I recognize them is 'cause well . . ."

"Well, what?" Brett asked.

"C'mon, look at these pics? How the hell did you get them to pose like this?"

"I have my ways."

"Why're you looking for them?" another asked.

Yeah, these girls had been drinking. "I'm not looking for them, I'm trying to find out more about them. I know where they all are right now."

"That's really weird."

Brett gave her her best sly grin. "I've never been accused of normality."

"If they're dancers, why don't you ask the girls here; after all, they'd probably know more than us," the second woman said.

Duh. From the mouths of babes. "Thanks a lot girls," Brett said, deliberately using a term she knew they'd hate. When Sarah brought their drinks, she said, "Enjoy your drinks," as she headed back to the dancers' dressing room.

But Cindy grabbed her arm. "So if you're so smart, where are they?"

Brett grinned at her. "You don't want to know."

"Yeah, I do."

"You really don't know me, then, if you insist on asking after I've told you not to." Brett ran a hand down Cindy's cheek. "Three of the girls are either in the morgue or in their graves. The last one works for me." She turned and left. Brett was in her element here, among these sorts of people.

"Hey, you, nobody's allowed back there," some guy said when she tried to walk behind the bar and into the back room. Brett looked up to where he stood on a small ladder, adjusting the spotlight to be used for the dancers. She thought about bribery, but he

166

was probably the new owner. She thought about just slipping in, but decided instead to find a spot to stand, or a table to sit at, if that was possible in this crowd, and watch the talent.

The place had changed since she'd last been there—now the dancers weren't just "Girls! Girls! Girls!" but there were also some boys and queens as well. She wasn't too interested in them; after all, they had a couple of good male strippers at the theater, but choosing them was more Frankie's province than hers, though she had always been intrigued by all the basic mechanics of pornography, erotica, and its sale, uses and distribution.

And they just plain out didn't do drag shows at the Paradise Theater.

The first female dancer she saw went by the name Amber and had long, red hair and a shapely, yet slender frame. What most attracted Brett was the way she moved, undulating her hips to the beat of the music, using her entire body to lock every eye in the room onto her, luring them with both suggestive moves and glances. She might be just an amateur, but she had some great natural talent.

"Hot damn, she's good," Brett murmured to the woman next to her. "Better'n anyone I remember."

"Oh, she came in a coupla weeks ago to dance for a woman's birthday. I guess they talked her into coming back."

Brett went to the dance floor, put a ten in her teeth and knelt on the floor. Amber danced up to her and leaned down to take the money, but Brett pulled back, trying to tease her into playing. The crowd hollered at this, a few laughing their encouragement. Amber stood back, hands on hips, and brought one high-heeled shoe up to gently push Brett in the chest.

Brett played along, flying onto her back. Amber dropped to the floor and crawled over to her, then on top of her, rubbing her body against Brett's, until she pulled the bill from Brett's teeth with her own and took it with her hand to place into her cleavage, then kissed Brett long and hard on the mouth, her body pressed into Brett's.

She was the only dancer that night worth looking into further for business, because Erika, the new Miss Rainbow Room, couldn't dance for crap. Apparently, someone liked how she looked or something. Brett knew they had to have better talent somewhere.

When Brett went after girls for the theatre, they had to look like Barbie, have big tits, an incredible ass, or know how to do business and have a good enough body to follow through on it. She had to go after the women her customers would like.

18

The spotlight dude was nowhere to be seen, so Brett went through the cut in the bar and into the back room. She strode through it like she knew where she was going, which she kind of did because she had been back there a few times before, but now she glanced around for Amber, figuring she'd catch her first, then Erika, since she might as well be thorough in her questioning.

Of course, if she was thorough, she'd also have a talk with the new owner—especially considering what Cindy's butches had just said—that all the victims had danced at the Rainbow Room. But they were all fairly tanked, so Brett didn't know how seriously to take their remarks. In fact, she should talk to all the performers, but she wasn't sure how far she could get with some of them.

But she found both Erika and Amber in the bathroom, near the stall. Apparently they had staked out the area as their own territory in the jumbled confusion of people getting dressed and changing costumes for the show. She really couldn't blame them—a place of one's own could be a wonderful thing in such a group of people.

Amber caught sight of Brett over her shoulder in the mirror where she was touching up her make-up. "Trouble maker."

"Always and forever," Brett replied, leaning in the doorway.

Amber continued playing with her make-up. "You know, you're not gonna see anymore back here than you will out there." Brett remained silent, knowing Amber was playing with her and not liking it. Women didn't play with her unless she allowed them to. She'd get the upper hand.

Amber again met her eyes in the mirror. "Oh, playing the strong, silent type, huh?"

Erika, who was rolling a fishnet stocking up along her leg, stifled a giggle.

Amber turned and looked at Erika. "Oh, c'mon, doesn't she seem like she should be swinging from vines in the jungle, pounding on her chest and screaming?"

Erika seemed to approve of what she saw. "Don't mind her, she's not used to working the gay bar scene."

"Ah, I see, so a throng of hairy, dirty, smelly, drunken men is better. Obviously I was miscalculating the equation." Brett stepped around Amber. "New Miss Rainbow Room, eh? Nice." She let her eyes say everything else.

"So the big, bad butch likes what she sees," Amber said from behind her.

Brett had her hooked, and right now she was just squirming on the line, waiting for Brett to reel her in.

"Should I bother asking what you want?" Erika asked.

"Name's Brett, and I'm looking for some info about a couple of girls." She pulled the photos from her back pocket.

"Uh huh, sure," Erika said, taking the pictures with a suggestive smile. Her eyes wandered over the pictures, taking in every detail of each one.

"Do you know any of them?"

Erika laughed. "What sort of a weird trip is this?" She leaned around Brett to look at Amber, handing her the pictures. "She wants to know if we know these dancers."

She heard Amber's deep, rich laugh behind her. "What a perv!"

Brett grabbed the photos, pocketed them, and leaned back against the wall. "So, what can you tell me about them?"

Erika shrugged. "'Sides that they're whores?"

"What do you mean by that?"

"Who the fuck else would pose like that for you?" Amber asked.

Brett wheeled around. "So you've posed like this yourself?"

Amber turned a particularly bright shade of red. "No," she said to the floor.

"I didn't know any of them too well." Erika said, pulling the pictures from Brett's pocket. "This one did dance here occasionally," she said, referring to Nicola. "The others came through once or twice—they thought it'd be easier to dance for chicks, which it is, but girls don't pay so much, you don't do big-time lap dances, and dykes just don't buy hookers that much."

Amber took the pictures and glanced through them. "I don't really think any of these girls would waste too much time here."

"What makes you say that?"

"They look straight. Straight, pretty sleazy, maybe users. They

171

probably don't have regular jobs so they just dance and hook. You can't make living wages here. This is just for fun. Well, some of the dancers here make some fun money, but that's it."

If Brett's senses weren't lying, neither of these women had even had a drink so far that night. They both sounded and acted stone-cold sober, and there wasn't a hint of a smell of alcohol about them. "So you're just here for the fun of it?"

"Great way to meet girls, and it's a turn-on to take your clothes off in front of all these women."

"Without demeaning oneself," Amber added.

"Huh?" Brett asked.

"We just go down to panties and bras, or g-strings and pasties, here—we don't have to get naked or play with ourselves or anything like that."

"And it's just for girls," Erika said. "Kind of a turn on, all in all. Stripping for women."

"So why're you looking for these girls?" Amber asked. "I mean, I could understand if you were looking for just one, you know like maybe if you had something for a particular girl, but four of them is kinda kinky, wouldn't you say?"

"I don't know," Brett replied, "would you?" She raised an eyebrow and grinned. She couldn't resist playing.

"Whatever," Amber said turning away.

Brett wouldn't let her get away that easily. "All except one of these girls has been killed within the last month."

"So you're a cop?" Amber said, turning back around. "You don't look like one."

"You know a lot of cops?"

"Not really. I just know the dyke cops that come in here, flashing their guns and badges as if they were their dicks or something."

"So what's your point?" Brett asked, facing off with Amber, just inches from her.

"I think she's just curious why you're asking all these questions," Erika said.

"They've all worked for me. I liked Nicola, she was a good girl, so I'd like to know who killed her." She leaned back against the wall. "So neither of you ever did anything more with any of these girls?"

"No, not my type at all," Erika said.

"What's your type?"

"You."

"Let me see if I've got this right," Amber said. "You're not a cop, in fact you're a bar owner or something, but you're wondering about these girls. These girls you have disgustingly intimate pictures of. Did you have anything more to do with any of them?"

"No, I'm just a curious sort, and I don't like anyone taking out my girls."

"Your girls. Rather possessive, aren't you?"

Brett chose to ignore the fiery redhead, instead settling her hands on Erika's hips. "So you have no idea why anyone from around here would go after these girls?"

"Nope."

"You've never witnessed any strange behavior then?"

Amber laughed out loud. "This place is filled with it—straight folks looking for lesbians to join them, straight boys trying to get laid, possessive butches losing it when somebody looks at their woman . . . We got it all."

Erika looked behind her at Amber, then back at Brett. "But we've never seen anything that might be considered really threatening. No stalking or anything like that. Nothing beyond the usual stupidity."

173

"And what about you?" Brett asked Amber.

"Hey, I've only been working here a little while."

"That's not an answer."

She sighed. "Erika, why are we even wasting our time with this woman?"

"I like her."

"Well, Amber, have you ever noticed anything strange?"

"No, not really. Nothing suspicious. Nothing anymore suspicious than some bull asking about dancers who've recently been killed."

Brett smiled, then guided Erika around next to her so she could look directly at Amber. "You never answered my earlier questions about if you ever had anything going with any of the girls," Brett asked Amber. She loved being able to touch these women like this. She could imagine the two of them together. She wanted to be there to watch it.

"No, I didn't. How's that for an answer? They're not my type either," Amber replied.

"And are big, hairy, smelly, drunken men your type, then?"

"Lemme guess, Brett, you're one of those butches who think you're every woman's type. No better than a man, really."

"But, unlike so many men, I try to pick bed partners..." She let her gaze slowly drift over Amber. "...with some taste, judgment and class." She glanced down at the pictures. "So you don't remember anything about this one?" she said, again showing the photo of Victoria.

Erika glanced at it, then looked at Amber. "Hold on, wasn't she here that one night, like a year ago, when that cop got drunk and tried to shoot someone?"

"What cop?" Brett asked.

"Oh, just some possessive, drunken bull who wanted to show

her shit. And I don't remember," Amber replied. "I don't think it was her, but then again, I didn't see quite this much of her."

"The cop?"

"No, the girl," Amber sighed resignedly. "About a year ago, this girl danced a few weekends, then stopped showing up."

"Is that usual here—for someone to dance a while and then stop?"

"Sure. They decide the money's not good enough, or it just isn't their thing."

"But wasn't that the girl," Erika said, "you thought was looking, or asking, for someone in particular?" She was saying it as if she were trying to remember.

Amber shrugged. "I really can't remember."

"Hold on—can I see those pictures again?" When Brett handed them over, she went directly to the one of Victoria. "This was the girl," she said, tapping the picture with her finger. "She was here like a year ago for a few weeks, asking questions and doing some dances, and then suddenly she disappeared."

"Are you sure about that? This is the same girl?"

"Yeah, Victoria Nelson, right?"

"Victoria Nelson?" Brett repeated, slack-jawed. Storm's real name was Pamela Nelson.

"Yes."

"What sort of questions was she asking?"

Erika glanced up, her eyes unfocused and wandering, like she was trying to remember something. She moved her hands about, then finally said, without looking at Brett, "I think she was asking about some guy. Some guy who owned a bar, maybe."

"What makes you think that?"

"I'm not thinking, I'm just trying to remember." She met

175

Brett's eyes. "I think she was looking for some guy named Higgins."

Brett stared at her for a moment, wondering if there was anything she could do to make her remember any better. To fix her memory. Finally, she pulled a business card from her pocket and handed it to Erika. "If you do remember, or think of anything else, give me a call."

Erika took the card, which stated simply "Paradise Enterprises, Brett Higgins, Manager," with her work and pager numbers, as well as the address of the theatre. She looked down at the card, then pulled her wallet from her purse, and deliberately put the card into it. "So you're Higgins, huh?"

"You're not sure who she was looking for, so how can I possibly proclaim to be the one?"

Erika ran her hand through Brett's hair, finally resting her arm on Brett's shoulder. "If you weren't the one, why would you be asking about her?"

"Coincidence, or you're stalking her," Amber said.

"Why don't you stick around after the show? Maybe we could talk more then? After all, I might remember something?" Erika said.

"Looking for a better place to dance?" Brett grinned.

"Honey, in real life, I'm in banking. I do just fine." She again picked up her purse and opened it. "You've shown me yours, so I guess I'll show you mine." When she pulled her business card from it, a long strand of glassy-looking green beads came with it and dropped to the floor. "Shit," she said, leaning down to pick them up.

Brett beat her to it, retrieving the beads from the floor before she could. "Interesting," she said.

"It's a rosary, okay? I'm a Catholic and it was a first communion gift from my godmother."

"I know what it is," Brett said, meeting her eyes, "I was just noticing how long it is. Aren't most rosaries only five decades long?" She gave a little smile, knowing she was surprising the two women.

"Yes, they are," Erika said, clearly impressed with Brett's knowledge. "This type isn't very common at all. It's the Rosary of the Seven Joys of the Blessed Virgin Mary, so it has seven decades, with an ending of two Hail Marys, and then an Our Father and one last Hail Mary." She apparently realized how she sounded, because she quickly stuffed the beads back into her purse and offered Brett her business card again.

"Just how common is such a rosary?" Brett asked.

Erika shrugged. "It's not the sort of thing you can just pick up at any store. My godmother had this especially made for me because she wanted to encourage me to ponder the more wonderful mysteries of life." She pulled the rosary from her purse and gently caressed the beads. "I've never seen another one like it."

"You haven't?" Brett asked.

"No, I haven't. Have you?"

"Yes. Did your godmother have any more of those made?"

Erika shook her head. "I told you, I've never seen another one like it. She used my birthstone for the beads. It's not that exciting."

Brett put her hand next to Erika's, to also hold the rosary. "Yes, it is."

"Freak," Amber said.

Erika seemed to see how serious Brett was. "I really have never seen another like it—and I went to Catholic school, okay? I mean, you can get these things made, or even make them yourself. All you have to do is buy the parts. I'm sure that's what my godmother did."

"What's your godmother's name?"

"Teresa Delaski. She died nine years ago."

"Oh," Brett said, letting her hand fall to her side. She took the business card Erika had laid down on the counter. Looking at it, she said, "If you've got such a great day job, why do you work here?"

Erika shrugged her lovely shoulders. "Spare change. For the kicks. Gets me as many dates as I want. You're only young once. That enough?"

"Maybe I will hang around." Brett said, knowing she wanted to leave. She couldn't believe she'd hit such a hot lead that turned against her.

19

Brett spent the next hour cruising the bar, asking more questions. Nicola was the only one who was really remembered, and was generally well-liked and considered pretty hot. The other girls got the "she might've danced here," bit, or else, "where can I find her?" thing.

Overall, what Brett got the most of was fascination with the pictures. Some women stared, all but drooling, whereas other women were disgusted with them. More the latter than the former, overall, actually.

When Erika danced again, Brett tipped her, teasing her with a bill stuck in the front of her pants. Brett danced Erika around the floor, until, much to the crowd's enjoyment, Erika pinned Brett against the wall and claimed her prize—as well as a very deep kiss.

When Brett moved off the dance floor, she noticed Amber standing by the door to the back area, watching. She hadn't tipped Amber this time around.

After the show, Brett sipped her beer, waiting for Erika. But instead of the blonde, Amber came over and sat across from her. She had switched from her revealing costume into a light, simple sundress and sandals. Her long hair floated freely and her face looked a little red, like she had scrubbed off the heavy make-up and applied a light brushing of powder and lip liner instead.

"Do you two do everything together?" Brett asked, eyeing Amber's body once again.

"Actually, Erika got paged—her mother had a flat downtown, so she had to go get her. She asked me to stand in for her, and let you know that she really would like to have that drink with you sometime."

"Ah, so you're the unwilling replacement?" When Amber didn't answer, Brett met her gaze with her own and continued, "What's your poison?"

"Corona with a lime."

Brett caught the passing waitress, a cute little butch who doubled as a very efficient bouncer, and ordered the beers, paying for them as well.

Amber reached over and took Erika's business card from Brett's pocket, quickly writing on the back of it. "I think Erika would like you to have it."

Brett took the card, noted what appeared to be a home phone number on the back, and repocketed it. She then leaned back and nodded toward the dance floor. "You like this song?"

Amber stood and Brett took her elbow to lead her to the dance floor. Once there, they both started moving to the fast beat of the Erasure song that was playing, but once it smoothed over into the slightly slower fast beat of *We Are Family*, Brett took her hands and led her around the floor, using moves adapted from swing dancing. She twirled and dipped Amber, who followed beautifully, even when Brett pressed their bodies together.

After a half-hour, the DJ slipped into slower notes, beginning with *I'll Always Love You*. Brett had begun to pull Amber to her, but that particular song was hers and Allie's. She couldn't dance it with another woman. She suddenly remembered the first time she and Allie danced to that song—at the Affirmations' Youth Prom, right before they broke up. It was also the first slow dance they shared after they got back together five years later.

Brett pulled away and Amber looked up, questioning. She had already been resting her head on Brett's shoulder.

"I . . . I've got to get going," Brett said, quickly glancing at her watch. Amber's brilliant green eyes clouded over. Brett squeezed her hand and rushed out the door.

● ● ●

Chantel was already in the dressing room when Angela entered for the last show of the night. "So, are you and Tempest going to let me make any money tonight?" Chantel asked nonchalantly, putting on her make-up. She already had her beautiful, full-figured body in her costume.

"What do you mean?" Angela asked. "We've always worked well together in the past." She put her bag down and started undressing. She wished she had curves like Chantel.

Chantel looked up at Angela. "Shit, babe, I'm sorry. I just don't like that Victoria at all. She tries to hog all the money, men and everything else she can get her hands on."

"What do you mean by that?"

"Have you seen the way Brett looks at her?"

Angela made a face. Chantel laughed. "You got the hots for Brett, baby? Join the line." With that simple line, Chantel made it clear that most of Brett's dancers adored her, and maybe more.

Angela wanted to hit Chantel.

But just then, the first subject of their conversation entered, so Angela withheld her reply.

"Silence?" Victoria said. "Talking about me again?" She looked closely first at Angela, and then at Chantel.

"Why does everything have to be about you?" Chantel asked angrily.

"I was just joking, but it looks like I hit the nail on the head," Victoria said.

"Brett ain't here now, so you can just chill," Chantel said. "Even if she can't tell, I know you're after her ass."

"What do you mean by that?" Angela asked again.

"I just told you—have you seen the way Brett looks at her?"

"So she likes me, what can I say?" Victoria said, obviously getting upset.

"Don't play me like that. You do everything you can to get her to like you." Chantel said.

"I like pleasing my employer. Maybe you should watch and learn."

"But why do you do so much to get Brett to notice you?" Angela asked, wearing only her sexy, skimpy, lacy, bikini under-wear and bra.

Victoria put her bag down, making it obvious she would be

changing on this level of the dressing room. "Like I told you, I like making a good impression on the boss. What else can I say?"

Chantel finished putting on her make-up, glanced at her watch, and stood up. They only had a few minutes before the show was to begin. "You're a pure brown-noser."

"So? It's a good way to make sure one has a place to work," Victoria said, taking off her blouse and peeling her jeans off.

"What is your story, anyway?" Angela asked, taking off her bra and underwear.

"What do you mean by that?"

"I'm not buying that story you gave Brett."

"What's to buy? It's the truth." Victoria faced off with Angela, clearly looking at her naked body.

"Then why are you so hot after Brett?" Chantel asked, hands on her hips.

"What would you say if I said she's hot and can't wait until she fucks my brains out?" Victoria said, peeling off her undergarments so she stood naked with the two other women.

"I'd say she wouldn't have much to do," Chantel replied.

They heard the music rise in the auditorium—Chantel's cue.

"Knock 'em dead," Victoria said.

"We're not done yet," Chantel said to Victoria, almost a warning, then left.

"What do you want?" Angela asked Victoria once they were alone.

"You're up next, why don't you get ready?"

"Because I want you to answer my question."

"I think it's because you like being naked with me." Victoria slowly inched closer to Angela. "I know it's a turn on to me to be naked in front of others, and I think you're enjoying that, *and* enjoying seeing me naked." She took a deep breath to bring

183

attention to her breasts. Her hands were at her sides, and her legs were slightly apart. Opened enough so that Angela could see everything, including just how turned on Victoria was.

Angela, suddenly feeling self-conscious about her nakedness, quickly turned to reach for her bag and costume, but Victoria grabbed her hip and turned her around to face her. Angela immediately flattened herself against the wall, as far from Victoria as she could get.

"You have a very nice body."

Angela quickly put her bag between them and pulled out her costume. "You'll do anything to keep anybody from questioning you. Why?" She quickly slipped the flimsy red negligee over herself as if it were a shield.

Victoria perched on the make-up table with her thighs slightly spread. Her breasts were firm and unsagging, her rouged nipples testifying to her love of attention to her body. She leaned back against her arms, letting her legs fall open even more. "Why would you think that?"

Angela kept her eyes off of her, trying to ignore Victoria's glistening invitation. "You're trying to seduce Brett. You've thrown yourself at her, and keep taking your clothes off in front of her. I just want to know why." She tried to concentrate on the big mirror and applying her make-up.

Victoria popped off the counter like a cat and began pulling on her costume. "I'll think about telling you that when you tell me why you won't let yourself do what you want."

"And what's that?"

"Enjoy women."

Angela took a deep breath. Victoria took the moment and sprang toward her. "Why are you so afraid?"

"I'm not afraid!"

Victoria took Angela's hands and laid them on her breasts. Angela immediately jerked them away.

"Why are you doing this?" Angela asked.

"Because I've seen the way you watch Chantel, and me, and Brett . . . I saw how you looked at Allie this afternoon, even."

Angela turned away. "You don't know what you're talking about."

"If there's one thing I know in this whole, fucked-up life of mine, it's people. And Angela, anyone who's paying attention knows you're in love with Brett Higgins."

Angela didn't look at Victoria.

Victoria put her hands on Angela's waist, holding her in place. "I know what I saw this afternoon. You weren't repulsed by what I was doing, you weren't defensive of Brett or Allie. You were jealous —jealous of Allie being with Brett, jealous of what they were obviously doing when I interrupted them. You felt hatred at that moment, didn't you, Angela, darling?"

Angela looked down into Victoria's eyes. Then pulled away abruptly.

But Victoria caught her before she could escape. Victoria pressed her against the door and whispered into her ear, "You're in love with Brett. Admit it."

Angela was taller and stronger than Victoria, so with one massive push she shoved her back and onto her butt. Facing her, she screamed, "No! I'm not!" Then she towered over Victoria, who lay on the floor, "You think you know it all, yet you can't understand me and it's driving you crazy. Just . . . just go screw yourself, okay?" With that, she left the dressing room, and immediately fell under the leering gaze of Don, the night clerk. She slipped into the auditorium, sitting in a chair near the back so as to not interrupt Chantel's set.

Chantel was just finishing up her last song and preparing to go out to give lap dances, so she was on stage, naked.

And that was when it happened—the music was fading, and the stage lights were being dimmed while Chantel retrieved her g-string—and a big, dark-haired man yelled out drunkenly, "Hey baby! You don't need that!"

Chantel ignored him, so he rushed over to grab her g-string from her before she could put it on.

Angela jumped to her feet and ran to the box office. "Don! Don!" she yelled, pounding on the door. Don was half-asleep. "We've got a problem! Get the guard!" Angela knew there was an intercom linking the box office directly to the shack of the guard who watched the parking lot.

Angela charged back into the auditorium and raced to the front to help Chantel fend off her assailant. A few men from the audience had already bolted out the back door, not wanting to be caught at the theatre during any sort of incident.

The man was solidly packed muscle, so he considered Angela and Chantel a threesome instead of an annoyance.

But just as he was trying to rip off Angela's costume, a big, beefy hand reached out and grabbed the guy by the shoulder, yanking him around.

"What the hell?" he said just as a fist slammed into his face and sent him plummeting to the floor, where his head hit with a solid thunk. He was out cold.

Frankie used the panty hose Victoria handed him to tie the guy's wrists behind his back while he was unconscious.

"Are you two all right?" Victoria asked, helping Angela and Chantel to right their few bits of clothes, "I knew Frankie was upstairs, so I had Don call for him."

"Is everything okay in here?" the guard asked, shining his flashlight around.

"Yeah. I got it under control," Frankie said, hefting the fellow to his feet and practically carrying him out of the theatre. "You girls all right?" he asked the dancers, who all nodded. "Then get back to work, we still got some boys here for a show."

• • •

"Let's do it," Randi said, climbing out of the car with Allie at The Naked Truth. She looked at the guard and, lowering her voice, said, "How are you doing?"

"Watch the car for my baby, will you?" Allie said, putting a five into the guard's hands. "He's had a little too much to drink already, and I'm just gettin' started." She grabbed Randi's arm and led her into the bar. "Don't talk. Nice try, but your voice isn't deep enough."

"And Brett's is?"

"Yes." She took Randi's arm, leading her while trying to make it look as if Randi was leading her—basically like she always had to do with butches.

Randi pushed money into the bouncer's hand, led Allie in without a word, and looked for a table. She spotted one near the stage and led Allie over. "I'll get us drinks," she said just above the music.

Allie looked around, absorbing the music, the flashing lights, the three topless girls onstage . . .

One of the girls had her legs wrapped around a pole and was sliding down it, another was gyrating to the music, while the last pressed herself into the second girl's back, sliding up and down her body, her hands finding, and examining, all her curves. Allie noted that there were three more girls already in the audience selling lap dances.

187

After all, it was Friday, one of the busiest times for places like this. This was a great time to make a lot of money as a dancer.

Randi returned with a beer for herself and a Cosmopolitan for Allie.

"I smell pig," a woman said, walking up to their table and looking down at them.

"'Scuse me?" Allie said.

"You're a coupla cops, aren't you? What're you doing here?" She leaned down and growled at them, so nobody else could hear, "I pay all my bills on time."

"You pay your bills?" Randi asked, leaning toward the woman.

"My pay-offs, so I don't get disturbed. So I don't get the likes of you in here causing trouble."

"I don't know what you're talking about," Allie said, leaning back and not watching her volume, though she doubted anybody could overhear them over the din.

"Honey, I may be straight, but I know a femme and a butch when I see them."

"Then maybe you're not as straight as you claim to be," Randi said.

The redhead pulled out the chair next to Allie, turned it around, and sat down. Allie supposed this was how she thought a man would sit. "Well, I had some help. I'd know Brett Higgins' girlfriend anywhere."

"We've never met," Allie said.

"Tina O'Rourke. Your girlfriend and I have a history," Tina replied. Then she turned to Randi. "And I know you're a cop. So why don't you two tell me why you're sniffing around my club?"

"We're looking for information on some murdered girls," Randi said, turning official now that she realized their cover had been blown.

Tina gave a signal to one of the waitresses. "Yeah, Max, my manager, told me about that. I've got the information you're looking for in the office. Though Brett should've warned me the other day when we ran into each other. I would've had everything here for you earlier."

Brett was right, Allie thought—Tina was playing with them.

"Do you know any of these women?" Randi asked, getting to the point and placing the pictures on the table. All four pictures, including Victoria.

Tina gave them a cursory glance. "Of course I know those two," she said, indicating Sylver and Desiree. She tapped the photo of Nicola. "I assume she's the one who danced at the Paradise." The waitress arrived with her Scotch on the rocks, and Tina slipped her five and said, "Thanks." She took a sip.

"What about this last one? Have you ever seen her?" Randi asked, pushing her line of inquiry.

Tina pulled over the picture of Victoria, staring at it. "Yeah, I know her." She pushed the picture away and looked at Randi, taking another sip of her Scotch. "You two should understand that a lot of girls come and go. Some are regular at one place, others dance a week, or weekend, at one place, then move on to another. They move around and they go all around. There's a few who go from town to town, but most of what we get here are girls who work all in and around Detroit. Anybody who pays attention sees them all at some point or another."

"So what about her?" Randi asked, again pushing forward the picture of Victoria.

Tina pulled it toward her, then looked at Randi. "Your friend Brett keeps seeing the good in these girls. I, and most other owners, see the trash. They're no good, except for the money they make us. They're the dregs of society."

189

"She's not my friend," Randi said.

Tina grinned, then looked from Randi to Allie, "A little dissension in the ranks, huh?"

"Well?" Randi said.

"I think all of these girls danced here at one time or another, and at just about every other joint in Detroit. This girl here," Tina tapped the picture, "now she's only been around a year or so, but she's a bit strange. She knows how to dance, I mean really dance, and she's got a great body, but there's something wrong about her." She met both Randi's and Allie's eyes, a grin pulling at her lips.

"What do you mean?" Allie asked before Randi could say anything.

"By what?"

"Hold on," Randi said. "You make it sound like being able to dance is a criminal offense."

"Most strippers don't dance, they just take off their clothes and show their bodies. It's a job, and they know what the men want, and they don't give them anything more than that. This girl knows how to dance, it's like she's studied it—ballet or something. And she goes the extra mile; the boys love her."

"If they love her, then what's the problem?" Allie asked.

"No problem, just strange is all," Tina said, then added, to Randi's questioning look, "you don't know a lot about this all, huh? Well let me tell you, we love girls who show up, do their job, bring the customers in and make them happy."

"You keep saying she's strange, how so?" Allie asked. The situation was getting weird.

"She asked too many questions. She was looking for someone."

"Who?"

Tina looked at Allie, right into her eyes. "Your girlfriend."

"Ms. O'Rourke, what do you mean by that?" Allie asked, taking a deep gulp of her drink.

"Tina. We all go by first names in this business, as you should know," Tina said. "And I meant what I said. This chick was looking for Brett Higgins."

"How do you know that? How can you be sure?"

Tina leaned back, shaking her long hair back over her shoulder. "She asked me if I knew 'a Brett'."

"Did she ask anything else?" Randi asked.

"She asked a lot of specific questions about Brett—like what she was like, what her past was. How long she'd been around. That sort of thing." She shrugged and turned to Allie. "If I had to guess, I'd say she had a bone to pick with your girlfriend."

"What made you think that?" Randi asked.

Tina gave the two women a sly look, as if assessing them. "Her attitude when she was asking the questions. And I'm sorry, Officer, I didn't catch your name?"

Randi stared at her.

"In fact, I've not actually seen either of your badges. You are here on police business, I assume?"

"Detective Randi McMartin," Randi said, pulling out her badge as nonchalantly as possible, so nobody else would notice. She pointed to Allie. "She's just helping me out because of Brett's connection to Nicola."

"Randi and . . . Allie? That is what she calls you, isn't it?" Tina asked, looking at Allie. "Isn't it?" Allie finally bowed her head slightly in acknowledgement, realizing Tina wouldn't let it go. Tina turned back to Randi. "McMartin? Hmmm, let's see, you're the one who brought Brett down a few years ago, aren't you?" She was smiling now. When Randi didn't respond, she continued, "Unless I'm mistaken, unless you arrest me you have no way to make me answer any questions. So we're just having a nice conversation, wherein we chat about different things of interest to both of us, unless . . .?"

"Yes, I'm the one," Randi finally acknowledged.

"You seem to have some sort of a peculiar interest in Brett," Allie said to Tina, trying to steer the conversation away from the personal. The last thing she needed was for someone to rehash the bad blood between Brett and Randi.

"Yes, I do. She put my Dad away after all, so I'm curious."

"Earlier Max mentioned a couple of trouble-makers you get around here," Randi said, bringing the conversation back to the business at hand. "Jim Peterson and Stan."

"Yes, they come in sometimes, causing trouble."

"Do you happen to know Stan's last name?"

Tina nodded. "Dubrowski. But you're barking up the wrong tree looking at them."

"Why's that?"

"The other detectives told me neither of my girls was raped. If either of them did anything, they would've raped the girls—before or after. Sick sons-of-bitches."

"I'd like to see those copies of your contact sheets and schedules Max promised me," Randi said, not knowing how to respond to that.

"Of course. I'm always as helpful as I can be to law officers," Tina said, standing. "If you just follow me, I've got them in the office." She led them into the office, where she pulled them out of her briefcase and handed them to Randi.

"I don't see Tempest on here," Allie said, glancing through the sheets.

"Huh?"

"Tempest—Victoria—the girl who asked about Brett," Randi said.

192

"She danced here as Exotica," Tina said, pointing out Victoria's name on her contact sheet, next to the stage name Exotica.

"But she's at the Paradise right now as Tempest," Allie said.

"Girls change their stage names. Sometimes they end up at a club where someone's already dancing under their chosen name, so they have to pick something different. Or maybe they just don't want to be remembered. Wouldn't it be so nice if we could all just keep changing our names every time we wanted to be forgotten?"

"So she just suddenly decided to be known as Tempest?" Randi pressed, glancing at Allie.

Tina smiled, as if she understood far too well. "Either that or somebody else picked it out for her." She looked at Allie. "I get it now, your concern." She looked at Randi. "You two can be quite a puzzle, you know?"

"What do you mean?" Allie asked, trying to keep her composure.

"Brett must have picked the name Tempest for her. And I want to know why. Probably as much as you do." She turned out the light in the office and signaled for them to leave. "After all, I do have a bone to pick with her." She grinned at them. Besides wanting to seem malicious and enigmatic, she was also hiding her own personal joke: That Victoria also mentioned one other detail about Brett— that she was lovers with a dancer about a decade ago. A dancer named Pamela Nelson, who happened to be Victoria Nelson's older sister.

20

Victoria was walking out to the street. Don was inside closing up for the night. Victoria knew she needed to find a cab, or else it would be a long, lonesome, rather scary walk back to her place. She couldn't believe the guard was nowhere to be found. The theatre's employees seemed to be far from on top of things, despite what Brett had ordered.

She spotted a cab heading toward her, which was practically a miracle. Detroit had nowhere near the number of cabs of other large metropolitan areas. She began to lift her arm to signal for it when she felt one arm wrap around her waist and pull her away from the street, while another arm brought her upraised hand down to her side.

She screamed.

"Let's get a drink," a woman's voice whispered in her ear.

"What's going on?" an authoritative voice said, stepping out of a curbside car. The guard was there after all.

• • •

"Have you found out any more about her?" Allie asked, walking into the bedroom. It was way past 2:00 a.m., but Brett was sitting up, reading.

"Huh?"

"Victoria. She's gone out of her way to track you down. Why?"

"What do you mean?"

Allie sat down next to her. "There's something not right about her."

Brett sat up in bed, tossing the covers off. She was wearing a T-shirt and black silk boxers. "I know that. I know she's been lying to me—she told me she's new in town, and now I find out that she's been here for a while."

"She's been here a while? How'd you find out?"

"Angela told me she'd seen her a while ago at the Rainbow Room, so I went there tonight, and some people recognized her. But how did you find out she was asking about me?"

"Tina O'Rourke. She also told me that Victoria's been around here for a while."

Brett groaned. "Oh, god, babe, I'm sorry—I know how Tina feels about me, so I'm sure she wasn't exactly nice to you."

Allie sighed and leaned against her. "You're right there. So did you find out anything else interesting tonight?"

"Well, I found out you're right—Tempest really is Storm's sister."

Allie gasped. "Did she admit it to you?"

"No, but one of the dancers at the Rainbow Room told me that when she was there, she was calling herself Victoria Nelson, and Victoria herself told me she'd just come up from Indiana—and that's where Storm was from as well."

"So do you know what's she after yet?"

"Not yet, but I will find out."

Allie wrapped her arms around Brett, snuggling in closely. "Watch out. With the way she's been acting, there's no telling what she's up to."

Brett ran her hand over Allie's hair. "I know, baby, I know."

Allie leaned up so that she could look directly into Brett's eyes. "I'm serious, Brett. For all we know, she just might be out to avenge her sister's death."

"Well, we know I had nothing to do with that, so I really have nothing to worry about."

"You don't know what Victoria is thinking. Just as Randi blamed you for her brother's death, even though you didn't pull the trigger, so too might Victoria blame you for Storm's."

"I'll watch out, I swear, baby. Did you guys find out anything else?"

"There's a couple of regular trouble-makers over at The Naked Truth that Randi wants to look into. Stan Dubrowski and Jim Peterson. Tina's sure they're not behind it, though."

"Why's that?"

"Because none of the girls were raped."

Brett nodded sagely. "That makes sense. Oh, I saw one of those strange rosaries tonight. You know, the ones that were tied around the dead girls' wrists."

"Who had it? Where were you at?"

"I was at the Rainbow Room. One of the dancers I spoke with there had it—it fell out of her purse when she was giving me her business card."

"Oh my god, Brett—did she have any explanation for it?" Allie was remembering the notes she had written earlier about the possible killer, how he, or she, perhaps had been unable to lift the bodies into the Dumpsters.

"Yeah, she said her godmother, who died years ago, gave it to her for her First Holy Communion. She has no idea where the woman got it or anything, so I think it's pretty much a dead end."

"Unless she's our guy."

Brett pulled the business card she was using as a bookmark out and handed it to Allie. "I got this, in case you want to find out more about her.

Allie reached over to grab the phone by the bed.

"Who're you calling at this hour?"

"Randi," Allie said, dialing.

While Allie filled Randi in on these details, Brett began teasing Allie, slowly unbuttoning her blouse, undoing her jeans.

"Stop it," Allie whispered urgently, then, into the phone, "That's right," confirming the phone number Randi repeated back to her.

When she got off the phone a few minutes later, she swatted Brett playfully. "I cannot believe you!"

Brett put on her best puppy-dog look and said, innocently, "What'd I do?"

Allie swatted her again. "Don't give me that look—I can't believe you of all people would do that to me when I was talking to Randi!" A devilish glint lit her eye. "I guess I'll have to make you pay for that now." In the blink of an eye she grabbed the

197

handcuffs Brett kept in the nightstand and secured both of Brett's hands above her head to the headboard.

She had never done anything like this before, but she knew the only way she could both ensure the safety of the girls at the Paradise, as well as Brett's safety against Victoria, was if she took matters into her own hands.

But she couldn't do that unless she could do this.

She slowly strode over to the CD player they kept in the bedroom and slipped in some music. Taking a deep gulp of air, she let the music take over her body, and began swaying her hips to it.

She turned around to face Brett, running her fingers down the opened blouse, then slowly running them back up before pushing it off her shoulders and letting it drop to the floor. She ran her fingers over the tops of her breasts, just above her red satin bra.

Brett's eyes were glued to her, her breathing becoming heavier with Allie's every move.

Allie had taken off her shoes as soon as she entered the house, so when she turned around so her back faced Brett, and slowly slid her jeans down her hips, and then her legs, all she had to do was also pull off her socks to be left wearing only her underwear.

She turned back to face Brett, played her fingers over the top of her panties, teasing down the elastic to make Brett think about what lay just a little lower. She ran her fingers lightly over her crotch, touching herself through the thin material.

She had never been able to dance, or strip, for Brett. Nor was she able to masturbate for her. Why did butches so love to see femmes masturbating, she wondered briefly, before continuing her sensuous dance. She lowered her bra straps down her shoulders, pulling the material down a bit before she ran her thumbs over her already hardening nipples.

Brett was still on the bed, her eyes hot with passion. Allie knew

Brett wanted to see her touch herself. Allie realized with a sensual thrill that she had complete power over Brett at that moment. It was exciting, she was exciting.

Allie reached up and undid her bra, letting it slowly reveal her full breasts. Her nipples welcomed the cool air, puckering up even more. Still moving to the music, she cupped her breasts, squeezing the nipples.

Then she did something she'd never even tried before—she lifted her breasts and let her tongue snake out and caress first one nipple, then the other. And she kept her eyes on Brett. She had always thought she was too vanilla, too goody two shoes to do anything like this. But now that she was doing it, it felt so naughty it was good. She was being bad and it was really hot. Having Brett watch her like this was turning her on beyond belief.

Brett seemed to forget she was handcuffed. She was completely in Allie's thrall.

Allie had total power over her. And she liked the feeling.

Still dancing, she slipped her fingers back into her panties, and then she slipped them lower still, till she could feel just how turned on she was. She slid her fingers through her wetness and slipped one slick finger into her mouth to slowly suck it.

Brett lay on the bed, all but salivating.

Allie slid her panties off, and tossed them at Brett, who squirmed to try to get her teeth on them without taking her eyes off Allie. Allie knew she wanted to smell them.

Allie stood at the end of the bed, her legs slightly spread, her arms at her sides, and stared down at Brett. She reached between her own legs with both her hands, pulling herself open, and then fingered herself lightly.

"Oh, god, Allie," Brett moaned in a parched voice, "why don't you come over here and let me do that?"

"What? Don't you want to see me touch myself?" She had just planned on dancing for Brett, but it felt so good, she couldn't stop.

She straddled Brett's legs and sat back, one hand caressing herself, the other playing with her own nipple. "Isn't this something you've begged me for? Something you've pleaded for?" Allie slid two fingers up inside herself, then pulled them out and let Brett suck them.

Allie pulled her fingers from Brett's mouth and grinned evilly. She'd give Brett everything tonight. She leaned forward, her breast inches away from Brett's mouth, and grabbed the pillows from the other side of the bed.

She liked having Brett's undivided attention—and this time she was calling the shots.

She put the pillows at Brett's feet, and sat on Brett's legs, her own legs spread out in front of her. She then reached inside of the bedside table again and pulled out a dildo. They had a few, but Allie just grabbed one of the middle-sized ones. She couldn't imagine doing this with Brett's favorite, the largest of them (which was also Allie's favorite, when Brett used it on her).

Allie brought it up to her lips, and sucked it in and out, in and out. She couldn't believe she was doing this—let alone with the lights on. She felt a twinge of anxiety and embarrassment. "You do want to see me do this, don't you?" She had never been able to give Brett a blow job when she was packing hard.

"Oh, yes . . . yes . . ." Brett murmured, her eyes meeting Allie's, then trailing down over her naked body.

Allie suddenly realized why women did this. She reached between her legs, caressing her own wetness, feeling how swollen she was, and then she ran those same fingers along the green and black latex toy. She leaned back against the pillows she had propped up, and slid the dildo up into herself.

200

Brett and she both gasped at the same moment.

Allie took the dildo into her left hand, pushing it in, and pulling it out, slowly, enjoying the way it was filling her. Then she brought her right hand down between her legs, and lay her index finger along her clit, feeling it throbbing beneath her own finger.

And while she fucked herself with the dildo, she ran her finger up and down herself, knowing she couldn't make herself come too quickly. She wanted to fully tease Brett. A sudden thrill of excitement pulsed through her at the thought of making herself come while Brett watched.

She increased the pace with each of her hands, pushing and pulling more and more quickly with her left hand, while her right hand beat her hard clit back and forth, back and forth, ever more rapidly.

She was sweating as the energy and excitement gathered. She was so turned on now that she wished she could expose herself even more to Brett. Her hips were wiggling at their insistence. She wished she had a third hand to squeeze her nipples with.

She pushed the dildo in all the way and left it there so she could use both her hands to tease her nipples, squeezing them hard and rough, the way Brett would if she weren't handcuffed.

She pulled the dildo out and then reached down to open her lips up wide, showing Brett everything. She was shaking and hot and knew she was about to climax.

"Oh, god," she heard herself moan when she ran her fingers up and down her clit. "Oh, god . . ."

She inserted the dildo again and began fucking herself with it, hard, while she continued her hard and fast movements against her clit.

"Oh, god, oh god!" she screamed, bucking on Brett's legs.

• • •

Victoria and Angela sat in a nearly empty Highland Park bar. Victoria lifted her glass to indicate to the bartender that she wanted another Slow Comfortable Screw. "I don't understand you," she finally said to Angela, who was slowly sipping a white Zinfandel.

"I don't you, either."

"Why did you grab me like that?" The guard hadn't wanted the dancers to have to walk around the building by themselves, so he had been waiting in his car by the entrance. Victoria had just been hailing a cab, so he hadn't worried. When Angela approached, he hadn't worried either—until Victoria screamed.

"I had to catch you before you left."

"But why?"

"I want to know why you're after Brett like you are. I want to know what you're hiding."

"You're really messed up," Victoria said, downing her drink and heading toward the door.

"I know you've been in town a while!"

Victoria stopped. "What's your point?"

Angela walked over to her. "So you admit it?"

"I'm not admitting anything; I'm just curious about what you're after."

"The truth. That's all." Angela went back to the bar and her wine.

Victoria sat down and lifted her glass, which the bartender promptly replaced. Victoria didn't usually drink much, but she was wondering what Angela was about. "What do you think the truth is?"

"Well, I know you're definitely hiding a few things, including how long you've been in town."

"So maybe I did. People sometimes take kindly to somebody who's new."

"And sometimes they really don't like strangers. So you were taking an even bigger chance telling her you're new in town." She sipped her drink. "You did it for some particular reason concerning Brett."

"What if I did?" She knew she ought to slow down her drinking, but it was relaxing after the past few tumultuous weeks.

"I think you came to town to track her down, and are now setting her up for something. I'm wondering what it is."

"Have you ever lost anyone you loved?"

Angela nodded slowly. "My parents died years ago. My grandmother raised me."

"Then you might understand me. I lost my sister years ago. She was my entire life." Victoria downed her drink and signaled the bartender, who was chatting with the only other people in the place, a foursome at the far end of the bar, for another, which he immediately brought. "He gets a good tip." She stared at the bottles behind the bar, lined up like little soldiers, without really seeing them. "She ran away from home, our home in Indiana, when I was quite young. She'd send letters to me at a friend's house."

"Where had your sister gone?"

"Detroit. She became a dancer. In my young mind I thought she was a ballerina, but now I know the truth." She twirled her straw, staring into her golden drink as if it were a mirror to the past. "She said her boss was wonderful—tall, dark, handsome . . . Charming, kind, smart. I thought she'd marry him, because I knew she was dating him. It was that boss who had her going back to school, getting her GED and going to college. I felt almost as if I knew him."

"What happened?"

203

"The letters stopped coming. I kept waiting and waiting, but they had just stopped. I think I finally accepted it all at once—she was dead, someone had killed her, and she hadn't been a ballerina. It just came to me one day and I knew."

"And you came up to Michigan."

"I came up to Michigan." She threw back the rest of her drink, laid a twenty and a ten on the bar, and went to the door. She turned around just as she was leaving and looked at Angela. "My sister was the only person in this whole fucked-up world I ever loved. She meant everything to me."

● ● ●

Brett was panting as she fought against the handcuffs connecting her to the headboard. Allie was still laying back against the pillows, with her legs folded beneath it.

"Oh, god, woman," Brett finally said, "that was so fucking hot."

Allie pulled herself up, slowly sliding the dildo out of herself. Her clit was swollen and her nipples hard as she slid it back in and out, reveling in Brett's eyes on her. "So you liked that, huh?"

Brett pulled against the cuffs again. "Why don't you let me out and I'll show you just how much I liked it."

Allie ran her legs up Brett's muscular legs. "How about I just show you how much I enjoyed doing that for you?" She hooked her thumbs into Brett's boxers. "Or I could just show other ways it affected me instead." She lay down on top of Brett, rubbing her naked body over Brett's.

Brett groaned. "Please, please let me touch you."

"It's nice to hear you beg for a change," Allie whispered, her lips on Brett's neck.

204

Brett leaned her head up, allowing Allie greater access to her neck. "Oh god, baby . . ." Allie pushed up her T-shirt, nibbling upward.

"Oh, why don't you let me touch you?" Her breath was coming in hard pants as Allie lightly caressed her breasts, nibbling at her nipples and sending hard shocks of sensation coursing through her.

"You want to touch me?"

"Yes, oh yes . . ."

Allie stood up on the bed near the headboard, right over Brett's head, right where Brett's hands were cuffed. She lowered herself just enough to slide two of Brett's fingers into her hot, wet, cunt. She slowly fucked herself with Brett's fingers, while Brett moaned, trying to move her hands and head.

Allie then lowered herself to straddle Brett's face, allowing Brett to taste her, but then, even though she wanted to ride Brett's tongue over another orgasmic wave, she had to leave Brett wanting.

She straddled Brett's hips and slowly pulled off Brett's boxers, casually tossing them to the side. Then she ran a finger along the collar of Brett's T. "This has got to go." She reached into the drawer of Brett's bedside table and pulled out her Swiss Army Knife.

She opened up the longest blade, which Brett kept razor sharp. She had an identical knife in her car.

"You . . . you can't," Brett breathed, as Allie caressed the flat side of the blade along her cheek.

"I can do anything I like, now that you're all tied up," Allie said. Brett had once used the knife in her car to cut off Allie's panties when she didn't think she had adequate maneuvering room.

205

She used the knife to neatly slice Brett's T-shirt off her, leaving her as naked as Allie was. Allie wanted to see just how wet Brett was, how turned on she had gotten watching Allie strip, but she also wanted to take her time.

She lay between Brett's legs, first caressing Brett's nipples with her tongue, and then lowering herself, so that her breasts lay against Brett's wetness.

"Oh, god, Allie," Brett moaned. It had been a long time since Allie had touched her like this—not because Allie didn't want to—but because Brett wouldn't let her. Brett told herself that she got all the satisfaction she needed from making love to Allie. In truth, she didn't think she deserved it.

Giving herself to another never came easy for Brett Higgins.

Allie stood up, beside the bed, staring down at the handcuffed Brett. Brett felt exposed, and pulled her legs up to cover herself, but Allie pushed her back, laying her own warmth next to Brett. Half on top of Brett, Allie was entwined with her. Brett could feel the damp triangle of hair between Allie's legs against her thigh. She nudged her leg up against Allie, but Allie raised herself from Brett's leg.

"You behave now," Allie said. She draped her long, silky hair over Brett, then leaned down and cupped Brett's breast with her hand while she flicked her tongue over her nipple.

"Oh, god," Brett groaned, wanting to keep her legs closed and wanting to spread them wide open.

Allie grabbed one nipple between her teeth while squeezing the other between her thumb and forefinger. She twisted it hard, and bit down while still flicking her tongue over the other rock-hard bit of flesh. Allie sent heat coursing throughout Brett's body and down to her cunt, still hot and swollen from watching Allie.

Allie's hands were warm on her body, Allie's tongue was tasting her flesh, and now, *Allie's* fingers were exploring *her* cunt. Allie in control turning her on.

"Oh Brett, you are so hot," Allie moaned as Brett arched first her breasts and then her cunt up, her entire body squirming. "Open them up for me, baby," Allie said, trailing her hair over Brett's chest as she went down to kneel between Brett's legs.

Part of Brett wanted to pull away, wanted to run away, but a larger part wanted to stay—wanted to give herself to Allie. Wanted Allie to take her.

Allie spread Brett's legs open. She looked down at her. Ran her fingers through her wetness. Slipped a finger up inside of her. She grinned and leaned down over Brett, grabbing first one nipple, then the other, between her teeth, and tugging. She then ran her tongue down Brett's body, between her legs and over her swollen clit.

"Oh god!" Brett yelled as a bolt of electricity shot through her body. She lifted her butt off the bed as Allie stroked her tongue over her wetness and slid another finger into her. Brett kept her legs spread wide, exposing herself completely for Allie.

Allie's warm mouth and tongue knew just what Brett needed, and gave it to her. Brett loved feeling Allie inside her. She started trembling, heat flowing through her, energy gathering between her legs. She couldn't hold still. A surge burst through her cunt, swelling and taking over . . . Allie grabbed onto her, holding her . . . another surge shooting through her . . .

"Allie!"

• • •

Allie leaned up over Brett, her hair a silken screen around Brett's face as she unlocked the handcuffs. Brett wrapped her arms around Allie and pulled her close. She held her tightly in her arms and gently stroked that hair, enjoying the feeling of Allie's body on top of hers.

"Brett?" Allie said finally.

"Yes, baby?"

"I love you."

"I love you, too."

Allie paused. "I know you loved Storm, too."

Brett remained silent.

"And knowing you, in that great big teddy-bear heart you hide underneath this Mr. Tough Guy exterior, you love her sister, too."

"I don't even know her sister, if she is her sister. How can I love her?"

"Because she's Storm's sister. But I have to wonder why she's here?"

"What do you mean?"

Allie pushed herself up enough to kiss Brett. "Let's say she is Storm's sister. Why would she track you down?"

Brett smiled at Allie. "If she is Storm's sister, then Storm might've let her know about me and the Paradise. Oh god, baby . . ." Allie was running her hands lightly over Brett's body.

"But why would she come up here?"

"Oh, god baby, you feel so good . . . maybe to see how her sister spent her last days? Maybe to meet me?" Brett had begun letting her own hands wander over Allie's luscious curves. She was just regaining feeling in her hands and arms after the bondage.

"Then she'd tell you who she was." Allie put Brett's hand on her breast. Brett just kind've smiled deliriously up at her. "Should I just wrap you up in a blankie and let you sleep?"

"I'm just happy . . . but not quite satisfied . . ." Allie felt so good. Her body had filled out delightfully as she had gotten older. "What's worrying you, baby?"

"I was just . . ." she put her arms around Brett. "If Victoria is Storm's little sister, I can only think of one reason she'd track you down and yet . . . not identify herself to you."

"Why's that?"

"Please don't get upset, Brett."

"I'll try not to. Just tell me, Allie."

"Maybe she might think . . . well, what you yourself have sometimes thought. That you're responsible for Storm's death."

21

Saturday

In her office the next morning, Brett sat back in her chair and worked on the schedule for the next month. But her mind really wasn't on that. She was scared because she knew this guy struck twice at one club last week, and she was worried it would happen again this week.

And she knew she had been a damned idiot. A part of her was worried that the cops were watching her, trying to fit her for these killings as they had done before. She knew she was innocent, but she also knew that she had drawn attention to herself because she had covered Nicola's body.

She knew deep inside of herself that what she had done had been the right thing, had been the decent thing, but still she knew it had set her up as a suspect. By covering Nicola's nakedness with that one, simple blanket, she had screwed with the crime scene. Fibers the cops looked at as clues, could simply be shit from her trunk.

She had fucked up—but damnit, it had been the right thing to do!

Thankfully, she heard Frankie's heavy footsteps coming upstairs and called out, "Frankie?"

A moment later the big man poked his head into her office. "Yeah boss?"

"Have you ever heard of anyone named . . ." She paused while she pulled a piece of paper out of her wallet. The names Allie had given her the night before were on it. "Jim Peterson or Stan Dubrowski?"

"Shit yeah, boss. Dubrowski was just in here last night causing trouble!"

"What?"

"He tried to jump Chantel when she was on. Big guy. Good thing I was here, else who knows?"

"So what happened?"

"I knocked 'im out, and well . . ." he paused, as if embarrassed or searching for the right words.

"What did you do to him, Frankie?" Frankie and she had never been opposed to correcting other's ways—so long as they left no proof.

"I handed 'im over to the cops." He shrugged. "With all the shit goin' down around here, and that new guard . . . well, I figured that'd be the right thing to do."

"He ever been here before?"

"Not so I know 'bout it. They make trouble, they're outta here."

"What about the other guy, Peterson?"

"Ain't never heard of him."

"Thanks, Frankie." She dismissed him with a nod, and reached for her phone.

• • •

"Yeah, babe, it's me," Brett said, "I've got some news on those guys you asked me about last night—Peterson and Dubrowski."

"Yeah? What've you got?"

"Well, so far as we know, Peterson doesn't come here."

"What about Dubrowski?"

"You're gonna love this one—he was just here last night, causing trouble. Frankie was here, though, and took care of it."

"'Took care of it?' What do you mean, Brett? What did Frankie do?" Allie's heart was now racing a mile a minute. She was worried.

"Chill out, baby, he just grabbed the guy and turned him over to the cops."

"Oh. Okay."

"For chrissake's Allie, that's what we've always done with basic troublemakers."

Allie was relieved, with this outcome. She knew that wasn't all they ever did with troublemakers, though.

"But if you ask me, this all but puts him in the clear."

"How do you figure?"

"If he was about to off one of my girls, he wouldn't go making a spectacle of himself just before."

Allie paused. "I can understand that."

"Okay. By the way, Allie?"

"Yes?"

"What are you wearing?"

Allie laughed. "You are so bad!"

"Well?"

Allie looked down at herself. "I'm wearing a pair of jeans and my Las Vegas T-shirt."

"Hmmm. The one with the buttons on the front? Like a Polo shirt, but without the collar?"

"Yeah, that one."

"Mmmm. I love the way it shows off your collar bone."

"Brett, I'm going now," Allie said with a smile.

"Okay. Sure you aren't up for any phone sex?"

"I love you."

"Love you, too."

Allie hung up the phone and looked at the information she had keyed into the spreadsheet she was keeping of the investigation. Allie thought Brett was right, she didn't think the killer could be Dubrowski, either. And Tina did have a good point herself, against both Dubrowski and Peterson.

She wondered if any of the dancers had shown up at the theatre yet—if Brett was surrounded by beautiful, naked women at this very moment. Perhaps she should have given into Brett's idea of phone sex, even though she didn't think Brett was really serious about it.

Allie had always wondered if she was exciting enough for Brett. After all, she came from a mundane, hum-drum suburban childhood where nothing really exciting ever happened to her until Brett entered her life. She was the vanilla to Brett's Rocky Road.

But then last night . . . she had realized that she really did turn Brett on—that she really could rock Brett's world . . . and she had

213

also realized just how much power she could have over Brett. She had always realized she had a certain power over her butch (after all, she did wear the panties in the house), but . . . she had never before realized the extent of it.

All that left several questions in Allie's mind: Could she ever settle for someone like Randi, who although not Brett, could be exciting? After all, she was a cop, a Detective at that, and so her life was inherently exciting. Or could Brett really settle for somebody as plain as Allie? Somebody who wasn't very thrilling by nature, and didn't have an exciting life? But who could be exciting at times? Allie couldn't help but think about stripping for Brett, touching and fucking herself for Brett, and feel a surge of electricity run through her body. She wanted to find that excitement again.

Could Allie become everything Brett wanted and needed? Could she become as exciting as the women Brett was used to? Could she draw Brett in so Brett would want her and only her?

● ● ●

Allie showed up at the theatre that afternoon, pulling Brett into her office. "We need to talk," she said.

"What about? Have you found out anything new?"

"No, but I'm worried. He hit Friday and Sunday last week, so since he hit Thursday this week, he might do it tonight."

Brett sighed. "I know. I've told the guard to walk each girl out—I don't want them by themselves, or alone with Victoria either. At least, not until I know what's up with her."

"I know, and that's part of the reason."

"For what?"

"For what I'm about to propose. You see, if you up security any

214

more right now—not that I think that guard'll do much to deter whoever it is—he'll just put it off and strike later. And if Victoria is the killer, what I'm suggesting is bait she won't be able to turn down."

"What do you mean?"

"We've agreed if it's her, she must be here for some sort of revenge. It's the only logical explanation."

Brett nodded.

"So if she is trying to hurt you—by either framing you, or if she really wants to kill you, then . . . the best way for her to really hurt you is by killing me."

Brett simply stared at Allie.

"If it's Victoria, she won't be able to turn her back on me. If it's not, then, well . . . I'd be better prepared to deal with him then your other dancers."

"Are you suggesting what I think you're suggesting?"

"Think about it Brett—if it is Victoria, I may be able to force her hand. If it's not, then I'll be bait for whoever is doing it, as well as being able to watch out for the others."

"I've already told you—"

"Brett, your security guard was taking a nap when I got here. Why don't you ask Angela if she's gotten walked to her car lately?"

"What, exactly, is it you want to do?" Brett had thought hiring a "professional" security agency would ensure a reasonable guard. After all, she was paying three times as much for this schmuck as she had for the guy she brought in off the street. Obviously, many things were unchanged. People still didn't know how most security guards were unscreened/untrained idiots off the street.

"I want to dance for you."

"Are you nuts? You want to go out there and take off your clothes for all the perverts that come in here?"

"Brett, the cops can't or won't put somebody undercover here." Allie looked directly at her. "This way I'll be able to watch the girls and the customers. You can give me one of your guns, and I'll ask Angela to watch out for me while I'm onstage." Allie knew that sometimes Brett pulled in a fourth girl for the weekends, so the addition of Allie as a dancer wouldn't arouse suspicion.

"Is Randi behind this? I mean, I know she's wanted to see you naked again for years!"

"No! Brett—this is all my idea. Randi doesn't know anything about it!" The idea had come to Allie last night. She knew a sudden change in other staff would create questions, and the only way to really be bait was as a dancer. She had stripped for Brett last night, which she figured might make her seem a bit more exciting to Brett. After all, her lover did seem to have a thing about dancers. And Brett had certainly enjoyed her private little show the night before—the show that Allie knew she had to do if she stood any chance of stripping in public.

Brett sat back, assessing Allie. Allie could tell from her expression that she was remembering the times she had asked Allie to do a striptease for her, and Allie had bashfully declined, although last night was an extreme exception. Brett was probably convincing herself that as soon as Allie got onstage, she'd be unable to go through with it. After all, that was probably the only way Brett would agree to such a thing.

And Allie was right in her thoughts on Brett's thinking, on all counts.

"Okay, fine. I'll let Tim know, and you can start at the next show, seeing as how the one-thirty performance is already underway. Unless you want to put it off, that is?"

Allie almost wished Brett would argue with her, but Brett did know that once Allie made up her mind, she pretty well stuck to it.

Allie gulped. "No, the next show is fine."

"Should we call Angela up here now to talk with her about it?"

"No . . . no . . . I'll talk to her by myself, if you don't mind."

Brett grinned at this, probably thinking Allie was having second thoughts.

• • •

Brett was sitting in her office surfing the Net. She was trying to decide what other enterprises she and Frankie should get involved with. There were so many to choose from. They could start making their own pornographic magazines and/or videos, or perhaps catch some of the escort service market, or else get involved with Internet pornography, like maybe a live Webcam of the stage.

Or that was what she had convinced herself she was doing. She had learned years ago that sometimes she fooled herself even better than she did anyone else.

At this moment, she knew she was purposefully avoiding thinking about Allie. About how sexy, intelligent, beautiful and . . . and . . . well downright playful Allie was. Allie was everything she had ever dreamed of, but she knew she could never have the woman of her dreams. She wasn't worthy.

She stopped, realizing what she had just thought.

Well, damnit, she was worthy. She had worked herself up from the bottom of the pile just for such a woman as Allie. She did the college thing . . . wanting to both raise herself above her surroundings as possible, and . . . well . . . she wanted to attract the right mate.

217

She had always dreamt of a lover who would accept her as she was—someone who could also fulfill her needs/wants/desires . . . but always knew that was impossible.

She picked up Allie's picture from her desk, it was the only one on her desk, and realized she had found a brilliant, drop-dead gorgeous woman who had wants and needs of her own—who wasn't dependent on Brett, but had a life she wanted and needed to fulfill of her own—yet wanted Brett to be a part of that future.

"Oh, fuck me and the horse I rode in on," Brett murmured to herself. She really hated having to realize herself. She had always known what she wanted, and thought it impossible, yet Allie was the impossible brought to life. Brains and beauty. Plus she could be sexy as all hell.

Brett sighed, wondering if she was bound to wander the earth alone, when she heard the sounds change from the auditorium below a while ago, signaling the start of the four-thirty show. Usually she ignored the shift change, but this time she listened with half an ear, paying attention as first Angela's and then Victoria's music played. And then she heard the swelling of Enigma, and knew that was Allie's music. She figured she should go down to see if Allie even made it to the stage. She sincerely doubted it.

Actually, she couldn't quite believe it.

"And now, for your added enjoyment, we're giving you a piece of Heaven!" Tim said over the loudspeaker as Brett walked downstairs.

Heaven. Good name. Apropos for Allie. The thought crossed Brett's mind without her really thinking about it.

She entered the box office and looked through the little window at the stage. She couldn't believe it. Allie was in the theatre, getting ready to go onstage! Brett felt like she was in some strange, twisted dream. Enigma was playing, and the woman she loved was walking up to the stage, about to take off all her clothes.

She bolted around and out to the auditorium, where she stood at the back, next to Angela and Victoria. Surprised they weren't in the audience doing lap dances, Brett could only assume they were just as interested in seeing Allie dance as she was.

"It's not like you haven't seen it before," Victoria whispered, apparently enjoying Brett's slack-jawed amazement. "You've seen her naked, and you've seen your girlfriends strip in this theatre before."

"It'll be good to know that someone reliable is actually watching out for us—even if she's not a cop or anything. At least she could get help if something happens," Angela said, keeping her body between Brett and Victoria.

"This is un-fucking-believable," Brett said.

"Now, I might pay to see *you* strip," Victoria said to Brett, giving her the eye around Angela.

"And she does have what it takes," Angela admitted, completely ignoring Victoria.

Brett looked at them, and met Victoria's teasing eyes. "You're enjoying this," she said.

"I'd heard you were very composed. This doesn't seem to be your week at all."

"I only let one other woman I loved dance on that stage, but that was only because it was the only help I could give her that she'd accept."

"Your way of 'helping' her was to have her strip, here?"

"She wouldn't accept a handout, not even from me. She was too proud. She'd make it on her terms, or not at all. She'd lost all

219

self-respect long before, and letting her pay her own way was the only way I could help her get it back." Brett paused, looking at the two women on either side of her, and remembering. She looked down at the ground. It really was all her fault. "It was all a very long time ago, and I wasn't the person I am now. I couldn't give her the commitment she wanted. She needed." Brett wanted to cry, but she couldn't.

"What happened?" Angela asked.

Brett looked up. "We broke up. And then she was killed."

Angela's eyes were full of understanding. "How horrible."

"By that time I had started dating Allie, and we broke up over it. We didn't get back together again until years later."

"It sounds like you really loved her."

"I did. I still do."

"Is that why you still have her picture in your office?" Victoria asked. Brett looked up and realized tears were running down Victoria's face. "When I was in your office earlier today, I noticed that one picture . . ."

"Of Frankie, Rick, Storm and me. Yeah. Allie's not too happy that I keep pictures of Storm, but she's learned she can't change the way I feel. She knows I loved her." Brett looked around the theatre and saw the men getting turned on by her girlfriend. Her nice girlfriend. Her sweet woman. Sweet and innocent.

Allie didn't look so sweet anymore. Brett could only remember with shame that she had taken Allie to her first adult theatre when she was seventeen. She had brought Allie here. She had forced Allie into this.

22

The slow, agonizingly religious tones of Enigma filled the auditorium as the lights hit the stage. Allie, already onstage, let her body move to the music, then turned around to face the men. She watched as they stared at her in rapt attention.

She was in control of them. She knew this deep down inside. She'd had two shots of vodka just before she went on to warm her up and give her this control. Or this illusion of control.

She undid the top button of her blouse. She continued moving, trying to forget that people were watching her, and just let the music take over. Sway to the music and slowly take her clothes off. Just like last night.

Brett's activities used to inspire Allie and get her excited. When they first met, Allie was in high school and was turned on by Brett's power. Now she couldn't believe she was involved with this woman.

Of course, she was now taking her clothes off for a theatre full of men. And would then have to give them lap dances.

They never trained her for this in the police academy.

If she could just get cocky, this would work. She could do this. After all, she couldn't turn chicken, not in front of Brett or the other dancers.

She had to do this.

She tried to imagine that she was dancing for Brett . . .

. . .for Randi . . .

. . .for women . . .

. . .and she moved to the music.

It was an adventure. Or it was supposed to be. She had, for the most part, enjoyed her undercover assignments when she was a cop, but she wasn't enjoying this one. But she was tired of being the good girl, and just wanted to be bad.

She had gotten Angela to agree to always be there when she was dancing—to watch out for her. After all, she had no place in her tiny costume to hide any sort of weapon.

She dropped her blouse to the floor.

She concentrated on the music, trying to hide in her own little world, inside of her head. She knew Brett was in the audience, and couldn't believe she was doing this, but she would show Brett she was capable of doing anything she set her mind to.

She undid her jeans, and ran her hands over her now-hardened nipples, enjoying the feel of them through the silk of her bra. She pressed the palm of her hand against her crotch.

She had watched the girls at the Paradise dance, and knew what they did. She knew she could do it, too. She wasn't as vanilla as everybody thought she was. She could be a bad girl, she could be a dancer.

Was this how Victoria felt when she danced? Was this how Storm had felt when she danced?

She knew the men, and Brett, were glued to her every movement. She knew they wanted to see more.

Wasn't this what Brett wanted?

Allie swayed to the music and slowly peeled the jeans from her body . . . And down they came . . . until she was wearing only her underwear.

A jolt shot through her when she realized she was taking it all off in front of other people. Strangers. Men. She suddenly felt ashamed and embarrassed and thought about turning and running off the stage, but she couldn't do that. Nor could she continue doing what she was doing.

She glanced out and realized she could see nearly every face in the darkness. She tried not to see the men, so she could pretend it was an auditorium full of butches watching her. She'd had a secret fantasy about stripping for a group of butches, a secret she'd never shared with Brett.

She tried to use the fact that she was not fulfilling her worst nightmare—making a total fool of herself in public. People would be laughing at her if she were, but instead, they silently watched her, mesmerized by her every movement.

She continued dancing, and reached up behind her to undo her bra and let it drop to the floor. She caressed her breasts, drawing her nipples into hardened little buds.

It felt good.

It felt bad.

It made Allie wet.

It was like the very naughtiest of her masturbation fantasies.

Allie peeled off her panties.

It made it all the more erotic that she was the only naked person in the room. Everyone else was fully clothed. It made Allie feel all the more exposed.

She tried to mimic the dancers she had seen—but she just couldn't open herself up and show herself off like they could. She took a deep breath, turned around and bent over, knowing how much of herself she was showing off by doing so.

She quickly stood and turned back to the audience.

"C'mon baby—show it to us!" someone yelled from the audience.

It was dangerous. And exciting.

She was exciting.

● ● ●

Brett couldn't believe Allie could do it, yet she was up there dancing, stripping. She was slowly peeling her clothes off when Brett sat down and met her eyes. A slow smile spread over Allie's face.

She had obviously been watching Angela and Victoria dance, because she seemed to have most of the moves down. Now, up onstage, she wasn't leaving anything to the imagination. She was buck-naked and showing it all off.

And then the dance was over and Allie was in the audience, still playing her part and giving lap dances to these perverts. At least she knew the rules—legally, she was supposed to keep on a top

224

and a bottom, and not let the boys touch her too much. She was making sure they all kept to that fine line.

Brett wanted to stand up and strangle the boys who tried to touch her girl, who bought lap dances from her and wanted her to do more than they paid for.

She hated all her customers.

It was torture to sit here and watch it, but it was as if she was in a trance: she couldn't move, she couldn't leave.

Allie was standing next to her. "You want a dance, stud?" she asked.

Brett looked up at her felt the shame of having brought Allie into this life.

She remembered how she had cheated on Allie with Storm, and with Kathy. She was as bad a junkie as some of her girls were. Except her drug was different—she got off on the power she had over women. She loved making them want her, making them give it all to her.

She was addicted to it.

Wordlessly, Allie straddled her, as if to give her a lap dance. Brett put her hands on Allie's hips, set her aside and fled the auditorium.

● ● ●

Brett stopped in the lobby. She couldn't believe Allie had actually gone through with it, that she had exposed herself that way. Brett had expected her to at least retreat backstage as soon as her performance was over, but Allie put her panties and bra back on and came into the audience to perform lap dances. Brett couldn't handle seeing her beloved Allie give lap dances to her customers.

"Hot new dancer?" Randi asked from just the other side of the turnstile.

"Sorry, Brett, she wouldn't leave," Tim said apologetically from the box office.

"What do you need, Randi?" Brett asked.

Randi hefted a file folder. "I've got some information for you."

"Let's go upstairs, then," Brett said, nodding to Tim to hit the button to allow Randi through the turnstile and let them in the office. Brett blocked the window to the auditorium while Randi passed through, then led them upstairs.

Brett sat down at her desk. "What have you got for me?"

Randi tossed the file folder she was carrying onto Brett's desk. "Copies of the schedules and contact sheets we got from Tina last night." She stood in front of Brett's desk. "Thought you might like to see them."

"Any special reason?"

"Looks like your new girl was dancing there last week."

Brett shook her head. Tina was really fucking with them. "Is there anything in particular you'd like me to do?"

"I just want you to know exactly what you're dealing with."

"Yeah, yeah—Allie's told me all about it. Victoria's come looking for me for some reason. I know she's been lying, but I will find out why, and just what she's up to. Is there anything else, Detective?"

"Has anyone called here looking for Karin Frost?"

"What sort of a question is that? You think the killer's playing some sort of a game?" Brett was in a bad mood after watching Allie, and Randi wasn't helping her at all.

"Her girlfriend wasn't at their place when I went by there the other day. She left a message on the machine saying she'd be home today, so I left a card and asked her to call me when she got home."

"And she hasn't called yet."

"No."

Brett shook her head. "I don't know."

"Is there anything you can remember about Nicola that might help?"

Brett stood. "If there was, I would've told you and Allie. I have work to do."

23

When Randi closed the door behind her, Tim only glanced up at her. She took a moment to look around the box office, noting that another dancer, Heaven, had been added below Chantel, Angela, Nicola (who was scratched out), and Tempest on the schedule on the clerk's desk.

She then went to look through the window and into the auditorium. She could see the porno movie playing on the screen in the theatre, as well as the voluptuous black woman dancing naked onstage in front of it.

"Can I help you with something?" Tim asked.

"Who's this new girl that's dancing?"

"Chantel? The one that's on now?"

"No, Heaven, this last girl on the list."

"Oh, her." He raised an eyebrow as if languishing in the memory of her. "Tall, blonde, man she's hot."

A tremor of fear swept through Randi. "What's her real name?"

"Oh, uh, it's Allie. She's Brett's girlfriend."

"Is she in the dressing room?" Randi asked, leaving the box office before he could stop her.

"I dunno. You can check, though," he said, obviously deciding that if she had been in Brett's office, she must be all right.

Randi stepped across to pound on the door, and almost immediately found herself face to face with Victoria. She had seen the woman from a distance, but at this close range, the resemblance to Storm made Randi feel as if she was facing a ghost.

"Can I help you?" Victoria asked when Randi didn't speak.

"Uh, yeah, I'm looking for Allie?"

"Randi?" Allie said, stepping around Victoria. "What are you doing here?"

"I could ask the same of you." Randi heard the clerk charging and admitting a customer behind her.

"You'd better come in here," Allie said, apparently noticing it as well, and pulling Randi by the arm into the dressing room.

"What's going on?" Randi asked as Allie closed the door behind her. "Please tell me you're not . . . you're not dancing here!"

"Randi, this is Victoria, and Angela."

"Hi. Do you think you could give us a minute?" Randi asked.

Allie gave Victoria and Angela a quick nod. Since they had danced first, they were already dressed and ready to go to dinner. "I'll meet you guys in the parking lot," she said.

"You'd better hurry, it's already six, so we don't have long before the seven-thirty show," Angela said, closing the door behind her.

"Are you trying to blow my cover?" Allie asked Randi as soon as the door was closed.

"Cover? What cover? Allie, you're not a cop!"

"And the cops aren't doing anything to keep these girls safe."

"But how are you going to do that?"

"I'm armed, Randi. I'll be walking the others out to their cars. This guy only seems to attack single girls."

"Then why'd you send them out, alone, now?"

"He only hits after closing."

"So why are you here, now?"

Allie sighed. Even Brett hadn't given her this many problems. She had understood Allie's plan fairly quickly. "Think of me as a worm, Randi."

"What do you mean by that?"

"I'm bait. If he comes in throughout the day, he'll see me here. It'll help convince him I'm just another dancer—so long as people like you don't pay any attention to me. If he sees me with a cop, it'll be over. He won't try anything."

Randi could not believe calm, sensible Allie was doing something so stupid.

"You guys won't do a stake-out, but even if you did, he might notice something's going on. This way I can try to lure him in."

"How's he going to know I'm a cop? It's not like I wear a uniform or anything."

"Randi, Tina didn't have any problems identifying us last night."

"She knew we were coming."

Allie shook her head. "It doesn't matter. You look too much like a cop."

Randi paused, digesting this and trying to figure out a reply. "Allie, did you get . . . well . . . y'know . . . naked, onstage?" she finally asked.

Allie turned away, clearly frustrated. "Randi, that's what dancers do here. I am now a dancer here."

"So that means you're not armed when you're onstage."

"Don't worry, Randi, I've got Angela watching me when I'm on."

"Angela—that tall brunette I just met?"

"Yes. Her."

Randi laid a hand on Allie's shoulder, turning her to face her. "Allie, you're not a cop. If you catch this guy, what are you going to do? You can't arrest him."

"I . . . I figured if he tried anything, we'd stop him. Then we'd call the police."

"Okay, he always hits late. What if I come back later, dressed like I was last night, and watch out for you? I won't talk to you or anything, just be on hand in case anything goes down."

Allie smiled lightly, then nodded. "I'll go out first, and you follow in a couple of minutes. I don't want anybody seeing us leaving together."

Randi's cell phone rang. "Randi McMartin," she said. Allie looked at her, and she nodded back, showing that she understood.

"Detective McMartin?" a woman's voice replied on the phone as Allie left.

"Yes."

"This is Jennifer Baranowski. You left a note for me to call you."

"Jenny?" Randi repeated, feeling the color drain from her face. She hated the bad news she had for this poor woman.

"Yeah. What's going on? Why were you in my apartment?"

"Ms. Baranowski, are you home right now?"

"Yes. What's this about?"

"I'm in Highland Park right now. Stay where you are and I'll be there in fifteen minutes."

• • •

"Hey boss, I heard you wanted to see me," Victoria said, entering Brett's office and sitting on the edge of her desk. Brett had asked to see Victoria because she knew that Victoria had been dancing at The Naked Truth when the other girls had been killed.

Brett looked up at her. Brett had left her blazer on because it covered her shoulder holster, and she wanted to be armed for this conversation with Victoria. After all, the only reason she could come up with for Victoria's behavior would be revenge, which meant she'd either try to frame Brett for the murders, or else kill her. Brett wasn't fond of either thought. "Why are you here?"

"You wanted to see me, didn't you?" She was still wearing her street clothes, but Brett was willing to bet she had undone an extra button on her blouse just for this visit. The clerk had probably caught her just as she was going out to dinner.

"Yes. But I meant, why are you at the Paradise? Why did you come to this particular theatre?" She stood up and went to stand near Victoria, looking down at her.

Victoria reached up to tidy Brett's tie. "I already told you yesterday, it looked like a good place. I do also like that you don't sell alcohol here, because that makes the customers a little more bearable. And you watch out for your dancers."

Brett brushed aside Victoria's hands and then went to look out the window while she lit a cigarette with the Zippo Storm had

232

given her. "So one day you woke up, maybe shortly after you graduated from high school, and . . .?"

"If you must know, I got out of that house as soon as I graduated. I couldn't wait to get away from that . . . that . . . prick."

"Your father?"

"Yes."

"Abusive?"

"In more ways than I can say."

"I'm sorry," Brett said, coming back from the window and lightly laying a hand on Victoria's shoulder. "So you . . . what? Caught a bus? I noticed you don't have a car . . ."

"I got on a bus."

"Why Michigan?"

She shrugged. "I could afford the ticket. It seemed like a better option than Ohio, and frankly, Chicago and New York scare me. They're so big and impersonal."

"So you arrived here, got off the bus, and came over to my theatre?"

"What is this, the Inquisition?"

"I'm not sure if you noticed, but a girl was just brutally murdered behind this theatre. I find her body, and then I was a dancer short, and you showed up. Pure coincidence?"

Victoria turned and looked at her in shock. "You think I killed her just so I could dance at this lousy place? Are you nuts?"

"Lousy? You just said it looked pretty good."

"It's not like I've got a lot of options. Frankly, even I know there's other places to dance at in this town."

"Have you danced at any of them?"

"I told you, I just got to town."

"And you've been lying to me ever since. While taking your clothes off for me every chance you get. What's your game?"

Victoria stood up and began unbuttoning her blouse. "Are you complaining? I thought it might be a job perk for you."

"You met my girlfriend yesterday. We've been together for quite a while, and we are monogamous."

"Like that means anything these days. If it did, the entire marriage-counseling industry would collapse." She dropped her blouse to the floor. She wore no bra.

"Do you know anything about love, Victoria? Well, I love Allie. I'm not some boy who goes chasing after whatever pussy's offered."

Victoria sighed and reached down to pick up her blouse. "I bet you used to, though," she said, glancing at her watch and turning to leave. She had to get to dinner so she could be back for the next show.

"Know that I'm watching you, and I know you've been lying to me ever since the day we met," Brett said.

Victoria paused half-way to the door, where she stood stock-still for a full minute before finally replying in a shaky voice, "How do you know that?"

"You didn't just get to town. You've been here a year, and I will find out why—why you've been lying to me. You can make it easier on both of us by just telling me what you're up to right now. Tell me Victoria."

Victoria looked at Brett with strangely bright eyes. "I have nothing to say to you."

After Victoria left, Brett walked to the door to see what had frozen Victoria in her tracks, and realized that it must've been the picture of Storm.

● ● ●

"What's going on?" Jenny accosted Randi as soon as she arrived at the small apartment.

"Ms. Baranowski, I'm afraid I have some bad news for you." The woman looked exactly as she had in the photographs Randi had seen earlier.

"Then why don't you tell me already? And while you're at it, please explain why the hell you were in my apartment?"

"You might want to sit down, Ms. Baranowski . . ."

"I'll sit down when I feel like it. Now explain."

"I . . . I don't know how to say this. It's about Karin."

Jenny sat down. "What . . . she didn't get arrested for something, did she?" she asked almost hopefully.

"I'm afraid not."

"When she wasn't here when I got home, I was surprised, but figured she was at work. I . . . I . . . didn't let myself think anything bad had happened. What happened? Where is she?"

"Where is she?" Randi repeated.

"Which hospital?"

Jenny was doing everything possible to deny what she had to know. "Ms. Baranowski, I'm sorry to tell you that Karin Frost passed away Thursday morning."

Jenny was silent. She stared blankly at Randi. "No," she finally said. "You're confused. You've got the wrong woman. It's not Karin."

"She was killed behind the Paradise Theatre Wednesday night after closing, when she got off work. Her parents and employer IDed the body. Jenny, your girlfriend is dead."

It was a good five minutes that Jenny stared at the floor in front of her. She jumped to her feet screaming, throwing books and milk crates. "No! No! It can't be! NO!"

235

Randi grabbed Jenny, trying to hold her, but Jenny slammed her against the wall.

"Why! Goddamnit! You're a cop—why couldn't you guys do anything?"

Randi held Jenny tightly as she crumpled against her, sobbing. She rubbed her back, cooing soothing sounds to her. She led her to the sofa and sat her down.

When Jenny finally calmed down, it was a sudden transition—she yanked away from the very unbutch embrace, wiped her face on her sleeve, and blew her nose with a napkin. "Goddamnit. Goddamnit. She always said that she could make more money than I could without a degree. She said this was the only way that made sense—she puts me through college, so I'll become an engineer, and then I'll put her through school so she can become a teacher." She stood up, strode into the kitchen, pulled a glass and a bottle of cheap whiskey from a cupboard, poured herself a tall, straight one, and downed it.

"I tried to make her quit when she told me about that other girl. But she said her club was a long ways from that one, and if anything else happened, she would quit," Jenny said, returning to the living room and Randi, poured herself another and sat down with it and the bottle.

"What other girl?"

"Up in Warren. That businessman's luncheon joint . . . you know the place—all topless, all the time."

"Charlie's?" Randi suggested.

"Yeah, that's the place. It was like six months ago, but I knew it was no accident—it's the same freak, isn't it?"

Brett had mentioned it to her. The girl's name was . . . Randi couldn't place it. But it wasn't related to this series. Of that she was sure, so she shook her head. "No, it's not."

"So you mean's there's several guys wandering out there, killing dancers? Can't be. It's the same asshole, and you guys have just been sitting on your butts—what is it? Do you think they're scum? You just don't understand what they go through to do what they do!"

"Jenny, the murders were very different, and there was six months between that murder and this series."

"Series?"

"This one's killed three girls in a week, each one with a scalpel to the neck. That girl, the one at Charlie's, suffered a severe head injury."

"Oh God!" She poured another glass of whiskey. She downed it and poured a third. She stood, almost as tall as Brett, and looked down at Randi. She was wearing old, torn jeans, a clean T-shirt and heavy workboots. She was an imposing woman, and was well on her way to getting drunk.

Randi laid a hand on the glass. "Jenny, you're getting drunk."

"Damn right I am! What the fuck else am I gonna do?" She slammed her fist into the wall. "Don't you understand that my life is over? Karin and I were supposed to grow old together—we were supposed to end up as a funny little couple of old-maid aunts." She picked up the glass, pulling it away from Randi, and downed it.

"I'm sorry. I really am."

Jenny finally looked at Randi. She was drunk. "I get it now. Why you told me. Why you came down here like you've got a shred of decency. You're a dyke, too."

"Jenny, how did you know about the dancer in Warren? Did Karin ever dance there?"

"No. But she knew some girls who did." She leaned drunkenly against Randi. "Exotica and Starr and Expose and . . . and . . . I

237

can't remember any more."

"Exotica was dancing there then?"

"Yeah. She and Karin were friends . . . Maybe it was her that told Karin about the girl found next to the Dumpster."

"Jenny is there someone I can call for you? Someone to come over?"

"No, no . . . I won't be alone, I'll call some friends . . . two favors, though . . . before you leave . . ."

"What do you need?"

"Go into the kitchen, find all the knives and take 'em with you."

"What? You want me to take your knives?"

Jenny sat down, finishing off the bottle of booze, straight from the bottle. She nodded. "Yeah. So take 'em with you and . . . here's my wallet, go get me a bottle of something."

"I think you've had enough."

Jenny looked up. "If you don't get me another, as soon as you leave I'll go get myself one, and we both know I'd be driving drunk. Karin'd kill me. Go get me another one, so I can get drunk enough to sleep through tomorrow. I'll call somebody to come over."

"Can't she pick one up?"

"I'll sober up before then." She staggered to her feet and picked up her car keys.

Randi took them from her. "I'll do it."

24

Brett fixed herself a drink and kicked back at her desk with the *Adult Entertainment News*. She turned a couple of pages and threw the magazine against the wall. She needed to can Victoria. The girl had given her more than enough reasons to do so. By getting rid of her, Brett could then be even more careful about her and her movements. Victoria gone would give Brett some piece of mind.

She went downstairs. "Did Victoria go to dinner right after talking with me?"

"Yeah. But she came right back."

"So she's here now?"

"Yeah in the dressing room."

"Just come right in, why don't you?" Victoria said when Brett entered without knocking. Her eyes were red, as if she'd been crying. The sight of Storm crying melted all of Brett's intentions. Even as she told herself that it wasn't Storm.

"Why aren't you at dinner?"

"I just picked up a ham and Swiss from across the street," she said, indicating the untouched sandwich on the counter in front of her. "Is that a problem, boss?"

"No, no problem," Brett said, sitting down and throwing her legs up on the counter. She couldn't look directly at the woman. "If there's something you want to talk about, something you want to know, you shouldn't be afraid to ask me."

"What the hell are you talking about?"

"I loved your sister, very much." She didn't know where the words were coming from.

Victoria paused, then said, "I don't know what you're talking about."

Brett looked at her, tempted to tell her to just leave, now. Leave this town, this state. But she knew, she had learned, that she had to deal with the past before she could move forward with the future. And she had to know what Victoria was up to, because as every moment passed, she was looking more and more like their killer. "Why don't you tell me the truth this time, instead of more lies? In case you haven't noticed, I do have most of it figured out already."

Victoria looked over at Brett. "What makes you think I've told you anything but the truth?"

"Because I know you've been in town for months. Probably at least a year. You didn't just blow in a week or so ago, like you've said. You've been here, and you've been asking about me. Looking for me."

"So what's your point?"

"It looks quite suspicious. I mean, you start hanging around the clubs, and then these girls start dying."

Victoria shrugged. "Coincidence. I didn't have anything to do with their deaths."

"Why should I believe that? I mean, you've even lied about your name."

"How do you know that?"

"I know your name isn't Victoria Smith, or Jones, or whatever you claim it is."

"Then what is it?"

"Victoria Nelson."

Victoria just stared at her.

"I saw it, but didn't get it, when I first saw you. Frankie saw it, as well, and so did Allie. They were the ones who pointed out that you had to be her sister. You're so much like her. She was sweet and naïve when she showed up here. I knew she was underage, but if I didn't give her a job, she'd go out hooking and get into even more trouble. At least here, I could keep an eye on her." She pulled out a cigarette, lit it, and handed the lighter to Victoria. "She gave me this."

The simple inscription read, "To my soulmate, Love, Pamela."

"I don't know why you're here, though. Maybe it's to find out more about your sister. I know she was happy most of the time I was around her." Brett remembered reading that some people wanted to ensure their loved ones had been happy and loved. And she could give that much to Victoria, truthfully and honestly. She smiled. "She loved going to the zoo. She could spend hours in the penguin house, watching their antics. She loved that they mated

241

for life. She thought that was so cool." Brett shook her head slowly, remembering each image vividly. "By the time we left, I had to give her my jacket and hold her as tightly as possible, because she was always frozen. She'd forgotten everything while watching those little tuxedoed beasties."

Victoria kept staring at her. "You really did love her, didn't you?"

Brett looked up, into her eyes, so much like Storm's, yet so different. "Yes. I did. Every morning I walk into my office and I see her smiling face, and I realize how much I screwed up to have lost her." And then, more to herself, "My beautiful, sweet, Storm."

"Did you always call her Storm, instead of Pammy, or Pam, or Pamela?"

"Most times, yes. The first time I met her, I saw the Storm in her eyes, and gave her that stage name. She seemed to like it just fine."

"Is that why you decided to call me Tempest?"

Brett nodded sadly. "Yes. You reminded me of her. I saw you, and thought I was looking at a ghost."

Victoria looked at her and was no longer the femme fatale. Instead, she was the shy girl Brett knew her sister had been. "She sent me a few postcards and letters after she ran away. She didn't say much, I was too young, and it took me a while to figure it all out. Years in fact."

"How did you?"

"I kept everything she sent me in a very secret spot. She wrote to me at a friend's address and that's the only way I got anything at all." She looked up at Brett with tears in her eyes. "She left me. I loved her and she left me. Anything I had of hers was precious. My most precious possessions were the things she left me. She had written to me about you, so when I was about sixteen, I started trying to find out what happened to her."

Brett almost broke into a sweat forcing herself not to go to this woman who was so obviously in need. She just wanted to hold her and make everything all right.

"I was young. She said she got a job as a dancer, and I had these thoughts of her being a ballerina. It was something she'd always wanted to do. She said her boss, who was tall, dark, handsome and charming, was helping her. She was going to school and I thought the boss who was helping her was her fiancée." She again looked at Brett. "She described you perfectly, told me your name was Brett, and it took me a while to discover you weren't a guy. On a whim one day I searched her name on the Net and found a newspaper article on her death. It didn't give many details at all, so I came here to find out what really happened."

"I'm sorry," Brett said. Questions were eating away at her, but she couldn't ask them now.

"Don't be." She knelt at Brett's feet and took Brett's hands in her own. "I came to Detroit wanting to find this guy she had fallen for. I didn't know how to make any money, and I fell into dancing, and that's when I started to hear about you. I tracked you down, and, once I did that, once I knew who you were and what you did, I thought you had to be behind her death."

Brett touched Victoria's face. "And what do you think now?"

Victoria pulled away, looking up at the ceiling. Then slowly, she nodded. "I came here with nothing to lose. I'll never go anywhere in life, and I have no family that I want. The only thing I ever had in my life that was worth anything was Pammy. Dad got rid of her, and then I was all alone. But I dreamt of the day Pammy'd come and take me away. Knowing that she was dead made me realize I had nothing at all."

"So why did you come to the Paradise?"

Victoria looked directly into her eyes. "I wanted to meet you, and I wanted to kill you. Then kill myself."

Brett couldn't help but smile. "And just how were you going to do this?"

"Very simply," Victoria said. She reached into her handbag and pulled out a gun. Then she pointed it at Brett.

Brett couldn't believe she'd let her guard down. She did have her gun on her. But she'd have to get to it before Victoria killed her. She slowly, automatically, raised her own hands up, showing them to be empty. Her right hand was now closer to her shoulder holster.

Victoria held the gun lightly in her hand, as if weighing it, and Brett had a brief thought that she might be able to distract her long enough to pull out her own gun. "I had nothing to do with your sister's death. I can't tell you how many years I spent longing for her, wishing for her back. I'd give anything that it had been me and not her who got killed."

Could she dive out of the way of Victoria's shot? Could she knock the gun out of her hand before she pulled the trigger? Why hadn't she listened to Allie—why hadn't she kept her guard up around Victoria?

Victoria stared at Brett. "I saw the picture in your office. If you'd wanted me to see it, you would have placed it more prominently. But you didn't."

Whenever Brett or someone she loved was in jeopardy, Brett was quick and decisive in her response, but this time she was frozen. She couldn't attack Victoria, because she'd probably kill her in the process, and she couldn't do that. She was screwed.

"From that, and everything you've said," Victoria continued, "I know there's really only one person I can blame for her death."

She met Brett's eyes over the gun. "Besides the person who pulled the trigger, that is."

"And you think that person is me?" Brett asked, not blinking.

Victoria lowered the gun. "No. I don't." She shook her head sadly. "The only person I can really blame is our father." She took the gun by its barrel and handed it to Brett. "After all, I do know that Pammy loved penguins. She loved any creature, and always pointed out to me the ones who mated for life. She went on about penguins for a while. Our parents never took us to the zoo. She always wanted to see them." She leaned forward, crying.

Breathing a sigh of relief, Brett pulled Victoria into her arms, gently taking the gun and pocketing it, slipping on the safety. She didn't know what to do, so she kept Victoria talking. "You're so very young, just like she was."

"She was only sixteen when she ran away. I'm nineteen."

"Nineteen. God, gotta buy you a walker soon." She was rewarded with a tremulous smile from Victoria. She made a pact with herself. Nothing would befall this young woman who was all she had left of her beloved Storm.

Victoria nestled into Brett's arms, crying quietly. Brett held her tight, her own eyes tearing up as she smoothed Victoria's silky hair.

"Make me a promise," Brett finally said.

"What?" Victoria said in a voice hoarse with crying.

"Let me help you. Promise not to kill yourself."

Victoria pulled away. "What do I have to live for?"

"Everything Pamela lived for." She ran her hand down Victoria's cheek. "Except maybe for a baby sister. But she was going to college, trying to make something of herself, and you can pick up where she left off. You can make yourself into the woman who can go back, years from now, and tell your father to go fuck himself, like Pammy always wanted to do."

245

Brett now knew the murders had nothing to do with Victoria. Which meant there was still a cold-blooded killer on the loose, one who just might target one of her dancers tonight.

"Brett? Brett? Are you all right?" Victoria said in a quiet voice, putting her hands gently on Brett's shoulders.Brett reached up and took one of Victoria's unbelievably soft hands in her own, gently kissing it. "I need to find the asshole who's killing dancers, 'cause he's not going to take you from me, too." She stroked her face. "Did you notice anything last week when you were at The Naked Truth?"

"I wasn't there last week. I was up at Charlie's."

"Victoria, I saw Tina's schedules. You were there."

"I'm not lying Brett. Call around and you'll find out there's another Exotica in town. I'm surprised you don't know her."

Brett smiled, relieved.

Victoria reached forward and pulled her gun from Brett's pocket. "I'd kinda like to have this."

• • •

Randi pulled out the old police file she had on Pamela Nelson, a.k.a. Storm, and used the contact numbers from that to call Victoria's parents.

A nervous-sounding woman answered the phone, "Nelson residence."

"Hello, is this Mrs. Nelson?"

"Yes, it is."

Randi would've liked to have seen her in person, but Indiana was a few hours' drive. She felt as if she was racing against the clock because every minute she wasted meant another minute Allie was on stage and in danger. "My name is Randi McMartin.

I'm with the Detroit Police and I have some questions for you about your daughter, Victoria."

"Oh my god, has something happened to her?"

Bingo. She was Storm's sister.

"Please tell me! I can't lose another daughter!"

"Victoria's all right, ma'am. I just have a few questions is all . . . But first of all, I know this is rather personal—may I ask your religion?"

There was a long pause. "Catholic. But what does this have to do with Victoria?"

When Randi hung up the phone a few minutes later, she called Danielle to cancel their date for tonight. She knew she shouldn't put Danielle off, but the woman was very understanding. Randi would call her to set up another date as soon as this special investigation was done.

"Just don't leave me hanging, honey," Danielle said.

"Oh, I know better than that," Randi said, and hung up. She glanced at her watch. Although this guy usually struck after closing, she wanted to get back to the theatre as soon as possible, just in case he decided to try something different.

But still, she had to carry through on her promise, and she wanted to check something else out. She still needed a little more information. She didn't know how many speed limits she broke, but she got up to the Warren police station in record time.

● ● ●

As soon as Allie returned from dinner, Brett had Tim call her. She needed to talk with her lover.

"Can I see you upstairs?" Brett asked her, leaning into the dressing room.

Allie looked up. "What is it?"

"Why don't we talk in my office?" She looked over at Angela. "Nothing personal, this is just between us, though . . . You understand?"

"Yes. I do. Allie, I'll go first, you go on up."

Allie nodded and followed Brett. "Are you trying to draw attention to me?" she asked once they were in Brett's office.

Brett shrugged. "I just thought we needed a chance to talk. I wanted to apologize for leaving you like that this afternoon."

"Goddamnit Brett, I was just doing my job—trying to blend in. You're not helping matters!"

"Allie . . ."

"What is it? It's not like you haven't dated dancers before." Allie fell into a full-fledged pout.

"Allie, I *used* to date dancers. I don't anymore. Quite frankly, I didn't like seeing you out there stripping for . . . them. My customers." She got up and wrapped her arms around Allie's waist. "You're mine. I don't want to share you with others."

Allie pulled away and turned her back on Brett. "Then why do I have to keep sharing you?"

Brett was stunned. How did Allie know?

"You're here all day with all these strippers, and don't even think about telling me that they don't flirt with you."

Oh. Okay. "Allie, I've done this for years. A naked woman isn't enough to turn my head." She walked up right behind Allie, not touching her, but whispering in her ear. "It takes more than a naked body to get my interest. I need a mind and a soul as well. I need a real woman."

"Then why have you always been so hot to get me to strip for you, and masturbate for you? Didn't you want me to act just like one of your dancers?" Allie faced Brett.

Brett grinned. "That was hot as hell." She remembered the point of the conversation. "But it was so hot only because it was you. I love you, baby, don't you realize that?"

"You've had other lovers dance here, so why does it get to you so much when I do it? I thought you liked watching dancers strip."

"But . . . it's you now. Don't you understand? You're mine, and I don't want to share you. I want you to strip for me, do things for me—just like I do things only for you."

"You're sounding awfully possessive." Brett might've taken this personally, except for the beautiful smile that lit Allie's face.

Brett realized what she had to say. She took Allie into her arms, feeling that wonderful body against hers. "Don't you get it? I love you—for your sexy body, your sensuous nature, your quick wit, sense of humor . . . The way you think, feel and are. I am possessive, because I adore you." She pulled back from Allie so she could look in her eyes. "Maybe I should've made you argue more before agreeing to let you dance here, but I realized you had your mind made up. All I'd do by saying no would've been to piss you off and make you determined to do it all the more."

25

Randi stared at the words in the detective's folder. Angela had been dancing at Charlie's when Luscious was killed. But so had Exotica. She remembered Allie saying Angela was watching out for her. Randi decided she had enough time to look into this woman a bit. She'd just have to make sure she made it back in time for the 10:30 show. The last show of the night. No one was likely to do anything before then.

Randi saw that the Warren documents listed Angela as living in Centerline, but Brett's had her living in Detroit. She decided to pull her up on the police computer in Warren and go to whatever address they listed as her residence.

Centerline was a city totally surrounded by the city of Warren. It was the hole in Warren's donut. Randi hated it because all the streets twisted and turned so it was almost impossible to find anything there, but still she went to the address listed on her paperwork: 1364 Crestwood Drive, Centerline.

Randi found the address and knocked on the door. An old, frail woman answered it. Randi hoped she hadn't woken her up.

"Hello," Randi said, "I was wondering if Angela was home?"

"I'm sorry, she isn't," the woman told Randi. "She's downtown. She works at the Christian youth center there."

"Oh really?" Randi asked, becoming aware that the woman, whose hair was pure white, was leaning heavily on the doorframe. She must've been well over 70.

"Oh yes, she's such a good girl. Always trying to help others. But—" and now she peered through her thick bifocals up and down the street, "I've just realized I don't have any idea who you are."

"I'm sorry, ma'am," Randi said, pulling out her badge, "I'm Detective Randi McMartin, with the Detroit Police."

"Oh?" she said, taking the badge in a shaking hand for a closer inspection. She looked up, frightened. "Nothing's happened to Angela, has it?"

"Oh, no, not at all ma'am. I'm here following up on some things pertaining to a case I'm working on."

"Oh, well it can't have anything to do with my Angela."

Randi quickly searched her mind for the right words. If this woman didn't know where Angela really worked, it wasn't Randi's job to set her straight. "It's more of an issue of where she works. The clients there."

"Oh . . ." the woman nodded her head sagely. "Of course. Though I don't suppose I'd be able to help you at all . . ." She looked rather hopeful though, as if this was the most exciting thing that would happen to her all day. As if Randi were the only person besides Angela that she would talk with today and she was about to lose her.

"Well, perhaps you might be able to," Randi said, quickly deciding she could spend a few minutes making this old woman's day more interesting. "Are you her mother?"

"Oh, dearie no!" the woman said. "I'm Ginny Malinowski, her grandmother," she looked inside. "Would you care to come in Detective? My old legs aren't what they used to be."

"Yes, thank you," Randi said, taking Ginny's hand to lead her to the couch. A cup of tea on the table next to it indicated she'd been sitting there when Randi had come to the door.

"Would you like a cup of tea, dear?" Ginny asked, once she was sitting.

"Oh, no thank you," Randi said, taking quick note of her surroundings. The place was a study in contrasts: the furnishings were worn, but obviously well cared for, and there was a riot of colors made by hand-made afghans, samplers, and embroidered pillows, but there was also a new TV in a new entertainment center with all new components. On the wall were pictures of Barry Goldwater and Ronald Reagan. Randi wanted to puke.

"That's Angela and her parents," Ginny said, getting off the couch to stand beside Randi, "And that's my Angela at her First Holy Communion, and graduating from high school . . ."

Randi lost the rest of the words as she tried to reconcile the sultry Angela she had seen at the theatre with the pious-looking girl in the photos, the one with her long, luscious hair in tight pigtails, thick glasses with dark, heavy frames on her face, no make-up, and dresses with high collars and low hemlines.

In all of the pictures, Angela looked about the same—pious. That was the only word Randi could think of to truly describe the appearance. She looked like somebody's old maid aunt, or maybe a particularly mousy librarian who never left her house except for work.

The last thing she looked like was an exotic dancer.

"You two must be very close," Randi finally said.

"Oh, of course. I mean, after her parents died, she came to live with me."

"Oh? Her parents are dead?"

Ginny looked very sad as she sat back on the couch. "They died when Angela was quite young. She came to live with me then, and has been with me ever since."

"What happened to them?" Randi asked.

"Oh, I don't like to talk about it."

Randi noticed how many pictures showed Ginny with Angela, and how the pictures of Angela and her parents stopped when Angela was indeed quite young.

"Oh, she's not like all these young kids these days. She pays for practically everything around this old house. I sometimes wish she'd get out more to have fun with people her own age, but she does work quite a bit. And with the way the kids at the center need her, she can be gone late into the night. But it is nice when she's able to slip out for lunch or dinner with me, though there's some weeks when she can spend a lot more time with me than others. In fact, just last week we went to Greenfield Village, and she always takes me to Mass every Sunday at the Shrine, even though there are churches that are closer."

"The Shrine?"

253

"The Shrine of the Little Flower, St. Therese. At Twelve and Woodward. It's such a beautiful church, just the way they used to build them. I understand it's recently become a National Shrine. That would've made Father Coughlin so proud."

"She sounds like a very good girl."

"She even occasionally takes me to my women's group there, if I can't find anybody else to drive me."

"Ginny, I hate to ask, but is there any way I can use your restroom? I think I had a little too much coffee with dinner."

"It's just down the hall and on the left."

Randi followed Ginny's instructions and found the bathroom, right across from what appeared to be three bedrooms. Randi took a slight detour to silently open the first door.

The room was painted in a fading yellow and was obviously where Ginny created all of her crafts. There was a brand-new sewing machine and an old dresser covered with plants. Randi envied Ginny her green thumb. There were also spools of thread and bolts of material on the shelves.

She silently closed that door and went into the next room, which was off-white and furnished with a double bed decorated with a colorful patchwork quilt. Ginny's wedding picture was on the dresser, along with more pictures of Angela and her parents. A new boom box sat on the dresser, next to a stack of CDs, including Chant and some Polish music. There was even one that had something to do with Pope John Paul II. On the bedside table was a bible and and a copy of the Limbaugh report.

In the third and last room was a twin bed neatly made with a homemade quilt and Raggedy Ann sheets. She looked around in amazement at the faded pink walls to realize she was in the bedroom of a child, a young girl. Looking above the bed, she also realized that every room in the house had a crucifix in it.

Quickly glancing through the dresser drawers, aware that she had already taken too much time, she couldn't find a single piece of apparel that looked as if it belonged to the Angela she knew. There wasn't a single thing an exotic dancer could wear here.

But there was a well-worn Bible, and a rosary, right next to the bed. The rosary was an ordinary five-decade, black beaded one.

It was the only room without any new furnishings or electronics.

Randi went to the bathroom, flushed the toilet and washed her hands. "Ginny, I thought of one other question," she said, walking back into the living room. She stopped dead in her tracks. There, in a corner on a small, square table, a 7-decade, green rosary was draped over a picture.

"What is it dear?" Ginny asked.

"Wha . . . who is that?" she asked, pointing to the picture.

Ginny picked up the faded print, automatically wrapping the rosary around her hand. "That's Father Coughlin. He founded the Shrine, you know. The new priests are nothing like him, and I miss him dreadfully. He even had his own radio show! And it was a good one, nothing like the ones these days!"

"What a beautiful rosary," Randi said. "May I?" Father Coughlin was known as the father of hate radio. He had a radio antenna built into the tower of the Shrine, so he could broadcast his anti-semitic, homophobic, misogynistic drivel that said that anyone who wasn't like him was going to hell.

Ginny handed it over for Randi to examine. "Angela gave that to me for my birthday."

"When was that?"

"Just a month ago . . . she gave me that and my DVD player."

Randi left as quickly and quietly as she could, running to her car once she was outside.

• • •

"What have I gotten myself into?" Allie asked the mirror. Already today she had seen more dick then she had seen in the rest of her life put together—and not just from the ever-present porno movies. Guys actually wanted her to suck it or . . . fuck them . . . right in the theatre. Some of these guys, these businessmen, would put on condoms so they could jerk off and not soil their expensive pants.

Allie again questioned her lover's line of work.

• • •

Brett put her feet up on her desk and sighed deeply, glancing at her watch. Of course Allie would have to decide to start this on a Saturday. They had more live shows on Saturday than on any other day of the week, including a late show they only did on Fridays and Saturdays.

Now that Allie was dancing, Brett was going to stick around until closing. There was no way she was going to risk having her dancers walk out with just the security guard

Brett couldn't bring herself to watch Allie dance again. She grabbed a bottle of Scotch and a glass, returned to her desk, poured a drink, turned on her computer, signed onto AOL and found her favorite lesbian chatroom, one for butches and femmes. She should find some work to do, but she couldn't concentrate on anything.

She opened her candy bar and began flirting online. She still couldn't believe she was doing such things.

• • •

Chantel was supposed to be on first, but she hadn't shown up after the 4:30 show, so that meant Allie was first, with Angela following her, and Victoria going on last.

Angela, true to her word, stayed at the back of the theatre while Allie danced, watching her. When Allie finished her dance and headed to the dressing room, Angela whispered quickly but urgently, "You'll wait for me, right?"

Angela was still onstage when Allie returned to the theatre a few moments later, fully clothed. Brett's small Beretta was in an ankle holster around her left ankle, hidden by her jeans.

As soon as Angela was done with her lap dances, which didn't take very long because there weren't many customers, and Victoria was onstage, Allie followed Angela to the dressing room.

"Thank you so much for everything you're doing," Angela said. "I really don't have a lot of confidence in either the clerks or the guard here to keep us safe."

Angela's cell-phone rang. She reached over, picked up her purse, and answered it. "Hello? . . . oh, hi *Babcia* . . . Who stopped by? . . . No, no, I have no idea what that was about . . . She left quickly? . . . I love you, too." She glanced at her watch, and quickly started dressing.

"Is something the matter?" Allie asked.

Angela turned to look at her. Staring at her for a moment before speaking. "That was my grandmother. I think I need to run over and check on her. I'll try to make it back for the last show— do you think you two could go on first, though?"

"Yes. Is something the matter with her?"

"I don't know. Do you think maybe you could walk me out to my car?"

"Oh, sure." Allie followed Angela, briefly wondering if she should let the clerk know what she was doing, but Angela was walking quickly, and he was engrossed in some silly TV show. She really couldn't believe the number of rejects Brett found to hire. She'd have to talk to her about that.

Once outside, Angela said to Allie, "You know, I really don't like that Victoria. I mean, she really does represent the worst type of dancer."

"What do you mean?"

"Well, there's some girls who are working hard to pull themselves up and out—you know, going to school and trying to make something more of themselves. Then there's the ones who are just bad. There's something wrong with them."

"I have noticed that Victoria really seems to enjoy taking her clothes off for Brett every chance she gets," Allie said, nodding to the guard, who sat in front in his car, that everything was all right.

"I originally thought it was the owners of these places who were to blame. They lure the men in from the streets, and they don't let the girls know they really do have other options. I thought that if someone talked to these girls, let them know what they were really doing and what they could be doing instead, it would be all right."

"Oh, god," Allie said with a laugh, "some of the girls really enjoy what they're doing. They like the fast, easy money. They could survive on Welfare, but they dance for their drug money. It's an awful system." She liked Angela. She was someone Allie could talk to. They were leaning against Angela's car in the far back corner of the lot. Allie was relieved to see Brett's vehicle nearby. The guard was nowhere to be seen.

"If the girls would stop dancing, all of these places would go out of business, and more families could stay together. So I got on the inside to do something about it."

258

"What do you mean?" Was Angela trying to explain that she wasn't really one of them? That didn't make any sense.

"I wanted to show them the error of their ways. Explain to them what they were doing—and how what they're doing effects others. I mean, it seemed like the only way to help!"

"I understand," Allie said. "Have you had any luck?" She had thought she was doing a lot to help keep these women safe, but Angela was obviously trying to do something too. Trying to get them to quit dancing. Allie realized that Angela had been thinking about it all. After all, there was no way Brett would close her business as long as women were willing to work for her.

"I tried talking to a girl, and she explained it all to me. Boldly. She told me why she, and others, dance—that they're not being forced into it, that they want to do it."

"But you've kept at it—that's great Angela!" Allie exclaimed, yet she started nervously looking around. This wasn't making any sense, yet Angela was one of the good girls.

"You want to know what else she did?"

"What?"

"She laughed at me."

"Oh, god, honey, I'm so sorry." She realized Angela was right, there was no good way to stop the entire cycle so long as men were willing to pay money for women. She moved to take Angela in her arms, but Angela pushed her away.

"It all happened so quickly . . . her words, her laughter, she was laughing at me. And then, and then . . . I guess she thought I was up to something, so she pulled out a knife . . ."

"Oh my god," Allie said, realization dawning. "Who was she? When did this happen?"

"I didn't even think, I just reacted—I pushed her back. It was an accident, I didn't mean to do it."

"Hold on, what are you telling me, Angela?" She wished the parking lot wasn't so desolate. It was off the main thoroughfare, hidden by the theatre.

"She fell back and her head hit the Dumpster. I tried to help her, but she was already dead, so I ran. I didn't know what else to do."

"Hold on, you killed a dancer?"

"I didn't mean to do it, it was an accident!" Tears were streaming down her face.

Allie breathed a sigh of relief. Angela was worried about a tragic accident. "Oh, god, Angela, it's all right . . . It was just an accident . . . We can just report it to the police . . ." She put her arms around the woman, drawing her near so her head rested on her shoulder.

"Allie, you still don't get it," Angela murmured into her shoulder, pushing away. "It happened, and there was nothing I could do about it, so I went home and I prayed and prayed and prayed, hoping for absolution." She looked directly into Allie's eyes. "What I found, instead, was the reason—the reason it happened!"

"Wha . . . what are you talking about, Angela?" Allie noticed that Angela's hand was draped casually over her purse. Allie looked into her eyes. They had a wild look to them. Allie tried to casually inch away.

"My parents died when I was very young, and my grandmother raised me. *Babcia* taught me right from wrong and I've seen what's happening to this country."

Allie waited for her to continue. She readjusted her weight so she could run, or fall into a defensive position if she had to. She cursed that she'd strapped her gun to her leg instead of putting it in her purse.

Angela moved with the speed and agility of a jungle cat, suddenly pouncing. Before Allie could even begin to respond, she'd pulled a short, sharp knife out of her purse. Its blade glistened in the moonlight. "And you're the worst of the lot." she said, pushing the X-acto knife against Allie's throat.

"I . . . I don't understand!" The knife was pricking Allie's throat. A drop of blood trickled down toward her blouse. She could see how Angela could easily kill the girls—she'd leave with them, when nobody else was around, and either pretend to be picking a piece of lint off of them, or just reach around them, and slice their throats with her X-acto knife. There'd hardly be any sound, and death would be quick.

"Of course you'd say that. You'd come up with any reason you could to keep me from helping you find redemption."

Redemption from what, Allie wondered. "But I'm not a dancer, really."

"But you came here to stop me from doing the Will of God. You see, that night, after I released Leslie from committing further debauchery and sin, I prayed and prayed and prayed for absolution. And the Lord showed me that I had pulled one girl away from a life of evil. Through me, God wanted to rid the streets of this trash."

"But Brett and Randi have been trying to stop you as well. And the rest of the police."

"I will deal with each in their own turn. I am on a mission of God, and so shall I prevail. I will have to leave here now—now that your friend Randi has taken to bothering *Babcia*, but I will save you first."

Allie's only hope was to keep Angela talking. She tried backing up, to put some space between the short, sharp, knife and her throat, but Angela kept it pressed tightly to her, until Allie's back was pressed against the car.

"Why . . . why the rosaries and leaving them nude and all that?" Allie whispered tensely.

"Killing them is the only way to save them, don't you see? So I had to give them whatever chance of redemption possible. I baptized them with holy water and sent them to their maker with His Mother's holiness in their hands. You see, by killing them, I am helping them. God told me so."

"You're no better than those who kill doctors and bomb clinics to stop abortion—who claim to want to stop the killing by killing themselves."

"Sometimes sacrifices must be made," Angela said, nodding sagely. "I have the deepest respect for those who endanger themselves, martyr themselves, in order to make the world a better place. I have taken their example as well." She smiled an evil little smile. "And now, I must send you to your final judgment."

"Hold on!" Allie cried, arching her neck back from the knife. "You haven't told me how you've picked these girls? Is it all random chance? Or does the Lord tell you who to kill?"

Angela shuddered slightly. "Once Leslie died, and I learned of my mission, I researched how best to help their souls to depart from the sins of the flesh. And I waited for God to give me a sign as to who would be next. It was only when He failed to do so that I realized He had already given me that sign."

"And what was the sign?"

"That women who own these clubs are the worst, because they should know better. They should stay home and raise children and support their men. So they are the worst. Those who even further forsake the Lord are even worse—those who copulate with other women as if they were men."

"I understand, not all those you've . . . released . . . were lesbians."

"When I first decided to embark on my mission of mercy, and show these girls the evil they were doing, I cast about for those most likely to see the error of their ways, those most willing to be redeemed. But as I learned about how these places operate, I also found out about more places where women tempt others. One night, I was dancing at The Rainbow Room, and I realized that those women were committing twice the sin—because they were dancing for other women. But when I started to talk with them, they all laughed at me, as if I were joking."

"And so now you are getting your revenge on those who laughed at you." Allie kept her talking, hoping Angela would loosen her grip, become distracted.

"Revenge is not mine to have. I am simply following the Lord's will. He showed me that night who had to be the first to go."

"But I wasn't there that night—and I've never laughed at you."

"You are the worst because you choose to dance—and you enjoy it! You enjoy the power it gives you, I can see it when I watch you dance!"

26

Randi raced down Eight Mile, trying to dial her cell-phone. When she called Allie's phone, she got an "All circuits are busy," message, and she didn't know Brett's or the Paradise's numbers. She wasn't going to stop to look them up.

● ● ●

Brett went downstairs to talk to Angela between shows.

"What's going on?" Victoria asked, fully clothed, sitting in a chair and putting on her boots.

"I wanted to talk with Allie and Angela."

"They're not here. They must've stepped out once they got done."

Brett didn't hear anything more. She was racing out to the parking lot, drawing her gun as she ran. She was probably just being over-protective.

She stopped in her tracks when she saw that Angela had Allie backed up against her car, a small knife to her throat. Even in the dim light, Brett could see blood on Allie's neck.

She heard the screeching of tires behind her, but her mind was numb. Suddenly, someone yanked the gun out of her hand.

"You kill Allie, and I kill Brett!" Victoria screamed, pointing the .357 at Brett's temple.

It was like slow motion as Angela turned toward the sound of Victoria's voice. Her face registered shock, disbelief. The hand that held the knife moved away from Allie's neck. Brett turned to stare at Victoria, then back at Angela and Allie.

"It'll make my job easier!" Angela laughed.

Allie jerked sideways away from the knife and slammed her arm hard against Angela's side. They fell to the ground, Allie on top of Angela, struggling to grab the X-acto knife. Screaming in rage, Angela swiped the knife toward Allie, its blade glinting sickeningly in the moonlight. Allie felt it cut her cheek.

When Brett saw the blood on Allie's cheek, it broke her seeming trance and she ran forward, ignoring the gun pointed at her. She kicked Angela's hand, sending the knife flying. It only served to make Angela more enraged. With an almost maniacal strength, she managed to flip Allie onto her back, her hands circling Allie's throat. Brett fell to a crouch and threw an arm around Angela's neck, making her break her grip on Allie.

"Police, freeze!" an authoritative voice yelled into the night.

Brett slammed her knee down on Angela's right hand, and secured her arm around her neck. She grabbed her other hand, which Angela was trying to use to get at Allie's eyes, with her left hand. When Allie managed to wiggle away, Brett twisted both of Angela's arms behind her before she slammed her fist against Angela's head, knocking her out cold.

Randi pulled the gun out of Victoria's hand. "What the hell were you doing with this?"

"I thought Angela was in love with Brett, so if I pointed it at Brett, she'd turn from Allie." She looked down at Angela and shrugged. "I guess I was wrong, though."

Brett looked up at Randi and said, "About fucking time you showed up."

About the Author

Therese Szymanski recently relocated from the Motor City to the Nation's Capital. In a blatantly obvious move, she would like to mention that she volunteers a few hundred hours a year for the Mautner Project for Lesbians with Cancer, her favorite non-profit organization (www.mautnerproject.org). An award-winning playwright, she believes in erotic freedom, and maximizing the erotic content of life.

She is the author of the Brett Higgins Mysteries/Motor City Thrillers. *When the Dancing Stops*, *When the Dead Speak*, *When Some Body Disappears* and *When Evil Changes Face*, a 2000 Lambda Literary Award Finalist, are available from Bella Books. Her short stories can be found in the Naiad anthologies *The Touch of Your Hand* and *The Very Thought of You*. Upcoming stories can be found in the Alyson anthology *Up All Night*, and Haworth Press's *Shadows of the Night: Queer Tales of the Uncanny and Unusual*. (She also has stories in Alyson Press's *Roughed Up* and *Sex Buddies*, and an upcoming one in *Frat Sex*, but those only came about as a dare.)

She is currently at work editing her first anthology. *Back to Basics: A Butch/Femme Erotic Journey* due out in 2004 from Bella Books.

Publications from
BELLA BOOKS, INC.
The best in contemporary lesbian fiction

P.O. Box 10543, Tallahassee, FL 32302
Phone: 800-729-4992
www.bellabooks.com

MAYBE NEXT TIME by Karin Kallmaker. 256 pp. Sabrina
Starling always believed in maybe next time . . . until now.
ISBN 1-931513-26-0 $12.95

WHEN GOOD GIRLS GO BAD: A Motor City Thriller by
Therese Szymanski. 230 pp. Brett, Randi, and Allie join forces
to stop a serial killer. ISBN 1-931513-11-2 12.95

A DAY TOO LONG: A Helen Black Mystery by Pat Welch.
328 pp. This time Helen's fate is in her own hands.
ISBN 1-931513-22-8 $12.95

THE RED LINE OF YARMALD by Diana Rivers. 256 pp.
The Hadra's only hope lies in a magical red line . . . Climactic
sequel to *Clouds of War.* ISBN 1-931513-23-6 $12.95

OUTSIDE THE FLOCK by Jackie Calhoun. 224 pp.
Jo embraces her new love and life. ISBN 1-931513-13-9 $12.95

LEGACY OF LOVE by Marianne K. Martin. 224 pp. Read the whole
Sage Bristo story. ISBN 1-931513-15-5 $12.95

STREET RULES: A Detective Franco Mystery by Baxter Clare.
304 pp. Gritty, fast-paced mystery with compelling Detective
L.A. Franco ISBN 1-931513-14-7 $12.95

RECOGNITION FACTOR: 4th Denise Cleever Thriller by
Claire McNab. 176 pp. Denise Cleever tracks a notorious
terrorist to America. ISBN 1-931513-24-4 $12.95

NORA AND LIZ by Nancy Garden. 296 pp. Lesbian romance
by the author of *Annie on My Mind.* ISBN 1931513-20-1 $12.95

MIDAS TOUCH by Frankie J. Jones. 208 pp. Sandra had
everything but love.   ISBN 1-931513-21-X $12.95

BEYOND ALL REASON by Peggy J. Herring. 240 pp. A
romance hotter than Texas.   ISBN 1-9513-25-2 $12.95

ACCIDENTAL MURDER: 14th Detective Inspector Carol
Ashton Mystery by Claire McNab. 208 pp.Carol Ashton
tracks an elusive killer.   ISBN 1-931513-16-3 $12.95

SEEDS OF FIRE:Tunnel of Light Trilogy, Book 2 by Karin
Kallmaker writing as Laura Adams. 274 pp. Intriguing sequel to
Sleight of Hand.   ISBN 1-931513-19-8 $12.95

DRIFTING AT THE BOTTOM OF THE WORLD by
Auden Bailey. 288 pp. Beautifully written first novel set in
Antarctica.   ISBN 1-931513-17-1 $12.95

CLOUDS OF WAR by Diana Rivers. 288 pp. Women unite
to defend Zelindar!   ISBN 1-931513-12-0 $12.95

DEATHS OF JOCASTA: 2nd Micky Knight Mystery by J.M.
Redmann. 408 pp. Sexy and intriguing Lambda Literary Award-
nominated mystery.   ISBN 1-931513-10-4 $12.95

LOVE IN THE BALANCE by Marianne K. Martin. 256 pp.
The classic lesbian love story, back in print! ISBN 1-931513-08-2 $12.95

THE COMFORT OF STRANGERS by Peggy J. Herring. 272 pp.
Lela's work was her passion . . . until now. ISBN 1-931513-09-0 $12.95

CHICKEN by Paula Martinac. 208 pp. Lynn finds that the
only thing harder than being in a lesbian relationship is ending
one.   ISBN 1-931513-07-4 $11.95

TAMARACK CREEK by Jackie Calhoun. 208 pp. An intriguing
story of love and danger.   ISBN 1-931513-06-6 $11.95

DEATH BY THE RIVERSIDE: 1st Micky Knight Mystery by
J.M. Redmann. 320 pp. Finally back in print, the book that
launched the Lambda Literary Award-winning Micky Knight
mystery series.   ISBN 1-931513-05-8 $11.95

EIGHTH DAY: A Cassidy James Mystery by Kate Calloway.
272 pp. In the eighth installment of the Cassidy James
mystery series, Cassidy goes undercover at a camp for troubled
teens.   ISBN 1-931513-04-X $11.95

MIRRORS by Marianne K. Martin. 208 pp. Jean Carson and Shayna Bradley fight for a future together. ISBN 1-931513-02-3 $11.95

THE ULTIMATE EXIT STRATEGY: A Virginia Kelly Mystery by Nikki Baker. 240 pp. The long-awaited return of the wickedly observant Virginia Kelly. ISBN 1-931513-03-1 $11.95

FOREVER AND THE NIGHT by Laura DeHart Young. 224 pp. Desire and passion ignite the frozen Arctic in this exciting sequel to the classic romantic adventure *Love on the Line*. ISBN 0-931513-00-7 $11.95

WINGED ISIS by Jean Stewart. 240 pp. The long-awaited sequel to *Warriors of Isis* and the fourth in the exciting Isis series. ISBN 1-931513-01-5 $11.95

ROOM FOR LOVE by Frankie J. Jones. 192 pp. Jo and Beth must overcome the past in order to have a future together. ISBN 0-9677753-9-6 $11.95

THE QUESTION OF SABOTAGE by Bonnie J. Morris. 144 pp. A charming, sexy tale of romance, intrigue, and coming of age. ISBN 0-9677753-8-8 $11.95

SLEIGHT OF HAND by Karin Kallmaker writing as Laura Adams. 256 pp. A journey of passion, heartbreak and triumph that reunites two women for a final chance at their destiny. ISBN 0-9677753-7-X $11.95

MOVING TARGETS: A Helen Black Mystery by Pat Welch. 240 pp. Helen must decide if getting to the bottom of a mystery is worth hitting bottom. ISBN 0-9677753-6-1 $11.95

CALM BEFORE THE STORM by Peggy J. Herring. 208 pp. Colonel Robicheaux retires from the military and comes out of the closet. ISBN 0-9677753-1-0 $12.95

OFF SEASON by Jackie Calhoun. 208 pp. Pam threatens Jenny and Rita's fledgling relationship. ISBN 0-9677753-0-2 $11.95

WHEN EVIL CHANGES FACE: A Motor City Thriller by Therese Szymanski. 240 pp. Brett Higgins is back in another heart-pounding thriller. ISBN 0-9677753-3-7 $11.95

BOLD COAST LOVE by Diana Tremain Braund. 208 pp. Jackie Claymont fights for her reputation and the right to love

THE WILD ONE by Lyn Denison. 176 pp. Rachel never
expected that Quinn's wild yearnings would change her life
forever.   ISBN 0-9677753-4-5 $12.95

SWEET FIRE by Saxon Bennett. 224 pp. Welcome to
Heroy—the town with the most lesbians per capita than any
other place on the planet!   ISBN 0-9677753-5-3 $11.95

Visit

Bella Books

at

BellaBooks.com

or call our toll-free number

1-800-729-4992